Just Daisy

DEBORAH LINN

Just Daisy, Copyright © 2021 by Deborah Linn

Interior Design by Judi Fennell at www.formatting4U.com

All rights reserved. No part of this publication may be reproduced, distributed, or transmitted in any form or by any means, including photocopying, recording, or other electronic or mechanical methods, without the prior written permission of the publisher, except in the case of brief quotations embodied in critical reviews and certain other noncommercial uses permitted by copyright law.

This book is a work of fiction. All names, characters, locations, and incidents are products of the authors' imaginations. Any resemblance to actual persons, things, living or dead, locales, or events is entirely coincidental.

ISBN: 978-1-737667-0-0-1

To my parents.
And to Aunt Marsha.

Mary! Happy Reading! —Deborah Hium

CHAPTER ONE

My dead mother's advice replays in my head as I slink past the slushie truck at the edge of Chicago's Gold Coast beach to wait for my best friend, Jordan Baker. My mom died three years ago. You'd think her voice wouldn't still nag at me like it does, but you'd be wrong. It's ingrained. At least this one piece of advice is.

"It's a blessing a woman can choose whom to love," Mom used to say. It was always followed by my dad who would tweak her nose and add, "So choose the top guy."

The top guy. As if it's that easy. If it were, I wouldn't be rereading the slushie menu to see if they've added Magic Invisibility Mango or Time Travel Tangerine since I was here last.

Not that I could slurp it down anyway. My stomach still hasn't settled from the bumpy landing at O'Hare Airport not two hours ago when I'd grabbed the barf bag only to have Grandma Betty slowly pull it away and return it to the seatback pocket in front of us. To Grandma Betty, public puking is unacceptable.

I spy Jordan in her adorable navy halter dress marching through the sand toward me. The nausea settles. I salute with a quick and cautious wave then scoot behind the far end of the truck where none of the other members of our senior class friend group can see me. They're gathered at our spot on the shoreline, the one where we back-to-school bash at the end of every summer. It's a tradition. I should be down there with them, but I'm not ready. I've been away all summer. I zoomed here as fast as I could from the airport, pausing at Grandma's to do nothing more than slide into my bikini and Tom's favorite pale blue sundress.

And send one text. One premature text.

And there goes my stomach again.

By the look on Jordan's face as she comes around the slushie truck, I can tell she's read the text. She doesn't hesitate before attacking me with a big hug. I think I broke her. She's malfunctioning. Jordan Baker doesn't hug.

She steps back and studies me with the most all-encompassing secret-mission smile I've ever seen on her movie star face. Her short, stacked brown bob hangs perfectly around her angular chin. Her dark eyes flash.

"Damn, Daisy. You look gorgeous and..."

"And what? What?"

"And sad. Why are you sad?"

"You got my text."

"Yeah, but that's not a reason to be sad."

"I'm breaking up with Tom."

"And that is reason for celebration."

"I'm gonna be sick."

"You absolutely are not." She takes my arm and guides me to a nearby bistro table, still out of sight of the congregated partiers down by the shore.

"How are you gonna do it? Have you practiced?" She rubs her hands together then rests her chin on her fists. She leans in, way too excited. But what did I expect?

"No. Not really. Wait. Don't you want to know why?" I'm dying to tell. Since grade school, Jordan and I haven't gone more than a week without contact. I've been away for two months.

"Want to know why what?" My cousin, Nick Carraway, has come upon us unnoticed. Nick looks exactly like a big gulp of healthy, fresh air except for the sloppy, fast-melting slushie he's trying to push back into the pink paper cup with the tip of his tongue.

"How'd you find us?" I ask, happy to see him, but not ready. Just not ready.

"Jordan." He shrugs and sucks the juices threatening to overflow.

Jordan shrugs, too, and pats the third chair beside her. "Daisy's breaking up with Tom," she tells Nick.

"Really? Why?" he asks and accepts her invitation to sit.

"Does it matter?" Jordan asks.

"I think it does," Nick says.

"Thank you," I say.

"The answer is obvious. She's met someone," Jordan says. She leans into him and licks his slushie.

"What makes you think that?" I ask. My heart clenches. I peek around the truck to the beach party. Does everyone know?

"Is it true? Who is he?" Nick asks, and I half expect him to slip out his phone to take notes for a salacious back-to-school story. Nick is the editor of our school newspaper and takes his job quite seriously. I'm sure he's been slouched over a computer screen all summer. His pale, untoned body proves it.

Jordan answers, "Of course it's true. Just look what two months on the Georgia coast has done for her. She's gorgeous, stunning, and so full of mystery. No one has heard from her. And why would they? She's been *otherwise engaged.*" She delivers the last part like it's the juiciest secret then reaches over and undoes the buttons on Nick's shirt, the sides of which fall open to reveal a pale peach V-neck t-shirt. She pats his chest, satisfied.

"Um. No one heard from me because Grandma didn't let me take my cell phone. You know this."

She flashes me a gossipy smile. "Are you claiming you weren't otherwise engaged?"

It's a beautiful breezy day. Cotton candy clouds rest in the soft sky. Heat flushes into my cheeks, but it's not from the sun. It's from a memory of *his* kisses, *his* hands, *his* ocean blue eyes that saw everything in me that I never even knew was there.

Nick leans back, wide-eyed and surprised. He always looks surprised. Surprised that people listen to him, surprised when they know what he's talking about, and more so when they don't know. He claims it's amusement rather than surprise, but I'm not so sure.

Nick turns to Jordan. "You're right. Look at her face. It reads *otherwise engaged* to me."

"How scandalous," Jordan teases.

"It would make a great story, wouldn't it?" Nick asks.

"Viral," Jordan answers.

"Stop it, guys. I'm right here, you know."

"Oh yes, we know, Daisy. We know everything. It's written all over your face." Jordan flutters a hand in my direction.

My fingers fly to my cheeks as if the whole story is typed there in bold font for all to see.

"Tom is gonna know, isn't he? This is terrible. He can't know. He can't." My chest tightens. My breath stops. I stand up and pace behind the truck.

I scan the party crowd and turn back from it and then to it again. My whole self feels pulled in as if on a rogue wave. All I want to do is paddle furiously for shore, but not this shore. I long for the beautiful beaches of Tybee Island where I've spent the last eight weeks in the arms of the most beautiful boy in the world who made me forget that this shore and this top guy existed.

"It's true? There's someone else?" Nick asks again, this time staring me down.

I gasp. I am drowning. Absolutely drowning. I know this because pictures of my life are flashing before me. I see the look on my dad's face the day I brought home Tom Buchanan, East Eggerton Academy's Top Guy, to meet him. I swear my dad had nearly popped a champagne cork. It was after a big game. We were only freshmen, but Tom had started at quarterback because the senior veteran was injured. I think if Daddy were alive and knew what I was planning now, he would pour the bubbly down the drain and light up a sad cigarette. Then Mom would cry because Daddy's smoking again.

"Relax, Daisy. Why can't Tom know? You're leaving him. Why does it matter?" Jordan asks.

"Tom will kill him. That's why."

"Kill him? Your secret summer love? All the way in Georgia? I doubt that," Jordan says.

"Then he'll kill me."

She swats the idea away. "No, he won't. Nick will protect you. Won't you Nick?"

Nick frowns as if he'd rather be pulled out to sea himself.

"Sit down, Daisy. It's gonna be fine. More than fine. Let's formulate a plan. It will all fall apart without a plan," Jordan insists.

"A plan does help." Nick pulls out his phone.

"Here, let's practice. We'll get the words right and it'll be easy. When Tom sees you, walk right up to him, put your hands on your hips, stick out your chest and say, 'It's over, Tom. You're out and'-- what's Beach Boy's name?"

"Jamie." His name floats from my lips like a lover's sigh. But it sounds foreign here like it doesn't quite belong in this world. I return to my seat.

Jordan takes up the speech again. She clears her throat, "You're out and Jamie's in." She sticks her nose up in the air to punctuate the finality of it.

Nick looks back and forth between us, waiting for my approval.

I sink into myself. "But that's a lie. Jamie's not really *in* at all. He's half a world away."

"Don't be dramatic. Tybee Island is only half a continent away." She laughs, but she's not really joking. I am dramatic. I'm nothing if not dramatic. I know this. I can't help it. Jamie knows it, too. He likes it. I smile at a memory. If I could jump back on a plane and fly to him this second, I would.

Suddenly, I understand the universe my parents lived in when they were still alive. I was never really part of it. I was merely an interesting tourist stop on their never-ending road trip. Every now and then, they'd pull over long enough to enjoy me, then they were off again. It's how I like to think of them. It's easier that way. After all, the last time I saw them, they were waving goodbye on their way to somewhere they never came back from. Sometimes I wonder if they even realize they didn't. They're still riding off into the perpetual sunset.

I could do that with Jamie. Join him on our island, hold hands in the sand, and never return. Just keep dreaming. There's something electric about the air around him. He energizes and mesmerizes me all at the same time. It's like a magic spell.

Something tugs my psyche back to reality.

"Besides, it's not like we're together anymore. We decided not to try long distance." My throat catches. I curl in my lips and bite down to keep from saying any more. If I speak one more word, I swear I'll burst out crying. The gash is still too fresh.

Just this morning before sunrise, before Grandma and I had to leave for the airport, Jamie had tapped on my window. We'd walked silently to the beach for promises, I'd thought, of ever-after. But that's not what had happened. Exactly.

"The universe brought us together," he'd said. "It will again. We don't need cell phones and social media. That's all fake anyway. What we have is too real." And then he'd kissed me in a way that made me believe. Even now, I still believe. When I close my eyes, he's right here.

"No long distance? Are you sure?" Jordan asks, disappointment dripping from her voice.

My heart slows to nearly nothing. "Yeah, I'm sure. But once a girl has lived that dream, it can't be undreamed."

"Undreamt," Nick says, and Jordan punches him. "What?" he says. "It's undreamt."

"Jamie sounds like the other half of your romantic soul." In the nearly ten years that I have known Jordan Baker, there are only a handful of times that I've ever heard her remove the hard edges from her voice. Today is one of them. Even the sharpness of her features melts a little.

I nod. She knows me. She gets it. Nick knows me, too, but he's a guy. He gets nothing. He just squints and then does that thing with his face that he does when he knows he's outnumbered by us.

Then he says, "Okay, but seriously, back to my first question. Why? If you break up with Tom, you're still not with this Jamie guy. Where does that leave you?"

"I know. But how can I be with Tom when I know there's Jamie? I don't see how…"

We all sit there for a second, waiting for an answer to come. Jordan raises her chin and glares in the air as if she can see straight through the slushie truck and down to the beach. "This is going to be intense."

"Tom is gonna hate me."

For half a second, she breaks form. "And just how would that change things?" She snaps her nose back into place so fast, I search the sky for some marionette string that might be controlling her movements. I should have known better. No one controls Jordan's movements but Jordan.

I close my eyes and breathe in the beach air. The Gold Coast shoreline is not Tybee Island. Not even close. I keep my eyes closed and try to recapture the magic of the summer. It's impossible. Already, the memories crumble in waves of disillusion. How long before I forget the taste of his lips, the undulating ocean blue of his eyes, the sunlight gathered in his golden hair? Even now the echo of his laugh retreats with the pounding of my mother's advice thundering through my brain. It's a blessing a woman can choose whom to love.

A different laugh, a raucous and arrogant one, rides the wind from the beach to my ear and startles me awake.

"It's Tom," I say, and all the stormy winds of the universe come crashing in on me at once.

My father's voice sounds clear and firm in my soul. *So, choose the top guy.*

CHAPTER TWO

I leave the table and head toward the inevitable. My sandaled feet hit softer sand with each step until Tom is clearly in view. I stop. My breath catches in my lungs. How could I have forgotten how--not gorgeous or sexy--how powerful he is. Those shoulders and arms belong more to a statue of Atlas than they do a senior in high school.

He's halfway between me and the party crowd when he looks up. He walks then runs across the beach. It all seems slow mo, his body separating the air before him as if he were throwing off tacklers in some ever-present football game.

And then, he's right here with us.

"Wow, Tom. You've really hulked up. Hit your growth spurt over the summer?" Jordan's snide disapproval shoots from behind me and into Tom. For a moment, he appears wounded, the wind knocked out of him, and I feel sorry for him. But it doesn't last.

"More like hit the weight room." He flexes, shifting that great pack of muscles chiseled into his chest and shoulders. He's tan, with a faint line across his biceps where his football shirt would have protected that beautiful skin from the sun until practice was over and he'd head to the beach. A sun-drenched sheen causes his whole body to appear as if it's molded from precious metal.

"And I appreciate every single second of it." Before I can catch the words, they tumble out, so quietly I don't realize anyone else can hear them at first. But no, they are out there.

He scoops me up and spins me around twice before setting me down.

"I hate that word--hulked up," he mumbles before a hungry smile spreads across his face.

A smile spreads across mine, too. I can't help it. He's very easy to look at. Tom has these dark, dark eyes, like balls of coal embedded in his statuesque head. Most of the time, they make him look dumb, like those eyes lead to nothing but emptiness. Every now and then, though, they shine like obsidian beads. Like now. He's entranced as he always is when I wear blue.

"God, you're beautiful." He plays with my hair. "I've never seen you this tan. Your hair is like blonder. Or something."

My bottom lip curls inward, and I bite down on it. My heart sighs. Jordan has moved to stand beside me, facing in. Nick is on the other side, forming a circular huddle of just the four of us. I feel rather than see Jordan's disapproval. I don't look at her, partly because I don't want to see that Jordan Baker glare and partly because I can't take my eyes off Tom. I haven't seen him all summer. At the beach, my eyes had grown used to the lean, towering frames of sand volleyball players and swimmers. My hands, too.

Without warning, Tom's lips hit up against mine as if he owns them. The spell is broken. I pull away, but his lips aggressively follow.

It is Jordan who physically pulls him off. "Jesus, Tom. Don't be gross."

"Daisy doesn't think it's gross, do you?" He slips his masculine hands around my waist to my butt and pulls me in.

"Maybe a little inappropriate. Everyone can see," I answer.

"What are they gonna do about it? I missed my woman. Did my woman miss me?" He brushes his lips on mine again.

Jordan pushes him away. "My woman? Toxic masculinity on display, ladies and gentlemen."

Tom slides his arm around my shoulders like a hungry python. "Of course, she's my woman. She sure isn't your woman. Not that I would mind seeing that."

"Seriously, Tom. Don't be gross," I punch his arm, but my fisted hand bounces right off. He's been at football camps most of the summer. In two months, I swear he's doubled in muscle mass.

We move toward the partiers and settle on a blanket under a big blue umbrella that Tom's prepared for us. It's all very surreal. I shiver against the remembrances of the cool Tybee breeze coming in off this morning's receding tide where nothing but water, a few beach bungalows, and a heavenly universe shared our space. Here, a million city folk posing for the Chicago skyline and a fake, cement ship housing tourist grub presses in on what should be an intimate homecoming, but it's not. It can't be. I'm leaving him.

My brain feels like it might short circuit at any moment. I close my eyes and picture that text I sent to Jordan earlier. I repeat it in my mind like a mantra. *I'm breaking up with Tom. I'm breaking up with Tom. I'm breaking up with Tom.* But it doesn't matter how many times the words replay, Mom and Dad's voices are louder, and when I look at him with his ripped muscles and six-pack abs, I'm deaf to anything but the Top Guyness of him.

Tom reclines on the towel and pulls me down nearly on top of him.

I hear Jordan release a short gasp. Then, "Daisy's got news for you, Tom." The edge is back in her voice.

But at the same time, Nick says, "Let's hit the water."

"Yes, let's." I scramble to throw off my sundress and sandals.

"Wait. What news?" Tom asks.

My breath stops again. I can't do it. This isn't right. It's not supposed to be Jordan leading the charge. It's supposed to be me, flippant and aloof, announcing the breakup with a toss of my hair. I open my mouth, but all that comes out is a stupid giggle. Jordan's eyes narrow. Nick's grow wide.

Tom jumps up and gawks at me. "Holy shit, Daisy."

"What? What?" Did I say it? Did my voice accidentally shout out the words, and I'm such a freak I didn't even know it? I try to remember to breathe.

"Is that what you wore this summer?"

"What?" I say again.

"That." Tom takes a step back and points at my top, then my bottoms, then wags his finger up and down at me like he might be scolding a dog.

"What's wrong?"

"Not a thing." Jordan's face lights up.

I look down then wrap my arms around my middle. I'm usually a one-piece kind of girl. Now I remember why. But on the island, it had been so easy. Jamie had suggested the two-piece from a boutique window. I had bought it immediately and soon owned a whole rotation of cute little two-piece suits.

Tom's face goes serious. "How many guys hit on you?"

"What?" I ask, my voice seductively low.

He narrows his black eyes at me like he could count the come-ons on my face. I hate it when he looks at me like that, like he owns me. I was never looked at like that on the island. Jamie's gaze was never one of ownership, more like belonging and oneness.

"How many hit on you? I know they did. I wasn't there, so how would they know not to?"

"They wouldn't." Jordan answers.

"Unless you stopped them. Did you stop them?" Tom's expression fades into a distant, false fantasy. I know what he's thinking. He's imagining all the things I might have done with all the guys who apparently flock to me every time he so much as turns his head in the other direction. All the guys I've supposedly liked and flirted with and kissed over the years even though I never have.

Not until Jamie, anyway.

Should I be jealous?" His voice lowers to match my whisper. There's a flush on his cheeks.

"Jealous? Of who?" I ask and hate that, this time, whatever he's imagining is probably pretty close to right.

Jordan gives an uncharacteristic snort from the blanket.

"They better have kept their hands off." His face is too close, but his voice is soft as if he's afraid release it. I set my fingers on his cheek. His jaw clenches under my touch. My mind travels back to a chilly night and an illicit campfire on the beach and my gorgeous other fish from another sea. *His* eyes were blue and flooded with emotion like waves on the shore.

For the first time, I recognize Tom's simmering vulnerability. I bite my lip so as not to smile in the face of it, but it's too deliciously tempting. All at once, I realize I changed on the coast. Now back, I've usurped his power, even if he doesn't realize it. I try it out, sliding down my hand and curving my fingers into his stone chest. "Maybe a little jealous."

"Dammit, Daisy. Did you at least cover up when you weren't in the water?" A seething whisper escapes.

"Why should I?" My own words surprise me. I don't talk to Tom like this. It's better to calm him, not to egg him on, but I don't care.

I'm breaking up with Tom. I'm breaking up with Tom.

"So guys don't look at you, that's why." He's pacing now, one hand fisted up and shoved into the palm of the other, our soft blanket twisting under his feet.

"So now they can't even look at me?" I ask.

Just Daisy

"Who is *they*?" He asks, stopping dead center.

"What?" Oh God. Here we go. He's gonna know. I swallow against the panic building in my brain and try to hold onto the power that is already receding like morning tide in the afternoon sun.

"You said so now *they* can't even look. Who exactly is *they*?"

Part of me wants to scream the name at him, but I can't. "Nobody, Tom. It's not like I was the only girl on the beach. There were better bodies to look at than mine."

"I doubt it," he says, and those black eyes scan me as if he can see through my suit. But the ownership now is tinged with something else. Maybe guilt? No, not که. Something else I can feel my heart sinking into.

But Jordan jumps up, plants her hands on hips and leans in very melodramatically. "What did you want her to wear at the beach, a muumuu?" She coughs out a tension-tearing laugh, and at that second, I love my best friend beyond measure. Siphoning her confidence, I follow her lead.

"I would never wear a muumuu, Jordan."

"I would hope not," she comes back.

"Can you even imagine?" We're performing now, and Tom can only watch. Nick stands up, too, hands uncomfortably shoved in his pockets.

"What did you wear? Let's hear it." Jordan's eyes grow like she is about to take in the juiciest gossip.

"I think I had a new bikini every day. A blue one to match my eyes. A green one, like money. A yellow one. With daisies right here." I point to my chest.

"And did they look?" She emphasizes *they*.

"Of course. They looked and I looked. Everybody looked at everybody." My hair flips like a lion tamer's whip.

We laugh. Nick gives a half-hearted *ha*. Tom is silent but looks, for a moment, like a circus strongman whose fake balloon weights have just floated away. He massages his fist, and his muscles bulge all the way to his hulking shoulders. I straighten my spine.

"Are you mocking me?" He asks.

"We don't need to. You're doing it to yourself," I answer.

"I'm mocking myself? That's just dumb, Daisy. You can't mock yourself." If *they* had bounced a beach ball off his head at that moment, his brainless skull might have exploded.

"You're making yourself look stupid."

"Oh yeah? I'm not the one throwing my body at every beach bum who--" He mumbles over the end.

Jamie's blue eyes float back to my mind. Beach bum. He wasn't a bum. He was more like--and I say this knowing how ridiculous it sounds--like a god.

"I don't have to listen to this, Tom. I don't need you to make me feel like I misbehaved, like I disobeyed simply because I enjoyed myself this summer. I don't need--"

"Maybe you don't need me at all. Is that what you're saying?"

"That's exactly what she's saying," Jordan answers for me.

Tom's eyes go cold. My skin goes hot. If I could, I would scoop up her words and jam them back down her throat.

The reality of actually leaving Tom hits me in a way I am not prepared for. It feels good to stand up to him, but I know it's not true that I don't need him. We've been together since freshman year. What am I without him? As Nick pointed out, leaving him doesn't leave me with Jamie. It only leaves me... alone.

"Daisy?" Tom's voice is soft like rose petals, like how he sounds when he realizes he's made me cry.

"Daisy." Jordan is adamant.

My heart sinks through the soles of my feet, clear to the center of the earth and leaks every ounce of conviction with it. When the sand doesn't obey my silent wish to open up and suck my physical body down, too, I frown in Nick's direction. Even though he's a guy, he's also my cousin. We've known each other forever, and I'm praying he's getting what I'm sending.

"So... um. Hey," Nick chimes in. Everyone looks at him. His pale face blushes.

"What, Nick?" Tom's demanding tone startles all of us.

Nick claps Tom on the shoulder and squeezes as if to say I'm here for ya, man. Tom sneers at him and shrugs it off like he might catch something. Again, I know what he's thinking when he makes that face, and it makes me hate him and pity him all at once.

"Uh... I've got news, too. Did you guys hear about the new guy?" Nick finally says.

"What? You got a crush on him or something?" Tom says.

Nick looks incredulous and shakes his head. "What's your problem, Tom?"

Just Daisy

"With what? With gays?" Tom gets in Nick's face.

"Stop it, Tom," I say. I want to jump in for Nick, but he holds his own. He doesn't flinch. He doesn't move. Tom smirks. My brain hurts. I'm watching the threads of the tapestry we've woven since freshman year unravel in front of me.

"I've heard of him," Jordan intervenes. "He's a senior. Emancipated. Access to the best weed. Plans to throw some ragers immediately."

Tom takes the bait and backs off. "A pothead? So not a football player."

Jordan laughs in his face. "Why, you worried about a little competition?"

"He's a swimmer. Or maybe tennis." Nick says, plunging his hands in his pockets and rocking back on his heels.

Tom leans into Jordan's face this time, "You're an ass, Jordan."

She rolls her eyes upward and elevates her chin, her signature I-don't-care-what-you-think Jordan gesture.

I gaze out to the shore's edge and consider plunging my body into the very bottom and holding my breath until they all leave when my name floats across the breeze to us.

"Daisy. Daisy. There you are." It's my grandma. Why am I not surprised?

I retrieve my sundress from the blanket and slip it on. It's over. Anything I might have planned for today's traitorous revelation is canceled. Grandma Betty's world offers no place for teen drama. Grandma's heart offers no place for me to contradict her son's (my dad's) wishes.

Tom Buchanan + Daisy Fay = my dad's wishes.

Even though Grandma Betty is walking through sand, she appears to glide, waving like a beauty queen with one hand and carrying a soft cooler with the other.

"I just couldn't let you come without some lunch. Here you go."

Tom takes the cooler and her elbow. Brushing aside stray sand pebbles with his foot, he lowers Grandma to the blanket.

"You're staying, aren't you?" He settles in beside her and unzips the cooler.

She taps his cheeks with her hand. "You are just the sweetest boy, Tom. We have missed you this summer. Haven't we missed him, Daisy?"

"Did you really?" He sounds like a pouting tween girl.

"Of course. Of course. Sit down, kids." She conducts us to the blanket where we acquiesce to her sandwiches and cookies and bottles of sweet tea. As I sip it down, the chill of it fills me with memories, already cold, of my beach and its lighthouse and the spot where I'd lounged with the love of my life, or so it had seemed at the time. That was just this morning, I keep telling myself. Just this morning when I'd felt his soft lips on mine and his hopeful arms pulling me into possibility and a universe of wishes.

But then Tom laughs at something Grandma says. He has a way with her that makes her so very happy. Then Nick nudges Jordan who throws sand on his pimento cheese sandwich. Nick's not Grandma's grandkid—he's distant relative from my mother's side—but Grandma treats all my friends as if they are.

The sun is high and hot in the sky, melting away the sweet memories of a summer that I'm not even sure was real. As I sip Grandma's sweet tea elixir, I realize there's no magic in this potion. It can't take me back to Tybee. Nothing can. You can't repeat the past.

Tom's muscular python arm snakes around my shoulders. I shiver and he wraps it tighter. He kisses my cheek. Jordan pretends not to see. Nick half-watches, trying to reserve judgment. I lean into Tom. I can't help it. He's here and solid and... very, very real.

And now it's not Mom's advice or Dad's quip or even Jamie's promise that tumbles in my haunted heart but Nick's earlier question. Without Tom, where does that leave me? The answer is I have no idea, but I'm not exactly sure what I am with him either, except for one thing. With Tom, there are no dreamy memories washed out to sea on the waves of longing and hope, no crumbling castles of sand that crush your soul. With him, I'm not alone.

CHAPTER THREE

When the counselor calls you into the office on the first day of school, you worry. Ms. Eckleburg caught me before I even made it to my locker. Now I'm standing in the middle of the office foyer waiting while she assures a pimply-faced, smelly freshman of his place in the world —at least of his place in East Eggerton Academy's world.

"Yes, I know you have Mr. Muldoon for biology and no, you can't trade out because your friend has Chrystie. It doesn't work that way in high school. You can't get what you want by whining."

A scrawny boy who looks closer to fifth grade than he does freshman screws his face like he might cry. I remember the first day Jordan and I entered those big, heavy doors. She'd marched in like a cadet and I had followed. What else was there to do? Jordan marches. I float like a soft petal on a rippling pond. Jordan's marching keeps me from spinning in circles.

Ms. Eckleburg pushes the boy out the door, sighs with her whole body, regains her smile and asks, "What can I do for you, Daisy?"

"You brought me in."

"Oh, yes. I have something for you."

More panicked students rush in. She shuffles papers on her desk while they line up. It's Schedule Central in here. I've had my individual plan of study set in stone since eighth grade. I'd nearly forgotten the need for Schedule Central.

I understand Ms. Eckleburg's annoyance. It's the same every year. School starts on a Thursday with freshmen and new students only, for orientation. They discover who is in what class and then storm the counselors office the next day to beg for changes, but all students are here today, Friday. Counselors don't have time or energy to deal with their insecurities.

My thoughts wander back to Nick's announcement of a new

student. His schedule is probably in that stack of papers Ms. Eckleburg has picked up and put down on her desk three times now. Not that I care what his schedule is.

After we'd left the beach and for the next several days, Jordan had droned on about New Guy more than she had the failed breakup attempt, probably as a way to keep from scolding me to death on my first night back. She'd revealed that rumors about him started a couple weeks ago when Lucille McKee brought her little sister to the school to enroll. She'd eavesdropped on the counselors' secretary disappointing Coach Wolfsheim that New Guy wouldn't be fulfilling the recently vacated tight-end position. No one has actually seen New Guy yet. Nevertheless, they are already planning their outfits for his parties.

I laugh inwardly that whoever this new senior is, his first experience with East Eggerton's student body had been orientation day with a bunch of freshmen. Whatever that experience had been though, it was nothing compared to what the populous would have in store for him if he was even close to what they were making him out to be.

"Ah. Here it is. Sorry about that." Ms. Eckleburg smiles, but her face sags from too many forced niceties. She shoves three colorful brochures at me with an impatient hand. I whisk them from her. Anything I can do to help.

The brochures advertise three universities. Cornell, St. Xavier University, and the University of Chicago. They are beautiful and glossy promises of the grand, new adventures that await us upon graduation.

"These are for me?" I ask.

"Of course." Ms. Eckleburg has a way of penetrating your soul through her round glasses. Her blue irises seem somehow big, like two gigantic glowing signs—the kind that decorate Times Square and follow you wherever you go.

A streak of yellow highlighter illuminates the words *Pre-law Program* on the back of one of the trifolds.

"This is for me?" I repeat, stunned.

Ms. Eckleburg sighs again, this time with a weary smile. Those irises lock on me.

"I see you, Daisy, even if you can't see yourself. I'll send you a pass next week and we can talk about it some more." Then she's off to calm the next schedule-panicked kid.

I see you. It's not the first time her observant words had both soothed and agitated me. She has a way of framing reality as a retouched photo that you don't mind looking at, but you also know you have to turn away at some point. The year my parents died, I'd spent more time in her office than in the classroom. I've come a long way since then. In some ways. Sometimes, it all feels like yesterday. Sometimes, it seems like another lifetime.

The pamphlets remind me I'm a senior. I suppose I should start thinking about my future, so I try to as I push through the door and into the hallway.

Pre-Law? Is it like a legal secretary? I'd never once in my entire life thought of myself as a secretary, doing the bidding of some power-hungry professional bullshitter. Then again, I haven't really thought of myself as anything. I've always just assumed I'd go to college, marry Tom, and spend afternoons on my parents' yacht. Now my yacht.

"There you are. Have you found him yet?" Jordan is pressed to perfection in her starched white button-down shirt and plaid uniform skirt. She catches me outside the counseling office. She has the most inspiring eyebrows, and I still don't know how her make-up is high-glam and yet her face seems so naked all at once.

"Tom? No, I--" I hold out the brochures to explain.

She cuts me off. "Oh, who cares about Tom? Have you seen the new guy?"

"No. Have you?"

"Not yet, but the day is young. Come on." She pulls me along.

"Where are we going? What's your first hour?"

"I have Government. You?"

"Choir."

"We have five minutes until first bell. We're on a mission." She marches. I float. The waves of students separate before us, but we don't find him.

I'm not really interested in finding him, but the vortex of Jordan's energy is impossible to resist.

"We'll try again at lunch," I reassure her.

"I plan to throw you two together and watch you fall madly in love," she says. It's more declaration than wish. She smiles with the self-confidence of a Hollywood superstar, as if it's a beautifully done deal. Jordan has forever reminded me of a Hollywood superstar, the old-fashioned kind, like she belongs to the black and white era of all those old movies she obsesses over, back when eyebrows and angular chins and drastic hair reigned.

"But I have Tom." I say his name, but my mind can only see my summer love and his sky-blue eyes.

"Tom who?" she asks. I giggle and shake my head at her.

"Even if it's *Tom who*, there's still--" I can't say his name. Saying it at home is one thing, but acknowledging his existence here, in the world I share with Tom...

My summer love's final words to me had promised that fate would bring us back together someday if we were truly meant to be. It's the reason he'd insisted on no long-distance trial. But the further I get from him, I have to wonder if fate believes in true love at all. Just look at what fate had dealt my parents, and there never was a more perfect love than Charles and Ginny Fay's.

Jordan's demeanor softens, "I know, Daisy, but I can't help wanting more for you."

I can't bear pity, so I lean in and play a vivacious dance with the notes of my voice.

"More for me? What about more for you? Maybe New Guy is your knight in shining armor."

"Do I look like I need a knight? I've got my own shining armor, thank you very much."

"Yes, you do. I don't know how you do it though. Everything washes off you like rain off a windshield."

"I'm Teflon, baby."

"See you at lunch," I say.

"And maybe we'll see him."

We start toward our classes, and I wonder with growing curiosity if New Guy is a singer. Then I remember something I need to ask Ms. Eckleburg. For three years, the volunteer hours graduation requirement has eluded me. Death of one's parents are considered special circumstances, but only for so long. I still have to do the hours even if I don't want to. Unless I can convince her that some of my summer activities count, I'm going to have to squeeze hours of envelope stuffing or homeless shelter cleaning into my senior year experience.

I shake free of a memory, swivel toward the office door and

freeze. A few inches above a current of bustling students, I see a wave of golden hair—briefly and then it's lost down the far corridor.

For a moment, I'm separated from myself. I'm back in the ocean evening with the cool wind brushing our skin, the wet sand enveloping our toes. I hear his laugh, only it doesn't erase all worry like it did then. It sticks in my heart like a wooden stake. Nevertheless, it sounds so real and so vibrant, I almost run after the blonde head like some kind of psycho.

The bell rings and I run to class wishing desperately I'd never come back to Chicago.

CHAPTER FOUR

Lunch is a madhouse. Swarms of green and gold uniformed students whizz around, searching for their proper landing spots. First day tagging of table tops is essential for rank and order. What is the private school experience without rank and order, after all? I find the corner most table and claim it. Jordan and Nick are late. He has student ambassador duties and she... she does what she wants.

Tom finds me first, and his python of an arm snakes around my shoulders. I don't remember this much PDA last year, but surely it was there. I try to squirm away, but Jordan and Nick arrive and squeeze in on the same side of the table as us.

"I need a view. Did you hear about the party?" she says and surveys the crowd.

"Tell me when you see him," Nick requests and bites into a sandwich.

"Who the hell are you looking for?" Tom's voice booms.

They shush him and answer in unison, "The new guy."

The second they say it, the back of that head pops in my mind again. And, of course, in my ridiculous, over-dramatic psyche, it's Jamie, fulfilling the promises of the universe. I unzip my lunch bag, trying to decide if I'm ravenous or nauseous.

"Jesus, I'm sick of him already," Tom snarks.

"You've seen him?" They turn on Tom like conjoined twins.

"God no. And I don't want to. What's the big fuckin' deal with him anyway?"

I retrieve an apple and prepare to stuff the whole thing in my mouth before I answer and reveal to the world what I'm imagining. What I couldn't stop thinking about for the first four hours of school. What I swear to God I need professional help to get past. New Guy isn't Blonde Guy and Blonde Guy isn't Summer Love.

The apple didn't make to the mouth in time. "I guess we'll find out what the big deal is when we find him, won't we?" *Crunch.* I chew slowly, trying not to cringe, and wait for Tom's comeback.

I've always marveled how all the unfortunate thoughts swimming in my head drift on my voice into open air often before I can dam them up. It was my mother who taught me that not everyone has such trouble with word control.

I was twelve when Dad had come home with a headache at the end of a particularly long day, and I'd prattled something at him.

Mom had leaned over and whispered, "You need to learn to know your thoughts before you speak them." She'd paused, kissed my head, and concluded once he'd left the room, "Not all thoughts are meant for speaking and not all spoken words are meant for thinking."

Tom doesn't comeback. Instead, he frowns at me like I'm speaking gibberish. "Whatever," he says and pulls out his phone to answer a text.

Jordan sits at attention. One eyebrow curves upward. "You're just jealous, Tom, because you aren't invited."

"Invited to what?" He downs the rest of his protein shake and grabs for Nick's peanuts.

Nick rescues the rest of his lunch and stuffs it in his bag. "I do see someone I need to talk to, though."

Jordan raises the other eyebrow and watches Nick walk across the lunchroom to a table of other newspaper nerds. He lowers himself down beside Owen Lees, staff reporter, who smiles too widely at his editor.

"Are they flirting?" I ask.

Jordan's face jerks to me with the precision of a synchronized swimmer. "They absolutely are not."

"Invited to what?" Tom growls louder, bringing me back to the present.

"The new guy's party, that's what. Tonight. After the scrimmage." Jordan answers.

"Why the hell would I want to go to that faggot's party?"

"Tom!" I push him, but he doesn't move.

"What?"

"That word." Jordan fires disapproval at him.

"Well, Nick did say he plays tennis." Tom shrugs. You can tell he thinks he's funny.

Jordan glances at Nick again, across the room. Owen cocks his head and close-mouth grins at Nick's face.

Jordan stands to leave. "You're disgusting, Tom. I'm going to New Guy's party and Daisy is welcome to join me. And he's a swimmer, not a tennis player. And he's also not what you called him." Then she leaves me sitting alone together with Tom like two shipwrecked tourists on a deserted island. Suddenly, I don't care if we are the last two people on Earth, I can't stand the weight of it anymore, and I lift his arm from around me.

"What is wrong with everyone?" His voice lowers.

"Don't talk like that, Tom."

"Like what?" He clearly doesn't know.

I shake my head and turn away.

"Why? Am I making myself look stupid again?" He sounds wounded, but I don't care. I'm too annoyed.

"You said it. I didn't."

His black eyes dart around as if he were considering his next play. "I just don't get why everyone's so crazy over some tennis player."

"Swimmer." A cool remembrance of evening swims rushes over me.

Tom growls in the back of his throat, and after a moment says, "I heard it's not a trust fund. I heard he deals."

I turn back to challenge him. "You can't know that."

Why am I getting so defensive? I don't know this guy. He's a new guy. He's not Jamie. Jamie is a world away.

"I also heard he's not emancipated. That he's faking his age to go back to high school. What freak does something like that?"

"Well, I hear he's a D1 level quarterback," I lie.

"No, you didn't."

"Maybe I did."

"I can tell when you're lying, Daisy." He doesn't even look up from the last of Nick's peanuts as he tosses them in his mouth.

The masses start to clear. The next bell will ring in two minutes. Quickly, my eyes move over the crowd for an unfamiliar face--one I've never, ever seen before that belongs to a swimmer I've never ever swum with before. Except for the freshmen, who barely register, all the students are familiar. They scrape their trays. Those who disperse in my direction smile and wave and say, "Hi Daisy." I smile back.

I can't remember what my next hour is, so I unzip my bag and fish out my paper schedule. It's wrapped around those glossy brochures, so I spread them on the table. Tom notices them. His thick, muscular fingers pick them up.

"What's this?"

"The counselor gave them to me this morning."

"This one isn't even D1. The other two are shit programs."

"I don't play football." The words drift out and I wonder if I'm making myself sound stupid.

"You're cheering for me. We settled this freshman year. We're a team. We go together and we don't go here."

Tom's dream isn't written in my individual plan of study, but it is certainly carved in my brain. He's right. We'd made this decision a long time ago on account of his cousin, Ed. His girlfriend had dumped him one sunny afternoon after a two-mile run when she'd received a text that she'd been accepted to Vassar. Something in Ed's pre-historic view of the world had crumbled that day. In his mind, he'd already bought the ring. He'd found his golden girl, and he was supposed to have been her god. Two years later, he was blowing through his daddy's dollars and crashing his cars into telephone poles until one night he drove into a ditch and never played football again.

I remember the glassy eyed expression on Tom's face when he'd told me the story. We'd only been together a month at the time, but he knew even then that what had happened to his cousin would never happen to us.

The bell rings. Tom throws the peanuts wrapper and the glossy promises in the trash can and heads down the hall. Two of his teammates find him. Their laughter carries through the corridor, then is swallowed by a classroom door.

Except for one bite of apple, I haven't touched my lunch. My hand moves to my empty stomach and stays there as I stand over those dumb brochures resting on a pile of Tom's refuse. The bell rings. I snatch up the top one, the one with streaks of yellow highlighter, and shove it back in my bag.

CHAPTER FIVE

Lucille McKee was born to be a cheerleader. So says her mother. But she's awful. She's horrible. The only thing she's got going for her is her energy. That and loads and loads of her daddy's money.

Unfortunately for us, her daddy's money is inexorably tied to her membership on our cheerleading squad. He pays for camps and uniforms and nice Christmas bonuses for our administration.

"Oh my gawd-uh. What is Myrtle's deal? She's like ignoring everybody. What the hell-uh." Lucille secures a green and gold sequined bow to the top of her pony-tailed head.

I'm in the gym, stretching with the squad in preparation for the First Day of School Pep Rally when Lucille lodges her complaint. I love, love, love the first pep rally of the year. After lunch, I'd decided to screw my head on right and focus on that. Not even Tom's disposal of my college pamphlets or Jordan's obsession with New Guy can ruin my excitement for it.

However, Lucille McKee's obnoxious whining might come close.

Lucille points at Myrtle Grey stretching several feet away from our group circle. It's unlike her, for sure. But I don't concur with Lucille's deduction. Myrtle's not ignoring us. She's avoiding us.

"What the hell-uh," Lucille repeats. "Aren't you gonna make her come over here like everyone else-uh?"

"I'll handle it, Luce." I'm watching Myrtle slump over her legs that are spread out in front of her in a wide V. She's not even trying to stretch, just folded over on herself like a discarded dinner napkin. Disapproval fumes from Lucille like a steeping teapot about to burst.

"Why don't you lead the rest of the stretches today?" I head over to Myrtle. I don't need to see Lucille to visualize the satisfied smugness of her expression.

Myrtle thrives on attention. She soaks it in like starfish soak in sun on a beach. Right now, however, she's more like a catfish out of water. Her shimmering red hair, reminiscent of a cartoon musical mermaid, should be tied back with one of our green and gold bows, but it's not. Instead, it hangs down over her face like a shroud. I grab an extra bow from our team bag and take it to her. I'm the captain. That's my job.

"Here's a bow for you." I lay it down beside her while she stretches from side to side.

"Thanks. I'll put it on in a minute."

After a pause, Myrtle raises her heart-shaped face to me. Her naturally full, red lips always part slightly as if in a perpetual puckered pout. Her cute, perky nose enhances bounteous, searching eyes. Her pale, freckled skin makes the purple and blue bruise around one of them even more shocking. It looks exactly like the shadow of a vicious fist.

"What happened?" I kneel beside her and begin brushing my fingers through her loose curls, pulling the strands into a ponytail.

Myrtle usually has this impressive vitality, an undercurrent of intense giddiness that practically boils under her skin. Her bosom outsizes her petite frame, making her appear thicker than she really is. She's our flyer--like a trapeze artist without anything to grab onto, only sisters to catch her descent.

"I fell," she answers.

I don't believe her.

"On what? It's a wonder you didn't blind yourself." I cringe at how much I sound like my grandmother. I guess that's what happens when you spend the summer together, just the two of us.

Well, the two of us and Jamie. My cheeks burn at the thought of him.

Suddenly, we aren't alone. Catherine, Myrtle's sister, has left her drum-line spot on the other side of the gym where the band is warming up. She crouches beside us and opens a make-up bag. I tie the green and gold ribbon in Myrtle's hair while Catherine dabs power on her cheekbone.

Catherine clucks, "Girl, who opens a door on their own face? I thought you were more graceful than that."

Myrtle side-eyes me. "I opened a door on my own face. Sometimes, I'm such a dork."

Deborah Linn

"So, you fell on a door?" I want to tell her how stupid she's making herself sound, but I can't. She's part of the team.

"I opened the door, and then I fell."

Something inside me wants to reach out and hug her. Instead, I offer a liberating laugh. "We're just glad that's out of your system. No falls today, right?"

"I promise." She smiles.

She and I aren't friends, really, but she's one of us. We're obligated. I'm obligated most of all because I'm captain. I wish I could focus more on finding out what really happened because I still don't believe her. But I can't. Part of me doesn't want to know. A flashback of an old Jack Nicholson movie that my dad loved to watch on repeat plays in my head and the words *you can't handle the truth* shake my conscience like a wagging finger.

The band director calls Catherine back. The look she gives me as she picks up her mallet makes me want to duck. I expected it to come flying at me any second.

As soon as Catherine is back in line, the band starts, and the students rush in. The squad gathers at one end of the gym. Our gymnasts flip all the way to the other side of the student section. East Eggerton is back, whatever individuality we might each have discovered over the summer beaten into submission with Catherine's mallet and habitual blasts of our fight song.

My girls run through our cheers as if their captain hadn't been MIA for the last couple months. Through every stunt, I can only think *Catch Myrtle, Catch Myrtle*. The chant fills my mind and keeps its promise. Myrtle keeps her promise, too. Her stunts are flawless, and the squad catches her every time.

When Coach Wolfsheim invites the football team captain to the floor, Tom winks as he struts past me. The crowd is crazy for him. At that moment, so am I. The undulating energy of the place vibrates between him and his fans, sweeping me into its enchanting rhythm.

My summers are usually spent at cheer practices and sleepovers. I shoot one hand in the air and shake my pom. I really have missed this. This crowd, they are my people. As they quiet their chant to hear Tom's pep talk, I'm reminded of my place in East Eggerton world. There's a symmetry to it, a balance. I look at the cliques in the stands, happy in their unspoken segregation. Our class has taken over the senior section, and all the other grades have filed in. It's how it's supposed to be. Everyone has a place.

Tom's place, for the moment, is in the middle of the gym floor, beside a line of coaches who beam with pride at what it means to have him quarterbacking their team this year. It means everything—for them and, in our senior year, for us. An eye-sweep of the crowd reminds me of the expectation of East Eggerton tradition. Football, homecoming, parties, parades, senior skip days. We are all are a part of that, each in our place. Tom and me, we're the power couple. East Eggerton doesn't do Power Singles, after all.

Tom ends his pep talk and the crowd roars. When he resumes his spot on the front row with his team and their envious hands reach to pat his back and fist bump his hands, he doesn't look at them. He looks straight at me, his graphite eyes writing promises on my heart. It's natural, like rereading an old book you've finished a dozen times. When being with him is like this, what I am without him doesn't matter.

The band beats out our pep song one final time. I flip a hip his way and hold my smile just the way he likes it. With the crash of a cymbal, summer is over.

When the rally ends, even though it's the first day, the gym empties quickly.

"Thanks," Myrtle manages a smile as she returns the bow to me.

"Keep it for the scrimmage tonight," I say, and shove all thoughts of her bruised face away. The make-up held, and she obviously wants to keep it that way.

Our gym is surrounded by a catwalk above it where championship banners line the walls. That's where Catherine waits for her sister. I swear she's shooting daggers at me while Myrtle jogs across the gym floor and up the stairs to her. There's someone else waiting there, too. Wilson George, with a dazed, expectant expression, leans against the top of the railing. Wilson has gained muscle since last year, too. His hair is longer and kind of flops around his face, but I know it's him. His signature slouch can't be mistaken.

He says something to Myrtle. She pauses, gives a complacent nod, and runs, giggling, with Catherine out the exit that leads to the parking lot. Wilson stares after her until the door closes behind her, and he's forced to leave or risk looking desperate. Finally, he heads the other way, through the door that leads back into the school.

Deborah Linn

My heart is still beating high from the energy of the day as I shrug our team bag onto my shoulder and turn for the locker room. Then the beating stops. At least that's how it feels. Myrtle and Catherine and Wilson are gone, but I'm not alone. There's someone else. My breath ceases, and I'm under water again, being pulled out on a powerful undertow of a rogue wave. I drop the bag because every ounce of strength is needed for the simple act of turning my body back around. I focus my eyes up to the catwalk and the exit doors.

His back is to me. He reaches for the door, the one leading to the parking lot, and pulls it open. Waves of golden sunlight break in and he walks out into it. As the door slowly sways to a close, blocking out the illumination of the day and leaving kaleidoscope diamonds in my eyes, I exhale. It's him. The new guy. Only he isn't new at all. Not to me.

CHAPTER SIX

At the end of last school year, when Grandma Betty had suggested a summer on the shore, I had balked at the idea. We hadn't been to the family island for three years--not since before the crash.

I say family island because that's how we refer to it. Tybee Island lies just off the Savannah coast. It's at Georgia's northernmost tip, and its signifying feature is a 250-year-old lighthouse which, along with its ancestors, has weathered storms and erosion, fire and war. It still stands—a beacon, a guiding light, a tourist attraction. A bauble.

The beachy breezes and golden sunsets of Tybee Island run through my family's bloodlines. Butler Avenue, the first boulevard on the island, was named after a distant relative whom my grandmother swears to remember. The memory is impossible, of course, but she surely knew his grandson whose family still owns one of the original grand, beachside homes. Supposedly, the home was a love gift some poor sap had built for his wife who had ultimately hated it and had refused to step foot in the place. That's how it ended up owned by my relative. Grandma Betty's branch of the tree had been practical and calculating enough to scoop up property during moments of tourist drought. They had transformed them into the lovely little successful summer places they are today.

My father grew up there. Thanks to the Air B-n-B wave, his childhood home is usually rented out to folks whose relatives never knew Tybee Island existed until they needed a vacation from the hustle of the city. To me, that house means vacation, but to my dad, it was the comfort of home.

I didn't want to go this past summer, but Grandma had insisted on it. A restorative, she'd called it. I still don't know if she meant for her or me, but one week after cheer camp, we landed on the family island and stayed there for the next two months.

It was on the second beach day that I saw him for the first time. Jamie Gatsby, as I came to know him later, with his sun-bleached hair and golden skin that virtually shimmered, stood three feet in front me, staring out at that historic beacon. I don't think I had ever really looked at the lighthouse before. It had simply always been a backdrop for a lifetime of family vacations. That hot day in June, with the cool breeze edging off the shore, I couldn't stop looking at it—not after I had followed his gaze to it.

I remember wondering at the time how on earth someone so gorgeous could be so mesmerized by anything other than a mirror. Even then, he fulfilled every promise of life and love I'd ever felt in the presence of my parents, and I didn't even know him yet.

"It's powerful, isn't it?" He asked without looking back at me.

"It's old," I joked.

"It's stalwart," he returned.

It's obsolete," I teased.

He turned and smiled at me in a way that every girl in the world wants to be smiled at. "It's ancient, like every tumultuous odyssey of every lovelorn mariner," he said.

It was the most ridiculously pretentious thing I'd ever heard, and I told him as much. "You're trying too hard," I said. Immediately, a nervous jitteriness ran over him but quickly disappeared.

"Are you new to the island?" I asked.

"Very," he answered.

"Would you like for me to show you around? The lighthouse isn't the only cool thing here." Suddenly, I remembered all the cool things of my childhood, and I wanted someone else to know them, too.

In Chicago, I would never have asked a stranger to allow me to show him around. Tybee was different. There were no strangers, only tourists, and new locals, like Jamie. We walked and talked and laughed until we eventually arrived at the neighborhood of quaint, old homes called the Mermaid Cottages.

"I don't think mermaids actually live there," I teased.

"Of course not. What do you think I was searching for near the lighthouse?"

"Oh, they wouldn't live there either. The lighthouse warns ships not to come too close. It guides them away from the shoreline, so they don't run aground. Mermaids are sirens. They sing sailors to their deaths. They are seductresses. They want the men to come to them."

At some point, my voice had taken on that enchanting rhythm it gets when I'm lost in a fantasy. Or so I've been told.

"They do, do they?" Jamie leaned his face close to mine. An urgency beat inside me. I willed him closer. He resisted. I knew, however, that if I wanted to, I could clamp down on the unuttered truth between us. He wanted to kiss me, too. He moved an inch more, and I flipped my hair in his face.

"Pirates mostly."

"What?" he asked.

"They seduced the pirates mostly. True story. Pirates scoured this island for hidey holes for their booty. If you search hard enough, you might just find yourself a treasure." I flipped back around and stared at his spellbound eyes.

"I think I already have."

My breath left me. I could fathom only one thing to say. "Are you a pirate?"

The dimple was back in his cheek and the solid layer of hair that fell in front of his face concealed one eye. For a second, I thought he might be.

"Are you asking if I'm a bad boy?" He cocked a sideways grin at me and shot flirtatiousness out from under his hair.

I mimicked the demeanor. "You know, when girls have the chance to choose the boy, they should always choose the best. I'm not sure dirty pirates with their ill-gotten gains are the best."

He stood straighter and raked his hair back in place. The sides were shorn short, so the top flopped or folded into place, depending on the posture of his neck.

"You seem the type who deserves the best," he said.

And that one statement gave credence to my mother's advice. The rays of the sun warmed us. I pulled a ball cap out of my bag and secured it on my head, pulling my hair through the hole in the back.

As I continued the tour of our family's history, I marveled at his interest. He seemed to evaluate all of it through its connection to me. I could see the admiration in his eyes as if the actual astounding presence of it somehow changed with my explanation of it. The soda shop where my grandfather had fallen in love with Grandma Betty became a tiny pearl on a long, expensive string. The place where the yachts had raced during the '96 Olympic Games and where my father had fallen in love at first sight with my mother became like the most precious gem.

By the end of the day, I had the idea that if he could, he would have wrapped my memories in the glittery awe of his vantage point and re-gifted them to me. Instead, he draped his long arm around me. I nestled in its crook. We shared a cotton-candy, licking the luscious sugar off each other's fingers and longing for the beautiful, golden Tybee Island sunset, not so the day could come to an end, but so the new one could begin.

"I want to spend every day with you." His eyes glimmered when he looked into mine.

"We have all summer." My face would not quit smiling, but the next day he didn't come to the beach. Nor the next day. Nor the next. All I could do was stare at that ancient pillar jutting out of my family's island and try not to cry.

I had never felt so dumb. I had known him for exactly one day. Grandma had scheduled herself in half a dozen recurring old-folks' activities. Also, she had insisted we leave our cell phones back home, so I didn't even have the means to conveniently cry on my best friend's shoulder. I was stuck at the beach with only my family's history and a long expanse of tourists as far as the eye could see. This was supposed to be a restorative. I had to find a way to not regret not kissing him. I had to find a way to forget the most gorgeous, funny, attentive guy I'd ever dreamed existed.

So, I joined a sea glass art class, a group who gathered on the shoreline every morning at the rise of the sun and the receding of the tide. We scavenged out shiny treasures, cleaned up the odd piece of trash, and scurried back to our airy hut to create wind chimes, framed art, and jewelry for a local shop. They sold our wares and donated the proceeds to the historical society. It was a class for tourists, mostly. While I talked casually with the Cohens from Colorado or the DaFontanos from Delaware, I took pride in my family's island. I felt like I was giving back somehow, like I wasn't searching for my place, but helping to sustain it.

Then one afternoon, he wandered into our hut as if he'd gone out for lattes. Whatever steady reality had started to build a rock-solid foundation inside me, flew away on a fairy's wing.

"I knew you'd wait," he said, and his flap of gorgeous hair fell forward to his face, clouding out his ocean-blue eyes.

I wanted to slap him. I wanted to, but I giggled. I couldn't help it. Some sort of happiness bubbled up within me and came out as this foolish giggle. Then he kissed me. It was on the cheek, sweet and innocent, and intoxicating. He stuffed a fifty into the donation jar in exchange for my latest masterpiece. He didn't need a bag, he said, and clasped the leather strand around his neck. On it hung my favorite stone--a vibrant green that seemed to dim and illuminate in an unsyncopated rhythm as it adjusted to the movements of his body. He rubbed it between his thumb and finger.

"It reminds me of you. I think I'll keep it."

"I made it," I said.

"That doesn't surprise me. You surprise me, but that doesn't."

Later, as we slurped lemon ices on the boardwalk, I asked him a question. "How is it that I surprise you? I mean you did say you knew I'd wait for you. Not that I waited, by the way."

"You waited." He smiled and nudged me.

I ignored him. "And you seemed to know which piece I made. So, how is it that I surprise you?"

He answered in a serious manner that I witnessed only once again all summer. "I always knew there would be someone like you waiting for me. No, that's not right. Not someone *like* you. Just you. Just Daisy."

"I don't follow. Where is the surprise?"

"Do you believe in manifestation?"

"You mean like if you believe it, you can achieve it kind of stuff?"

"Sort of. It's more like believing our lives into existence even if the rest of the world doesn't buy it."

I thought of the man whose failure of a house he'd sold to my ancestor. "I'm not sure I do."

"You should. You are a manifestation, Daisy."

I loved the way my name sounded coming from his lips, every intonation of it a new bloom.

He continued, "Sometimes, though, I forget that the universe works to give us our request even when we're focused on a different one. I asked for you a long time ago. I'd almost forgotten you were on your way."

"Now, I'm here." I had absolutely no freaking idea what he was talking about, but it sounded so beautiful, I couldn't not be a part of it. It was after that conversation that I noticed how easily my hand began slipping into his and how my worries erased at the touch of his palm on my back.

From here, I'm sure all the good love stories would have us frolicking alone together, splashing through the next six weeks isolated from humanity, but that's not what happened. He joined my art class, usually bringing lattes with him. We infiltrated a mean group of drunk sand volley ballers and kicked their butts. We held the limbo stick for a group of Florida grandmas, and, yes, we frolicked.

My favorite nights happened at the food truck court with its hanging strings of lights beckoning locals and tourists like a festive carnival. We dined on fish tacos and corn dogs with Ella, the daughter of our art teacher, and Cody, a Koch relative seeking solace for the summer. They were recent college graduates.

"What's your story, Jamie?" Cody asked one night, looking to feed his journalistic soul.

"Not much different than anyone else's," Jamie answered, and I realized I knew nothing about him.

Ella jumped in. "I saw you get on the shuttle last week. I don't usually ride it myself, but mom enjoys the ride. Keeps her close to the people, she says." Ella's family was insanely rich. Her mother had moved them to the island permanently when Ella was seven and her father died. We had that in common. Both of our dead fathers had taken very good care of us. Ella's mom poured her energy and money into historic projects and local people who needed a spiritual lift. Ella had disappeared into the city after high school but couldn't stay away. She was back for good, too.

"I don't mind the shuttle," Jamie answered. They were talking about the little bus that arrived three times a day to transport people across the bridge to Savannah's Central Station. Jamie seemed embarrassed.

"It's convenient," I offered.

"*You* ride the shuttle?" It seemed that I could surprise Jamie after all.

"From time to time. It's convenient," I repeated.

"I'd rather drive," Cody added, sipping his third rum and cola.

"Where were you off to? Shopping?" Ella laughed. Jamie didn't come off as a shopping for pleasure sort.

He smiled and a magical vibe exuded from him, encapsulating us and the blue music wafting over from the live band and the laughter of at least a hundred patrons enjoying the height of the season.

"I was picking up a few things. Did I tell you about my award?"

He pulled out a piece of folded, yellow cardstock and pressed it open on the table.

It was a certificate signed by the mayor of Savannah, titling Jamie as an "Everyday Hero".

"I saved a man once," he said.

Cody glanced Jamie over as if he were judging the credibility of the claim. For a moment, the nervous jitters of that first day vibrated through him. Jamie traced his finger over the letters on the certificate and moved his mouth around the words without actually stating them out loud. You'd have thought he was praying.

"You never told me," I accused.

"I didn't?"

"How did you do it?" I asked.

Cody answered. "I bet it was the Heimlich, huh?"

Jamie nodded.

"It usually is. Unless you're talking someone down from a bridge." Cody nodded his prematurely balding head.

"I've done that, too," Jamie said.

"What?" I smacked his shoulder.

Ella pulled at the collar of his V-neck tee and peeked inside. "Are you Spiderman and we don't know it? Do you have tights and a cape under there?"

"Spiderman doesn't wear a cape," Jamie and Cody scoffed simultaneously.

"You've saved two people?" I asked. I felt like a failure, like I should know this somehow.

"I saved one. The other one, I talked off a metaphorical bridge. Repeatedly. I'm not sure it's the same thing."

Honest consideration hung in the air.

"Everybody has someone like that, don't they?" Jamie finally asked, and I noticed a faint triangle of freckles beside his nose.

Did I have someone like that? I tried to think through everyone I knew, but they were gone to me. I could barely see Chicago. Confusion swirled in my brain as to what was real and what was simply the here and now. I focused hard on the freckle trio until my vision blurred. Jamie's hand wiped something off my cheek.

"Well, it calls for a round anyway." Cody's jovial laugh rang high above us. There wasn't much that didn't call for a round with Cody.

Ella jumped up and returned promptly with a tray full of fruity something-or-others. Jamie stared at them for what seemed like eternity. Quickly, he refolded his award and tucked it away.

Then he clinked his contraband concoction to mine. "Let's celebrate!"

Eventually Ella took Cody away for the night. "They're cute, aren't they?" They'd say the same of us, I'm sure, even though we were much younger, and they shouldn't have been buying us drinks.

Jamie pushed the balance of his alcoholic slushie to the center of the table. "She's bad for him," he answered.

"Bad for him? How? They're adorable."

"She just wants his money."

Laughter lifted out of me and mingled with the island music. "Money? Ella's rich. Her daddy left her a fortune."

"That's what she wants you to think." He was staring now, at nothing. "Her mom does all that charity work because she's waiting for a ninety-year-old billionaire to pluck her up like the prettiest rose."

Sometimes the way he spoke sounded like he was writing a book. I didn't believe him, although I had no reason not to.

"Have you seen where she lives?" he asked.

I hadn't, but I didn't answer. For three songs, he caressed my hands while I wondered when he had seen where she lives. Couples twirled in front of our table. How many of them were waiting to be plucked up? I pointed to a grey-haired vixen and her prince charming.

"What about them? Is she in it for the money?" She talked vibrantly to the couple beside her and fluttered her hand around like she was conducting a choir. Her partner looked at her like she was a pig on a spit, and he hadn't eaten for days.

"She's the rich one," Jamie answered. "She might play with him for a while, but she'll never marry him. It's different for women."

"Are you saying rich girls don't marry poor boys?" I'd meant it in jest, but the truth of it stung me.

"Not if they can help it. Their daddies won't let them."

"My daddy would like you, I think."

His face softened as if he'd settled into a decision. "Let's dance," he offered.

The town square had turned into a ballroom. He spun me in the middle then pulled me into him. It was a bit like cascading on a crashing sea, bumping into couples and laughing at the boldness of it all. The crashing was mostly me. He was a glorious dancer. I mean literally like what you see on the television show. Then the rhythm slowed, and we were two lovers lost on a riptide, floating into something from which there was no rescue.

Having Jamie's arms around me was the most natural and yet most exciting sensation. I clutched one of my hands on the back of his broad shoulder while he cradled the other in his leading hand. Under my fingers, his golden body churned with the potential vitality of a semi-dormant volcano. Yet, on the outside, he seemed cool as a rainbow after a refreshing shower.

"That choking man is not the only person you saved, Jamie," I said because my heart felt like it might burst if I didn't.

"What do you mean?" His soft breath whispered in my ear.

"You saved me, too."

"From what?" For the second time that night, surprise registered in his voice.

"I don't know. From myself. From—" *From Tom,* I thought. It was the first time I'd remembered Tom's existence since the day Jamie and I had gazed at the lighthouse together.

We stopped swaying. Jamie looked down at me. His beautiful face creased between his eyebrows. I'd never seen him worried before.

"What do you need saving from, Daisy? I'll save you from it. I won't let anything hurt you ever again."

I believed him. I couldn't have known then that no one can save you from yourself but you. I wouldn't learn until much later that before you can lift yourself up, you first must test just how far you're willing to let yourself fall.

"I miss my parents, Jamie."

"I know," he pulled me in, and we swayed again. I breathed him into me, and I swear—as cheesy as it sounds—our hearts joined in rhythm.

"I picture them happy, though. Alone on an island kind of like Tybee. Idyllic, golden, epic. I know they loved me. I know they did. But I always felt they loved each other more, like I was an afterthought more than a manifestation of their love. But when I'm with you, it doesn't seem to matter so much."

"You know why?" he asked.

"No, why?"

He stepped back, so he could see into my eyes. The green stone glowed between us. I smiled at him. His goofy grin put me immediately at ease.

"I already told you. I told you the first day we met. You aren't a manifestation of their love. You're a manifestation of mine."

Then he kissed me. Not on the cheek this time, but full on the lips, and all the rushing of the oceans and the smoldering of a thousand golden sunrises combined us. The island dream was ours. The ocean was ours. The world and all the stars were ours.

It wasn't until years later while hearing the news of an exhilarating, haunting death on the high seas of one member of a honeymoon party that I realized every word he'd said about Ella and Cody was true.

CHAPTER SEVEN

I am sitting on my bed in my cheer uniform, resisting the urge to stuff cheese dip and chips into my mouth as I desperately ramble all this to Jordan. I have to be at the football field in an hour, but nothing seems right.

"You really think it was him you saw leaving the gym after the pep rally?" Jordan asks, licking cheese off her fingers. She never dips the chips but can't resist the cheese. It's the only completely impulse-driven, non-calculated action in her repertoire.

"What I really think is that I'm losing my damn mind."

"How could it be him? How could it possibly be him? Wouldn't he have texted you or called if he was moving here?"

"We don't have each other's numbers."

"What?"

I shrug.

"How is *that* even possible?" she asks. She continues sucking her cheesy fingers.

"You know Grandma didn't let me bring my phone, and we were together nearly every day. At least part of every day. Evenings mostly." Except for the days he'd disappeared. There had been those. "There wouldn't have been a need to text even if I'd had my phone with me," I explain.

Confusion wrinkles every part of her, then her eyes find their spot on the ceiling. "How does one date someone without texting first?"

The answer evades even me, but the presence of a beach and a lighthouse and a history of hearts flowing together like water is surely involved.

"Were we dating?" I ask.

"Well, yes."

"Dating seems like it's meant to lead somewhere. I don't know if we were dating so much as we just were."

"Were what?" She seems annoyed.

"Just... were."

"But he did know you were leaving the island and coming home, right?" Jordan turns to me with astonishment.

"Yes. He knew. He said the universe would reunite us, that it had worked too hard to bring us together. It couldn't keep us apart. It would go against physics or something." My brain searches hard for his exact words.

I lift the green bead from where it dangles on my chest and extend it for Jordan to see.

"We were standing barefoot at the edge of the ocean when he clasped this around my neck. He said, 'Hang on to this for me, okay?' I asked him, 'Don't you want it anymore?'

"He said, 'I do. You can give it back to me when we reunite.' Then he stared at it for a long time. 'Or maybe not,' he said. 'I like looking at it on you. It's a beacon stronger than our lighthouse, a reminder of the dream you used to be and the truth of us now. As long as it hangs over your heart, we're still united.'"

A huge smile takes over my face. I fall back into my bed full of plump pillows and sigh like a ridiculous, lovestruck, soap opera diva.

"That. Is. The. Dumbest thing I've ever heard. That's dumber than Tom."

"Please don't. There is no comparison." I give in and stuff a few chips in my mouth.

"Ok, but if this guy is so great, why are you still with Tom? Daisy, none of this makes any sense at all."

"Love doesn't always make sense." Jamie's words float back to me like a deflated pool toy.

"How about social media?" Jordan grabs her cell from her back pocket.

"He doesn't believe in it."

"Now, isn't that convenient? Daisy, are you sure this guy even exists at all? Are you sure you didn't dream him?"

"Actually, no. The whole summer felt more like a dream than reality. But at the same time, it was more real than anything I've ever known."

I scoot back to my headboard, my mind swimming in a pool of hungry sharks. I continue. "His mom is dead, too. Did I tell you that?"

Just Daisy

"No. You didn't. You've hardly told me anything before today except the fact that you had a summer fling that made you want to dump Tom which is the smartest thing I've ever heard in my life."

"It wasn't like that. It's not that it made me want to dump Tom. It's just that when I'm with Jamie, the world makes sense. We are two castaways with only each other for survival."

"That's weird, Daisy. I'm just gonna tell you right now. No one fantasizes as much about being stranded on an island as you. It's an odd fantasy. You know that, don't you?" She keeps scrolling on her cell.

"I can't help it."

"Come on over to dry land once in a while. It's fine. Finer than the water, I promise. No tidal waves. No hurricanes. No beached whales. Just miles and miles of traffic jams and suburbs."

She scoots off the bed into the adjoining bathroom to wash her hands.

"Oh, now that's appealing. You'd rather be stranded in your car on a filthy highway? What about accidents?" I ask.

"At least I know there's indoor plumbing and probably a donut shop nearby. Besides, a good driver can avoid collisions."

I wait until she's in the bedroom again before I answer.

"Not everyone who thinks they're a good driver is actually a good driver, Jordan." The undammed words spill out and seep into the cracks of our conversation.

She cringes, obviously aware she's chosen the wrong metaphor.

"Look. Maybe you are remembering him wrong. Do you even have a picture?"

"I do." I jump off the bed. Jordan catches the cheesy bowl, and I run to my desk. From the middle drawer, I pull out a narrow strip of photo booth pics. In the pictures, we smile first at the camera, then at each other, then we're too lost in each other to smile.

I hand her the picture strip, and we plop back down on the bed.

"He is dreamy. Do people say that, dreamy?" Jordan asks.

"Only you, Jordan. But yes, that's the word. Dreamy."

"But you saw him from the back today. How do you know it's him? How could it possibly…"

I sigh. "I know. I mean I don't know."

Jordan wraps one of my curls around her forefinger then lets it spring back into place. "You, my love, are a mess. A real mess."

"You did say you wanted to throw me together with New Guy and make us fall madly in love. Maybe you're conspiring with the universe and don't even know it."

"If it gets you to dump Tom, I'll conspire with Hades, himself. Hell, I'd throw you together with Owen to keep you away from Tom."

I nudge her. "To keep Owen away from Nick?"

Jordan's eyes are big, and her glamour girl make-up accentuates them. When she rolls them at me, I nearly hold out my hand, ready to catch them should they fall right out of her head.

"Okay, let's make a plan. We need to find New Guy and see if he is, in fact, Mr. Dreamy," Jordan says.

"We'll hunt him down and peel off his mask like the police in a Scooby Doo cartoon." I bounce on my bed. We're fourth grade again, planning escapades we'll never take.

"Don't be dramatic, Daisy. We're just going to stalk him a little," she says.

"How?"

"Last name?

"G-a-t-s-b-y. Gatsby."

"Gatsby? Dear God."

"Yes, Gatsby. What's wrong with Gatsby?"

"Who ever heard of a name like that? It doesn't sound real. He sounds like an overdrawn character from a tawdry novel."

Her fingers fly over her phone. "Was he visiting Tybee, or does he live there?"

"Visiting. I think. Or just moved there." It's embarrassing how little I know.

"Is he from Savannah then?'

"He must be." I shrug.

She shakes her head. "Why must he be? You aren't and you were there."

Her eyes brighten and her lips curl into a smile similar to the Grinch when he gets his idea to pillage Whoville.

"Well, look at that. I found him. James Gatsby II. Savannah, Georgia, arrested for DUI. DUI?"

"Let me see." I grab her phone and click on the link. Relief floods my veins. The sad, craggy face staring back at me from that mug shot is definitely not my Jamie. I scan the associated news story.

Apparently, the guy had rammed his car through the front window of an unsuspecting bistro.

Jordan laughs and I toss the phone at her.

"Not funny."

"They have to be related though, don't you think? Is Jamie a Gatsby the third?"

"No way is that homeless looking hobo related to my dream boy."

She examines the guilty face. "I don't know…"

"No way."

She side-eyes me. "I guess we'll find out once we hunt him down."

"So, we're back to the Scooby Doo plan?"

"We're back to me going to his party. Unless he shows up at the scrimmage tonight and you turn around from celebrating one of Tom's world-ending touchdowns and he's just standing there in the bleachers in the middle of the student section with all the blessing of the manifesting universe shining down on him like a benediction. Ooo, wouldn't that be juicy?"

"Now, who's being dramatic?"

She swoons and falls on the bed.

"You know I can't go to the party. I'm with Tom after the game."

"Yeah, yeah. I know."

"But Jordan, what if it isn't Jamie? Then what?"

"My plan still holds. You think the universe is powerful? Just wait until I get a hold of your destiny." I've never seen her more determined, and I'm curiously afraid for a second.

"Then again, what if it *is* Jamie?" I ask.

Her head tilts back, and all the angles of her face point upward, but her eyes are narrowed and glance at me from their squinted corners.

"What if it is? What are you going to do about Tom?" Then she moves her gaze back to the ceiling again as if the answer were blazoned on the crown molding.

"I wish I were strong like you, Jordan, but I don't really know if I can leave him."

She doesn't budge. "Do you mean you can't be without him or that you can't physically open your mouth and tell him it's over?"

I can't answer. I don't know. And I don't know why. It should be so very uncomplicatedly simple, but fear snakes through me at even the idea of it.

Grandma Betty taps on my bedroom door.

"Are you coming home after the scrimmage, dear?" she asks, peeking her head in.

"Eventually, Grandma." A bleak understanding catches in my chest that my heart and the rest of me might be forever detached. It is already beating far away, basking in the golden sun, and I am here with the traffic jams and bad drivers and donut shops.

Jordan springs from the bed and hands her cell to grandma. "Take our picture, will you?"

Grandma adjusts the phone. She's a pro at this, very phone pic savvy for a grandma. Jordan poses beside me, and I'm once again a porcelain doll, part of a collection praised and admired by my movie starlet best friend. We smile. Grandma counts to three and returns the phone.

"I'll have a little something for you to eat when you get back." She scoops up the discarded chips and dip and carries them out the door.

"What's the picture for?" I ask and resume my make-up and hair.

"In case I lose you to the universe. I want some evidence of our friendship." Her laugh is low and calculated.

"Now, that's the dumbest thing *I've* ever heard."

Jordan picks up the photo booth strip and snaps a shot of it. "Well, I'm going to New Guy's party tonight. I'm going to solve the mystery, and then we'll know."

The soft rumble of a sleeping volcano floods my soul, and my ears fill with the noise of crashing waves. I barely hear her final words before we head out the door.

"A confident woman is a powerful thing, Daisy. The universe be damned."

CHAPTER EIGHT

"You better get it together, girl. Ms. Quinn is not happy-uh." Lucille snaps her fingers and purses her duck lips at me as she trots away to join her friends after the scrimmage. I can tell she's been holding that comment in since third quarter, but she stands at the other end of our line-up, too far away to nag me.

Ms. Quinn is our cheer coach, and Lucille is right. She's not happy. She reprimanded me three times for missing fight song cues from the band and once for forgetting to pull out the t-shirt cannons at halftime.

I couldn't help it. I was distracted. I thought I saw Jamie once at the beginning of the scrimmage, but it turned out to be Peter Jewett, a senior who thinks he's the next American Idol. He's tried out four times, but he was so stoned the last time, he couldn't remember the words to his song. They dismissed him and told him not to come back. It was his blond hair that had tricked me. I'd spent the next quarter trying to convince myself it had been him in the gym.

Now, most everyone is gone from the stands. With the crowd dispersed, my attention is drawn to Myrtle. She eagerly grabs one of the team bags.

When Myrtle walks over to me, I feel as surprised as Nick is on the daily over some sort of revelation. I'm always surprised by Myrtle--by her height that is. She fills space in a way that towers over, well, everything. In physical stature, however, she's short but not tiny. But not fat, either. The surplus curves of her body radiate a smoldering vitality that always makes me think I'd do that in a heartbeat if I were a guy. Plenty have, according to the rumors. The way she thrusts her bust forward and whips her luscious hair in the presence of any male within whiffing distance doesn't help dispel any of them.

"Wasn't that exciting?" She asks, her shiner shining at me through sweat-melted make-up.

I realize she means the scrimmage.

"It was a good one." I don't actually know that it was except for the final score. There was a time I would have tracked Tom's every throw until I realized one day what a time waster it was. He always replays every move for me in a masculine rush of words during a drive to somewhere after every game until we eventually end up at some party or in his basement, alone and unsupervised by parents or conscience.

"Tom was on fire, huh?" Her eyes light up. I check the score again. 42 - 21.

"I guess so."

"Guess so?" She lets loose an empty, envious laugh, and I stare at her.

Smudged mascara and eyeliner mingle with that bruise in a way that I can't discern what's real from what might be wiped away with a moistened cotton ball.

"Are you going to that party?" She changes the subject. "I mean are you and Tom going?"

Suddenly, my head hurts. How could I go to the party? But I want to. Of course, I want to. My brain has been talking itself into and out of believing what I saw since the pep rally. I want to know, and yet I don't. How would I deal with my two worlds crashing into each other like that? My whole being would feel exactly how Myrtle's eye looks.

"Myrtle, follow me." I take her into the bathroom under the bleachers with a warning from the SRO that they want everyone out now. I give him the thumbs up.

I pull my makeup bag from my purse. "Do you mind? I mean, if you are going to a party." Something inside me wants to bubble over in its own empty, envious laugh, but I clamp it down. Myrtle lets me fix her face, but she's embarrassed. So am I, though my foggy brain can't fathom why.

"So, are you guys going?" she asks.

"Probably not. Tom won't want to."

"Oh." She looks down. There's no way a door caused this bruise.

"Does it hurt?"

"Not anymore. It was stupid. Completely my own fault. Thanks for helping me hide it. Your makeup always looks so natural. How do you get like that?"

"I don't know. Practice, I guess." *I don't try as hard as you,* I think. Wow. How condescending. I press my lips together, a little disgusted at my place in the world.

"You're so lucky, Daisy."

"Lucky? How?" I layer on blush over the concealing mineral powder.

"Well, Tom, for one."

"Oh. Sure. I guess so."

That laugh again. "You guess so? It's not a guess. You are. He's…"

"The top guy." My voice sounds too snarky.

Her face scrunches. "That's one way to put it."

I add shadow, so guys will notice her eyes, not the bruise. I feel very big sister-ish. "Let me ask you something, Myrtle. Would you ever follow a guy to college just because he wants you to? Not because there's anything in it for you really. Only because that's what he wants. Would you do it?"

"Absolutely." She's bubbling now, those usually pursed lips smiling like she's been handed the final rose and some sexy bachelor is kneeling before her.

"Really? Just like that?"

"Of course. If a guy loves you enough to want you there with him, why not? You'd be a fool not to."

I'm done. I gather the brushes and stuff off the sink. She touches her eye socket bone as if she can distinguish its finish through her fingertips.

"You're beautiful," I say because I'm certain she needs to hear it.

"A beautiful fool, huh?" She whispers, examining her reflection in the dim mirror.

"Sometimes the best thing a girl can be in this life is a beautiful little fool." The words are remnants of something my mother used to say. They hang in the air between us, waiting for one of us to scoop them up like butterflies in a net.

Myrtle's body moves to their invisible rhythm. She breathes them in. "As long as you're a fool for love, nothing seems foolish at all." She finishes her perfected look with a subtle lip gloss and kisses at the mirror.

Three violent thumps on the bathroom door startle us. It's time to leave. I walk with her to the parking lot. Tom waits impatiently, leaning his punishing athleticism against the frame of his Hummer.

"Have fun at the party," I offer, but Myrtle is gone.

Tom opens the back door for my bags and then squeezes me in a victorious hug. He's happy. The night is his. I'm happy when he's happy. On the rare occasion of a genuine smile, his teeth shine like iridescent pearls. He kisses me hard on the lips, and I know I've completed his world by letting him.

He replays the scrimmage right there in the parking lot. His arm pumps with each remembered throw. He zigs and zags against imaginary enemies. Finally, he flexes and cries out like a Viking warrior.

I'm happy when he's happy.

"It's gonna be a great year," he says, exhaling like he's just run through the finish line.

Now I'm the one leaning against the car. He leans over me, a giant arm on each side. He does a standing push-up and plants his lips on mine. Behind him, I see something I've never seen before. Not in real life, anyway.

It's a circus-yellow, 1969 Ford Mustang Mach 1. I know a little about cars. My father loved to take me to the car shows and talk incessantly with men who knew more than he did about paint and parts. He never owned one. He had a yacht. Now, I have a yacht. I might rather have had the Mustang.

I know the car wasn't there before. I know with absolute certainty. I would have noticed on the way out of the stadium. It would have detoured me away from Tom.

The car is super cool, so cool at first, I don't see the driver opening the passenger side door for a tall, slender brunette whose style belongs seated in a roadster more than a muscle car. Before Jordan disappears into the dream of a vehicle, the driver leans into her and whispers something. She kisses his cheek and, with the unbridled giddiness of an underdog Oscar winner, hugs him. The driver closes the door, swoops his tanned hand through a layer of perfect blonde hair, and looks dead-on at me as he moves around his Mach 1 to the driver's side. As he lowers himself into position, a distinct squeal of excitement escapes into the atmosphere. It's Jordan, making a noise I didn't even know she was capable of. But that's not what causes my knees to crumble so that Tom literally has to catch me mid-fall.

I'm reminded of the first time I saw Jamie on Tybee and the distinct feeling that a band of mischievous fairies had just stolen every sense of reality from my brain and carried it away on their feathery wings. Tom's strength balances me, but for a moment, I'm not in East Eggerton's stadium parking lot. I'm on a beach, staring at a lighthouse with my big, beautiful fish. The universe has found a way. Anything can happen--anything at all. Even Jamie can happen. Excitement, fear, panic, exuberance shoot through me.

Then Jamie does something. He guns the motor in an obnoxious peacock display of testosterone. Jordan's odd squeal flies into the air as the car jettisons past us through several sparse rows of cars and out of the parking lot.

"What the fuck?" Tom shoves his middle finger in the air.

"Tom, don't." I pull his hand down.

"Why not? What a dumbass. Did you see that ridiculous car? Somebody's has-been father must be giving a joy ride to his gold-digging girlfriend."

"You don't know that." *What is Jordan doing with Jamie?*

"Yes, I do, Daisy. Who the hell else would drive a car that stupid?"

Why is Jordan hugging Jamie? Why is he running off with her and not me?

"I don't know. You drive a Hummer." The words are out before I can stop them. Again.

He leans aggressively in, his face an inch from mine. "You got a problem with my Hummer?"

Tom's hot breath invades my air. I turn to look after Jordan and Jamie. She looked pretty friendly for someone who wanted to throw me together with the very guy she's hugging, she's squealing over. Especially for someone who literally never squeals.

"Daisy!" Tom yells, but I ignore him. The car is too far away to see now, but I can't stop looking, wishing, wondering.

Jamie saw me. I know he saw me. He didn't smile. He didn't wave. He didn't do anything but put Jordan in his car and haul ass out of the parking lot. *A confident woman is a powerful thing, Daisy. The universe be damned.* Was she damning my universe?

"You didn't have a problem with my Hummer when I had you in the backseat of it." Tom leans in to kiss my neck.

Bile curdles in my stomach. I pull back.

"It's just that it's a cool car. My dad would've loved that car." I can hear him now. That's the kind of car a top guy drives, he would have said. I try to squirm out from under Tom.

"Yeah, well your dad didn't know shit about a real man's car. He drove a Lexus. Of course, he didn't have some gold-digging girlfriend he was trying to impress. That we know of." He mumbles out those last words, but not low enough. I hear them.

Apparently, I have no more control over my body than I do my words, because my hand shoots out and slaps his face.

He grabs my wrist, and before I know it, the oppressive weight of him is on me, pressing me into his ridiculous macho mobile. His face is so close, I can't even see it. "Don't ever fucking do that again."

If a body part could vocalize pain, my wrist would scream. The bones seem squeezed so tight, there's no blood flow. My fingers turn cold, my face hot.

"Tom, my wrist," I gasp, and he releases, but his hand moves to my throat.

"Did you hear me? Never again."

I nod and try to swallow. He lets go. I inhale against quivering lips, refusing to cry.

"Get in," he commands and stomps around to the driver's side door. I look around. There are fewer vehicles, it seems, than just minutes ago. Did any of them see us? Did any of them care? I scour the place for late leavers. Across the way, the SRO climbs into his cruiser and cruises off. I have no choice. I obey.

I know what's next. It's either hanging with the guys or it's his place. Either way, he'll want to celebrate. He'll want to relive his power on the football field in the rustled sheets of someone's bed, unhindered by clothes or morals.

I buckle in. His meaty hand finds my thigh. It's not a caress. It's a grip.

"I have a headache, Tom. Can you please take me home?"

"We'll take care of it at my house."

"Please." My voice wavers.

He smirks.

"You insulted my father, Tom. My dead father."

A very real pain shoots through my being. It's the first time I've ever used their deaths for manipulative purposes. What choice do I have? No one else is coming to my rescue, and I'd like to think if my dad were still alive, he would have.

"You know what? Fine. Sometimes you can be such a little bitch, you know that?"

He doesn't say another word until he pulls into the drive. He reaches over tentatively. "How's your head?" His voice is soft and inquisitive.

"I told you. It hurts."

"Daisy, don't be mad. I get worked up on the field. It's hard to come down." He leans to me and caresses my neck with his lips. I need air. I open the door.

"I'm not mad. I just have a headache."

"And that asshole just pissed me off."

"Because he drove through our parking lot?"

He pulls his hand back, and I prepare for it to swing my direction. He drops it to his lap instead. "Yeah," he mocks, "because he drove through our parking lot."

The stare-off lasts a full two minutes before I hear the vibration of his phone. He pulls it out and doesn't look at me again before I exit the Hummer and go inside.

CHAPTER NINE

It's Saturday morning, and I'm moping in bed. I haven't heard from Jordan. I fish my cell from a twisted bunch of blanket and text her again.

Come on, Jordan. I've resorted to VOICE MESSAGES.

I've left her three already.

No answer. Myrtle's giddy fool for love foolishness runs through my brain, and all I can think is that being a fool for friendship might be worse. Jordan knows it's Jamie. My heart clenches like I'm riding that beach roller coaster again and the wind is whipping my hair and Jamie is holding my hand, but the track divides and we slip apart.

I sink down in my pillows and pull the fluffy comforter tighter. Poor Tom.

Wait. Poor Tom? How am I possibly feeling sorry for him?

Last night, if Tom had had his way, we would have ended up in his basement bedroom in a very carnal celebration of his prowess. Ironically, it was really Jamie who saved me. When he screeched by in his party crasher of a car, the trajectory of the evening changed.

I remember his promise. *I won't let anything hurt you ever again.*

That car. That beautiful Mach 1. He didn't have that car on the island. At least he never mentioned it. We never rode in it. Of course, we never rode in any car. Yet, he really is here in Chicago, driving around and picking up girls in an automobile my father would have salivated over. The 1969 Mach 1 was more than a muscle car. It was built expressly to lure young drivers, mad with passion for speed and fashion. It was Ford's promise for the future.

I snatch a wad of tissues from beside my pillow and press them into my eyes. Not again. You'd think the tear ducts would be empty by now.

1969 Mustang Mach 1. Like the car matters. I mean it matters. Of course, it matters, but it's not how I remember him. It's not how I picture him, even now that I've seen him drive away, laughing with my friend. Heat crawls up my neck. My cheeks burn. My friend. My big, beautiful fish. And that trophy of a car. It's too weird to be true.

What really matters is that Jamie saw Tom hovering over me, close enough to kiss, and then he drove away with my best friend.

I pull the comforter all the way over my head. My phone buzzes. I grab it. It's not Jordan. It's Nick.

Get gussied up. I'm taking you to lunch.

Gussied? Sounds like something Gma Betty would say. LOL

She did. That's where I got it.

Sweet but I'm not really in a gussied up mood.

You will be. See you at noon.

Where?

I'll pick you up.

Grandma Betty does Zumba on Saturday afternoons. She'll be leaving in an hour. Tom is currently watching game film, so I'm not allowed to see him even if I wanted to, which I don't. Not right now. And Jamie, I'm starting to doubt the Jamie I remember even exists. But if he does, he rode off into the sunset last night with my best friend who apparently isn't speaking to me. My life is a pathetic mirage. So, I agree to lunch.

Is there anything worse than a pity-date with your cousin? Yes. A pity-date with your cousin the day after you see your best friend practically elope with the love of your life, abandoning you in a dark parking lot while you wrack your brain for ways to ward off celebratory sex with your top-guy boyfriend.

It takes me thirty whole minutes to drag my butt out of bed and into the shower. Only the incessant tapping of Grandma Betty on my door urging me to "get ready, Nicky's coming", gets me moving.

Apparently, he'd texted her, too. She won't leave until I'm up and at 'em, as she puts it.

When Nick arrives, he's tightlipped and boldly nervous. He doesn't drive me to Lucky Luca's Pizzeria as I'd imagined he would.

"Where are you taking me?" I ask.

"It's a secret."

"A secret? From whom? From me?"

"From the world, I think." He smiles with kind surprise. He looks good. His brown mop of hair appears ready to be tussled, as always, but his glasses are suspiciously as clean as his shaven face. His button-down shirt with the snap pockets on the chest is even pressed.

He pulls into Tuolomee Apartments, a new complex that suburbanites had initially petitioned against. An eyesore, they'd called it, beckoning the imposters and wanna-bes. Of course, it had all been worded much nicer to subdue the elitism and enhance the logic.

"Do they have pizza here?" I laugh. I have no idea why we're here, but my brain is too full to care.

"Pizza? No. Would that have been better? I didn't think of pizza."

"No. It's fine. Whatever you have planned is fine." My headache returns as Nick turns into a parking space already inhabited by an orange cone.

"Hold on," he demands, his assurance wavering. He jumps out, moves the cone, and jumps back in. With the car finally secure, he switches off the ignition.

He slaps his hands onto his thighs, releases a sigh and faces me. "Are you ready for this?"

"Well, you have me all gussied up. I'm guessing it's for more than stealing a reserved parking spot."

Although what it's for, I can't imagine. In fact, I try not to. It could only worsen the headache. Anyway, I trust Nick. He's family. He's blood. If nothing else, he's offering a distraction from Tom and Jamie and Jordan.

He frowns in confusion then looks at the discarded cone as if it might come to life and arrest him. "Stealing a parking spot? What, that?" He shrugs it away and we exit the car.

We power walk three flights up to the top apartment in the center tower of the bright and intruding complex. He knocks. No answer. Then he shakes loose a forgotten instruction and turns the handle.

Just Daisy

It's the flowers I notice first. The apartment itself is spacious and airy with big windows expanding the entire wall on the far side of the room. The curtain panels are drawn, but the light still gets in. It shines in waves over baskets and baskets of daisies--white, yellow, pink. They sit on glass side tables and on the granite tile floor. They nestle on top of fuzzy ottomans and into mirrored corners. They cascade down open-shelved bookcases, smiling out from between stacks of leather-bound journals and powdery classics.

"Nick? Are you in love with me?" I ask, turning my voice to song.

"Hold on," he says for the second time and disappears into what I assume is the kitchen.

I hear nothing at first, then it comes in hushed murmurs and spikes of Nick's reassurance. "She's nervous, too... You're being a child... She's come all this way..."

My breath stops. Through the doorway, he's waiting. I didn't hear his voice, but I'm as sure as the sun rising tomorrow. I don't mean to sneak up on them, but I can't help it. I step into the kitchen. There he is. He is everything I remember, even though his face is hidden under a blonde layer and a bent neck. His toned shoulders stretch my favorite tee across his swimmer's chest.

"Nick?" I ask because if I intone Jamie's name, it might break the spell. I might wake up amidst a cloud of fluffy comforter and pillows and cry because my heart still sits on a beach a world away.

Then Jamie lifts his eyes and smiles at me as if he's coming home from a long voyage.

"It's awfully good to see you again," I say.

"I'll leave you to it then," Nick says and starts to go.

Jamie fumbles. I grab Nick's hand. "You're leaving?"

"I have my own lunch date." He smiles and blushes.

"With Owen?" I ask.

"Owen? No." He seems hurt. I question him with my eyes. He squints.

"You don't have to go," Jamie finally speaks, looking at me but addressing Nick.

"I think I do," Nick is confident, more than we are, for sure. I reach out for Jamie. He pulls me into him, and all the stars fall into place.

"Enjoy lunch," Nick says, and with that, he's gone.

"I suppose he'll come back or am I your captive?" My voice finds him. I remember the way he'd pause when we would first come together every morning on the island and I'd call, "Good Morning" over the receding tide. It was like listening to the first beats of a favorite song, he'd said.

He pulls me in again and rests his chin on my head. He breathes in, slow and deep, as if trying to inhale every bit of us. I do, too.

"You smell like summer." My laugh tinkles off the glass orbs hanging over the kitchen island.

"Is this okay? Is this a good idea? Is it a mistake?" The shaking of his voice surprises me.

I pull away, so I can smile into his ocean blue eyes. "How could it possibly be a mistake? I think it's more like a miracle." I hear the music of my voice. It hasn't sounded so lovely since the island. I lean in, my lips eager for his.

He grabs my hand. "Let me show you around."

"Wait, wait. How are you here? Where is your dad? Are you alone? This is crazy. It's crazy good, but still. How on earth?" I'm laughing again because I actually don't care about any of it. I don't want to know. I only want Jamie and me and forever and for the world to disappear.

"Let me show you where I live, first," he insists.

We're two kids let loose in a playground. Tuolomee toys with us. We stroll around the lake in the center of the complex and throw a few balls with labradoodles in the dog park. A young couple tosses a volleyball over a net nearby, and I swear Jamie has somehow beamed Ella and Cody here, too. We walk past them on our way back around the lake. They're older and too formal to be an art teacher's daughter and a disillusioned trust-fund baby summering in Savannah. Jamie seems older, too. It's weird. He belongs in this glamorous resort with its virtual golf park, Pilates studio, and shiny finishes. Yet, at the same time, he doesn't. It's like he balances a timid toe in each world, and I'm his guiding beacon.

"I can't believe you're here." We're strolling the courtyard walking path. I keep looking at him, afraid he might dissolve in mid-air if I stop.

"Well, believe it." He kisses the back of my hand.

What's not to believe? Still, the Jamie rumors discussed at

Just Daisy

lunch—was that just yesterday—resound in my head. None of them are true, of course.

"Where's your father?" I ask.

"My father? What do you mean?"

"Isn't he here with you?"

"My father's dead, Daisy. You know that."

I flinch against an unwelcome memory of two matching caskets and the crying of a couple hundred mourners who have never once come by my grandma's house since the funeral.

"You didn't tell me that. I would have remembered." I stop walking and force him to look me in the eye.

"I did. We talked about it that day with Ella. Remember. Cody offered us each one of his stepfathers. He has enough of them." Jamie's laugh brought it all back.

"I thought it was your mother." I hate myself for remembering wrong. Who remembers something like that wrong? Me, of all people.

"No. Not my mother." His happy, forgiving smile soothes me. He swings our clasped hands between us as we continue to the club house.

"What do you think of the place?" he asks.

"It's paradise. Not an eyesore at all." I stand taller, somehow proud to have proven the suburbanite petitioners wrong. I look around at the brick, castle-esque buildings, with their windows gazing out like the eyes of knowing busy-bodies. I don't care. They don't know me. Jamie squeezes my hand. I smile at him. They don't know me at all. Maybe I don't even know me either because if I had asked myself three weeks ago if I'd ever in a million lifetimes find myself strolling with Jamie Gatsby around the lake of a rebellious, snobby little apartment compound, I would have laughed at myself for sounding so stupid.

"There's one more place I want to show you." He leads me to the club house and into the workout room. It's massive. Mirrored walls line the room filled with beeping treadmills and blue yoga mats and shiny barbells. Music pumps through speakers high on the wall. I wouldn't be surprised to see trapeze bars hanging from the ceiling. We make faces in the mirror. He flexes like a strong man, and I curtsey like a cute clown.

"I have a surprise for you," he says.

"Aren't you surprise enough?" I want to kiss him so badly, my lips ache.

He reaches a shaking hand toward me and gathers in his fingers my green sea glass bead hanging on its leather strand. His knuckles brush across my chest. I can't breathe. For a second, I want to shimmy out of my gussy little green sundress and press my body against his. I moisten my lips and wait.

He nods to the locker beside us. "Look in there."

He's killing me. That's the surprise. He's slowly trying to torture me to death by not kissing me. Why won't he just kiss me already? Swallowing my pride and my urges and every tingling sensation, I open the locker to find a bikini with a matching towel.

"I think I got the size right. Let's go for a swim." Nerves dance in my stomach. I'd spent my summer gazing at his half-naked bronze body shining against the backdrop of that ancient lighthouse and crashing waves, and I had mostly behaved myself. However, I'm utterly certain that in those two months, I'd used up every single ounce of willpower. I glance to the pool just on the other side of the glass wall. We would have it to ourselves.

Jamie moves his hand so his palm rests on my spaghetti-strapped shoulder. The warmth of a hundred summer days fills me.

"What if you see me in this bikini and you can't control yourself?" I risk and my voice undulates seductively.

"I'm sure I won't be able to."

He opens the locker beside mine and takes out my favorite trunks. He starts toward the men's locker room.

"Promise?" I whisper, but he hears me.

He turns back to me with a flirty grin that immediately disappears. In one move, his lips are on mine, his hands in my hair, his energy overwhelming me.

We never make it to the pool. I barely remember running back to his apartment, to his room. We never make it into our swimsuits, but we certainly make it out of our clothes. It is all a mad rush until he has me stripped from all pretenses, laying on his blue satin sheets. We don't leave the room for the rest of the afternoon.

At some point, I lean on one elbow and splay the fingers of my other hand on his gorgeous chest.

"How are you here? How is this possible?" I ask.

"I told you the universe would bring us back together."

"Wait. Did you plan this? Did you have it planned even then?"

His eyes search mine for the answer.

Just Daisy

"When you have money," he finally confesses, "you have choices. Just call it fate."

"I think you found a way to make your own fate."

"And yours," he says and kisses me like he doesn't ever want to stop, and I kiss him back because I don't want to either. Ever. And because I know it can't last. I've done a good job of ignoring that fact all day, but it churns up in me now.

The reality of what I've done hits me with the force of a speeding semi-truck. I have crossed over a line that I can't cross back. I fucked Jamie. The words sound too crass for the slow, sultry kisses and crashing waves of emotion we'd just experienced, but that's what it was. That's what Tom would call it. That's what he always called it when laughing about some locker room gossip he'd just heard. *Benny fucked Jacqueline last night. Did you hear?* Then he'd make a disgusting face and thrust his pelvis until I'd tell him to stop.

A few minutes ago, I was in another world, but now I understand there's no way people won't know. Jordan's ridiculous laughter from last night sounds in my head again. Jordan will know. She always knows everything. And then I remember. She was here last night. She'd kissed his cheek before he'd driven her here. Had she been with him?

Surely not. I mean, even though it would make great drama for a movie plot, surely, she wouldn't. But I hadn't heard from her. Was it out of guilt? Last night I had wondered what would happen if my two worlds collided. Now, I know. My brain would churn itself up like a hurricane and everything would turn to rubble.

I gasp. I sob.

"Daisy, why are you crying? Aren't you happy?" His lips are on my face, kissing away my tears.

Before I can catch them, the undammed words gush out. "It's all too beautiful, Jamie. It's just all too unbelievably--perfect."

"That's all I want for you. Perfection. Perfection and happiness."

A cell phone buzzes urgently on the side table. Jamie checks it.

"Nick is on his way. Should I tell him to wait?"

I cocoon the sheets around me. Reality begins to settle. "It's impossible, Jamie. This miracle you've created is impossible."

"Why?"

The words gush again, and when they do, I swear they visibly shake Jamie like he'd just been shot in the heart. "What about Tom?"

He recovers quickly and regards me from under that flap of unwavering hair. "Tom doesn't matter."

"He'll kill you, Jamie."

"You don't believe that."

"He'll ruin you."

"He can't."

"You don't know. He can do whatever he wants."

We're sitting now, facing each other, wrapped in blue satin and guilt. His hands slide down my cold arms until our fingers intertwine.

"Tom doesn't matter, Daisy, because you're mine now. You'll never be anyone else's."

CHAPTER TEN

We hear Nick's knock on the door. A glitch occurs, like pixelated images on a movie screen. I'm shaken back to reality. We hurry to make ourselves presentable again. I straighten my sundress and try to tame my hair; however, when we let Nick in, he knows at once.

"How was lunch?" I ask him. Jamie stands behind me, his arms around my waist.

"Obviously, pretty damn good." He nods.

We laugh for a minute until Jamie reaches for Nick's hand and shakes it like a couple of businessmen. "Thanks."

For a second, I feel invisible. Nick pulls something out of his pocket.

"I found this on the stairs." It's my cell phone, irretrievably cracked.

"I must have dropped it. Thanks."

"Sorry," he apologizes.

"It's kind of old anyway." We all nervously stare at the phone as if trying to compose its obituary.

"It's not your fault," I say to Nick.

"I hope not," he agrees.

In the awkward silence, I suddenly wish Jordan were here to stick her nose in the air and offer some brusk reassurance.

"Are you ready?" Nick asks me. The question seems so loaded, it takes a second to realize he's only saying it's time to go.

I turn to Jamie for one last kiss. "What now?" I hold up my phone and almost forget he'll be at school Monday. At my school. In my world. We must get through Sunday first, though. How are we gonna get through Sunday? How on earth will we manage Monday?

"We'll figure it out," he says. I believe him. I mean, he manifested this happy miracle. Anything could happen now.

Nick and I step through the door, but Jamie stops me.

"In fact," he says, then scoots off to his bedroom. He comes back holding a brand-new cell phone. It's one of those pre-paid ones, but at least it works.

"Wow. You really do work in miracles, don't you?" I smile at the incredibility of him.

"I happen to have an extra. It's already ready to go and everything. I'll text you tonight. It'll be secret. Just ours."

"Like a couple of spies," I giggle. Still in awe, I slide the new cell into my purse.

The awe doesn't last, though. When fresh air hits my face, the reality of everything does, too. By the time I buckle into Nick's Beemer, butterflies converge in my stomach. Not a mile down the road, I'm ready to throw up.

"I cheated on Tom." The words shoot from my soul and splatter in the air.

Nick chuckles. "Did you?"

"Don't Nick."

"Don't what?"

"Don't condescend," I say.

"I'm not. Maybe you didn't cheat on Tom."

With one hand, I finger the green glass bead. With the other, I pinch my thigh to make sure I'm awake and breathing. A stinging red mark appears. I cover it with the fabric of my skirt.

"What do you mean? I did. I know I did. I was there."

"Oh, you cheated, all right. But maybe it's Jamie you cheated on when you came back from Tybee and didn't dump Tom."

I look at him like he's crazy. Because he is.

He continues, "What I can't figure out is why you didn't. Jamie's kind of amazing, and he's obviously drunk in love with you."

The tears just keep coming. Nick gets tissues from his glove box and offers them to me.

"Can we not talk about it, please."

Nick fiddles with his cell, searching for a song, but gives up.

"What are you gonna do, Daisy?"

"I don't know."

"How do you not know?"

Knots pull tighter in my stomach, and all I can think of is the weight of Tom's arm on my neck and the way the nerve in his jaw pulses when he wants to kiss me or punish me, and how he pouts when I make fun of him and brightens when I kiss him back.

"I can't leave him."

"Who? Which one do you mean?"

I manage a whisper. "I said I don't want to talk about it."

He turns down the wrong street on purpose, taking the long way to Grandma's.

"Okay, what do you want to talk about?" Annoyance flavors his words.

"Tell me about your date." I wipe my face, knowing there's no salvaging it.

"You mean lunch?" Nick asks.

"Yes. lunch. Where'd you go?"

"Trimalchio's."

"Jordan loves that place." I remember I still haven't heard from her. I rub my fingers across the rough, cracked glass screen nestled in my lap.

"I know. That's why I took her there," he says.

"Wait. You were with Jordan?" I ask.

"Yeah, why?"

"I thought you were with Owen."

"I told you no. Why would it be Owen?"

"I saw you flirt--I mean chatting with him in the cafeteria yesterday." I twist the tissue around one finger, then another.

"Flirting? What the hell, Daisy?"

"Not flirting. Just chatting, Nicky. I didn't mean--" I stammer.

"Nick. Not Nicky. I'm not five and I'm not gay."

"You did just use the word amazing to refer to a guy." Oh hell. Why can't I ever control my tongue?

"Are you serious right now?" He's no longer annoyed. It's worse than annoyed.

I try really hard to focus on Nick and Jordan together, anything to escape the turbulent, raw tide of emotion swimming in my brain. But it's too weird. It's almost weirder than seeing her ride off in Jamie's muscle car. But at least I needn't worry about that now. That's something anyway.

I wrinkle my face and try to picture it in black and white, like one of Jordan's beloved old detective movies. "I'm sorry, Nick. I just never thought of you with Jordan. Jordan? Really?"

He doesn't answer right away. When I check his demeanor, I notice a red rage crawling up his neck. Finally, he growls, "We're with you like every single day. How did you not pick up on it? Are you that self-absorbed?"

"I'm not self-absorbed. Maybe you're misreading the signals." I don't even know why we're talking about this. How can I even think about Jordan and Nick right now?

"Maybe *I'm* misreading signals?" Nick growls.

"She would have said something. She would want me to know. Wouldn't she?" I don't even know if I believe what I'm saying at this point. I only know I need to be right about something.

I literally clap my hands over my mouth to cure my own stupidity. I glance at the world passing outside the passenger window. Between my swirling head and my tear-stained eyes, the view out the window blurs into a fantastical image. I've never done drugs, but I swear the fuzzy imprints of houses resemble an acid trip or one of those El Greco paintings we studied in art class last year. The front gate of a sprawling community rises up before us. Behind them stands my parent's home--my home once upon a time--now hollow as a discarded pirate's chest. Sometimes I forget it's there. Sometimes I can't think of anything else. Nick ignores the gates and drives around the bend back toward Grandma's.

Panic rumbles inside me. It feels like I'm losing everything all over again. I stare at Nick simply to remind myself that I'm not alone. Even if he's mad, at least he's still here, flesh and blood. Beginnings of scruff on his chin draw my gaze. I remember when he tried to grow a beard our freshman year. Now he can't seem to keep one away.

Nick notices me staring but misinterprets it.

"Jesus, Daisy, I'm not gay. I've never been gay. Obviously, Jordan knows that, even if you don't."

I'm jarred back to the present. If I understood why half the crap comes out of my mouth, I'd be a freaking genius. Did I really ever think Nick's gay? It's no secret Owen is. It's no secret Owen likes Nick. I guess I never really cared enough to ask if Nick likes Owen. But I'd never known Nick to really crush on anyone. I've defended him to Tom, but I don't know what I ever really believed. I chew on a cracked nail and attempt to mentally will the air around us into peaceful submission.

It must work. Nick's voice softens a little into the stern,

disappointed father. "Are you really gonna stay with Tom? After everything Jordan and I arranged for you and Jamie today? You're gonna choose Tom?" he says.

It's too much. A deluge of tears and fear and sickening confusion gush from me. I bend over and cry and cry and cry. Just minutes ago, I'd never been happier, and now, I've never felt more alone. Viciously, utterly alone.

Nick pulls into Grandma's drive, turns off the car and plants his palms on his thighs. He faces me and waits until I'm recovered. My breath comes in little spurts against a quivering lip.

He is calm now, and it's almost worse. "Listen, Daisy. Owen is my friend and a pretty damn good writer. So what if I want to mentor him so I can leave our newspaper in capable hands when I graduate? So what if I use amazing to describe a dude? So the fuck what? Jamie is... is... is different than every single basic white kid in our school. He possesses a sensitivity to the promises of life you don't find in East Eggerton. Hell, you don't find it in most people anywhere. He's a dreamer, Daisy. I knew it five minutes into a conversation with him. So, yes, I'm amazed. I do that. I get amazed by people and places and dreams. It's Jordan's favorite thing about me."

The look of surprise on Nick's face is of a new kind.

"Don't be mad, Nick. I can't stand it when you're mad."

"That's it? You can't stand it when I'm mad?"

For once in my life, I have no words. He shakes his head and then stares at the passenger side door handle as if willing it to move.

"Aren't you coming in?" My voice comes out in a squeak.

He scoffs. "I'm picking Jordan up for a movie. Then maybe I'll go fuck her brains out. Would that be manly enough for you?"

"That's not fair, Nick. I don't understand why you are so mad."

"I'm not mad. I'm just tired of everything being about you." Nick reaches across me, unlatches the door, and gives it a shove.

I want to stay put and force him to take me back to Jamie's bed to feel his presence beside me and reassurance of what's right, after all. Instead, I rush out of the car, back to my own bed and my own soft pillows. On my way to them, I toss my broken phone in the kitchen trash. On my bedroom door whiteboard, Grandma's funky scrawl warns me she isn't home and won't be until late, so I crawl into the comfort of my big, white blankets, longing for blue satin and him.

It was months later that Nick told me about the conversation he'd had with Jamie the next day.

"Don't expect too much of her," Nick had told Jamie. "You can't relive your island summer here in Chicago. It's not possible. That was a different time and place."

Jamie had disagreed. "You're wrong. It was perfect once. It will be again. She's just confused, that's all. She needs time."

"You can't relive the past," Nick had warned.

"Can't relive the past? Of course, you can. It's all any of us ever strive for, isn't it?" had been Jamie's naive response.

I remember staring out the window behind Nick at the restaurant and thinking of my parents, their smiling faces as they drove away, the carefree wave of my father's hand out the window, the ever-widening sinkhole in my heart when I'd heard the news of the crash.

When Nick revealed his conversation with Jamie to me, it had hit me with hurricane force that that's what I'd been doing for the last three years, searching for some different outcome over and over again. It's like when you reread *Little Women* hoping against hope that this time Beth won't die. My desperate heart regressed to fifteen again, but I wouldn't recede into the past. I would push ahead, sprout wings if I had to, and learn how to fly.

CHAPTER ELEVEN

The next morning, my whole body aches. What do I expect after I spent the entire day in bed reliving the way Jamie looks at me and then crying about it? Then crying about Tom. Then sneaking down to the kitchen for a handful of Double Stuf Oreos until I finally gave in and brought the whole package back to bed with me. Then being disgusted with my fatness. Then crying. Then sleeping. Then raging at myself for not just being happy, for God's sake. Then utterly missing Tybee with my whole being. Then crying some more.

When the sun unexpectedly and stubbornly rises this morning, I realize I can't go to church with Grandma. I just can't. The poor woman has suffered enough loss. I can't bear the thought of her watching her only grandchild go up in flames somewhere between the opening hymn and Pastor's sermon. Because that's exactly what would happen if I dared step foot in a church today. So, I lie and tell her I'm sick.

"Daisy, sweetheart, I've brewed you some tea. I'll just leave it here for you." Grandma comes in and sets a small tray of hot tea and honey on my bedside table. I sink deeper into my fluffy pillows and comforter. She's too nice. She deserves a better granddaughter.

She cups her hand on my forehead. "The ibuprofen must be working. No fever. You just get some rest, and I'll be back soon."

She trots around my queen-sized bed that feels so big it might swallow me whole. I almost wish it would. She fidgets with the ruffled curtains, pulling them tight against the daylight. My room is too soft. It's all fluffy ruffles and flowery pastels. I remember Grandma using the word *soothing* a million times when we had originally picked out the colors. Soothing, like a mother's lullaby that takes you away to dreams and unreality. Nothing that prepares you for the cold, stark world of East Eggerton Academy and Tom and Jamie and infidelity and...

She straightens my covers one more time.

"Thank you, Grandma. You're too good to me."

"No such thing as too good, sweetheart." She blows me a kiss and then she's gone to pray with all the decent, lovely people of good breeding who go to church on Sundays to face their sins, not lay at home in bed, wallowing in their own stupidness and drinking guilty tea.

I sit up and take a sip, but it's too hot. My tongue burns. Imagine my whole body burning like this if God ever found out what I did with Jamie behind Tom's back. Imagine if Tom ever found out. I shiver under the covers, but I'm not cold. I'm empty.

Which is weird because Jamie is here in Chicago. All the promises he made about the universe bringing us together came true. I should be miraculously happy, but it's just too weird. Jamie's here, but I can't be with him because there's Tom.

But I should be with Jamie. I know it to the depths of my soul. I should be with Jamie. Shouldn't I?

Yesterday, every happy kiss and carefree caress was tempered with an odd inner scale. Am I happy? Am I as happy as I should be? How could I not be? Who am I to ask for more? What more could I possibly ask for anyway? I mean when the entire universe pulls together to make my dreams come true, I'd be a fool to ask for more. What more even is there?

The answer thumped in my heart. There's Tom. There's Tom.

I'd have thought giving into Jamie's passion would've quieted the thumping. Instead, it only replaced it with burning, hot guilt.

Guilt that is not going to be assuaged with tea and honey. Cheating whores don't drink tea and honey. Cheating whores drink—.

They drink. That's what they do. They drink and lie and sleep with people other than their partners. I can't remember the last time I was drunk. Maybe the first time I drank, but after that I had been more careful, more sophisticated. A laugh lurches out of me and I announce to no one, "God, I'm sophisticated."

But right now, I want to be good and drunk. I don't care if it's 10:00 am on a Sunday. I'm already going to hell. I might as well be drunk when I get there.

I throw off my covers and throw on a sundress and sandals. I hurry before I can talk myself out of what I'm about to do. In ten minutes, I'm strolling through the grocery store with a cart. I have no idea why

I have a cart. I'm here for exactly two things. I swing around to the liquor aisles. I remember special occasions like Christmas and Easter when Charles and Ginny made mimosas and let me sneak little sips.

I find the refrigerated section. I grab the first chilled bottle of bubbly I see and then hurry away, nearly taking out the end cap display of some canned, fruity thing that resembles a child's drink. Seriously, what is wrong with people? Why would you put dancing fruit on a canned, alcoholic beverage? What seven-year-old wouldn't scoop that up accidentally at a backyard BBQ? I straighten everything back up before anyone can notice.

I run for the juice aisle. I can't stop staring at the one bottle in my cart. It's too obvious. No way will I get away with it. I need distraction items, like when you go in to buy emergency tampons, but you don't want the cashier to know they're emergency tampons, so you also buy shampoo and razors and toothpaste, so he'll think you are just restocking the bathroom.

What kind of items distract from an underage whore buying morning-after booze? I need something to make me seem older. Cleaning supplies? Office supplies? No. The champagne would be highlighted against paper clips and notepads.

Supplies for some kind of sophisticated get together? Book club? But I have no idea what kind of supplies one would need for a book club other than books. Baby shower stuff. That's it. I round the corner to the party supplies. Steamers, little plastic baby booties, balloons. I scoot over to the baby aisle. What's a baby shower without baby paraphernalia, right? Diapers, wipes, bottles, formula.

Wait a minute. I glance at the contents of my cart. This isn't right. The diapers are size five. The formula is for sensitive stomachs. How would the mom know the baby has a sensitive stomach before it's born? And size five can't be right. Does that mean five months?

I pace my cart up and down different aisles, thinking it through and panicking that some policeman will be scouring the pet aisle for dog food and arrest me when he sees my stash.

Maybe the new mom is a planner. She wants the sensitive stuff just in case. And the baby will still need diapers five months from now, right? So, she plans ahead. Clearly more than I do.

I head to the check-out and cross my fingers. The cashier at the far end of the store is someone I know. He graduated from Eggerton a few years ago. The janitor's kid, I think. He worked here back then, too. He's not really Eggerton blood. I splash on my widest smile and stick out my chest. This just might work.

His name tag says Ripley.

"Hi, Ripley. How are you? We've been missing you."

"What?" Dirty blonde is certainly the correct term for the long strands that he whips around his face to look up at me.

"Missing you. You know. Because you aren't there anymore."

"What? Where?" His glassy eyes try to focus.

Now I remember. He's a complete stoner. I almost answer, "At Eggerton." But I catch myself. I can't be twenty-one and still at Eggerton.

"Oh, nowhere. Everywhere. Just around, ya know. Around town. Uptown. Downtown. You know, around places. Like that."

Holy crap. This is stressful. How do people do this all the time? Tom makes it look so easy. He doesn't even have a fake ID like most of his friends. He just strolls in and gets what he wants. Am I such a spoiled princess that I don't even know how to buy my own champagne?

Ripley continues checking me out. There are two items left in the cart: diapers and champagne. Before I can stop myself, the words spew out.

"Kind of funny combination, huh? Diapers and champagne. Who would ever buy those? Unless you're hosting a baby shower. Which I am. Then, of course, you would need diapers and champagne. For the mimosas. I mean what else are you gonna serve at a baby shower, am I right?"

Oh. My. God. This cart full of baby shit is supposed to draw his attention *away* from the champagne.

"My sister had cupcakes at her baby shower," Ripley says in a stream of words so slow, you'd think he was a little drunk himself. He scans the diapers and picks up the bottle. He looks at it and then at me. He sets it on the counter like he's gonna think about something.

My face is on fire. My smile goes full Muppet at this point. I'm so busted.

"Hey, did we graduate together?" he asks.

"Um, maybe. What year did you graduate?"

He tells me. I quickly do the math.

"Yeah, we did," I lie. Because, again, that's what whores do. They drink and lie and...

"I thought so," he says and rings up the champagne.

Just Daisy

Relief floods my entire being. I pull out my debit card and shove it in the slot.

"Aren't you forgetting something?" Ripley asks.

Oh my god. Here it comes. He wants my ID. I look around for a security guard or a manager.

He continues, "You need orange juice for mimosas. My mom has them every morning for breakfast. I mean sometimes for lunch, too. But she usually has orange juice. Don't you need juice?"

My whole body shakes. I stare at the bottle. Its flowery gold label mocks me. Orange juiceless mimosas. I literally cannot do a damn thing for myself without screwing it up. I push the buttons on the machine and replace the card in my wristlet.

"We stocked up last time it was on sale," I answer.

I guess he buys it because I gather my bubbly and my cartful of ridiculous distraction items and escape.

An hour later, I've forgotten all about the baby shower when Jordan finds me in the tub, gripping a disintegrating wad of paper and sobbing into my bubble bath. The champagne is gone. All of it. Without so much as a consideration for juice. Or my sanity because I think I've lost it. Along with my eyesight. I think I've cried myself into semi-blindness cuz the world is like one big fuzzy fuzz ball and that looks sooooo sad and beautiful and makes me cry. *Hic.* And hiccup.

Jordan bangs open the door and looks down at me in the tub.

"Well, that's one way to handle it." She's so snarky. I try to hide under the bubbles, but she pulls me up.

I open my mouth to talk, but my face is kinda numb and something's wrong with my tongue.

"How dyou get in?" I ask, chewing on my tongue. Why is it so big? Is it always that big? I squint at Jordan and try to hold my head still.

"You know I know the code. My God. You are pathetic." She holds up the empty bottle of bubbly then dumps it in the trash shcan on the whole other side of the bassroom.

"I know. I'm a passetic whore," I say, only the words don't sound right.

"I wouldn't go that far," she huffs.

Then, I start sobbing all over again. I can't sop. I try and try, but I can't sop at all.

She checks her movie sar face in the mirror and says all mean like, "Don't blubber."

She comes back over to me, but somesing stops her. Iz the pile of diapers and stuff behind the door. I see a billion million emotions flash in her eyes. Or maybe one. The room is a little spinny, so I'm not sure.

"What's this?" she asks and holds up a package of baby butt wipes. I laugh at her cuz she pinches it between two fingers like it might infeck her.

Hic. Hic.

She drops it an comes zover to the tub an pries somesing from my hand. But iz okay. It wuz getting soggy anyways.

"And what's this? A list of boy and girl names?" she asks, peeling it aaaaall apart.

"Nope. Jus two names. Twos boyz namez. Boy an boy. Thaz all." I scoop up a handful of bubbles and blow them into the air. They make these tiny, little, itty, bitty irri... irrisessant... iridescent clouds.

Jordan plants her handz on her hip an' exhales at me with a very aloofy huffing noise. "Let me guess. Tom and Jamie? What? Are you trying to figure out who the baby daddy is? Really, Daisy."

"Ohhhhh nooooo. Noooo. Noooo." I swear I sound just like a whale. A prostituted whale. Is that a thing? "Jardon, Jodian. Jordan." I reach for her and practically slip out of the tub.

"What?" She's so tall. Like really tall. I twist my head up so I can see her face.

"Do they have prosisutes at Sea World?"

Suddenly, she's very close. She plunges her hand into my loverly bath and pulls my plug. She driez off with one of my softy, softy towels with D A I S I S Y mononogrammamed on the front then flings it at me. Right at my frowny sad face, and she marches out the door.

"Clean yourself up. I'm going to make coffee and eggs. I saw Grandma Betty at church. She'll be home in less than an hour. And she's bringing Tom." She yells it over her shoulder like a piss off coach or cop. Or parent. I guess. I don't have parens, so I don' know.

But wad I do know is I'm gonna vomit all over misslef if I don' make it to the toilet, so I flopsy out of the tub like a fuggin' mermaid and belly crawl across the floor.

CHAPTER TWELVE

The coffee works, for the most part. I'm still woozy and must be very still to keep the world from spinning. If I'm as pale as I feel, Grandma Betty will suspect, won't she? But she thinks I'm sick, so I guess it'll be okay.

But nothing feels okay at all. I'm perched on the downstairs sofa with Jordan, confessing and trying not to puke again.

"How very *Philadelphia Story* of you, Daisy," Jordan says as she hands me a refilled mug.

Philadelphia Story is one of Jordan's beloved Katharine Hepburn movies where the heroine gets drunk the night before her wedding because she knows she is marrying the wrong guy.

"It's not a movie, Jordan. It's real life. And in real life, I cheated on Tom. I mean really cheated." I take a fortifying sip and replace the mug on its coaster.

"You mean you didn't already do that this summer?"

"No. And don't worry. There's no need to figure out who the father is. No chance I'm not pregnant. I've been on birth control since freshman year. You know that."

I really do feel like a pathetic whore. Who gets on birth control as a freshman and doesn't even pretend it's to regulate periods? It was because Tom wanted to have sex, and I wanted to have Tom.

"I still don't see what the problem is. You're leaving Tom anyway," she says it so matter-of-fact, like it's already a done deal.

"Do you know what that paper was I was holding in the tub? It was a pros and cons list," I admit.

"Of Tom and Jamie? Do you mean pros for Jamie and cons for Tom? Because that's all I see." Her voice sounds just like Nick's yesterday.

"That's not fair. Tom has lots of pros. His muscles. His eyes and the way he looks at me when--"

"When he's not looking at someone else?" She always knows just how to turn it around, but I ignore her.

She continues. "Jamie moved half-way across the continent for you, Daisy. What does Tom do for you? When a guy moves heaven and earth for a girl, she ought to appreciate it, don't you think?"

I know where this is coming from, and it has nothing to do with Tom and Jamie. It has everything to do with Mr. and Mrs. Baker. Jordan's dad has moved heaven and earth and the moon and the stars for his wife for years. She drinks it away, sleeps it off in someone else's bed, and asks for more. Jordan never talks about it. Neither does her dad.

"Tom does stuff for me. Remember how he was there for me when mom and dad died. He was so patient and kind and understanding. I don't know what I would have done without him. He was everything I needed to get through it." Not that I'm through it. Not that anyone is ever through it.

"Gee, thanks." She juts her chin toward the ceiling. I can see she's truly hurt. Just like Nick.

I close my eyes and try to ignore the feeling that everything is spinning out of control. At this point, I'm not sure if it's champagne remnants or just what I've done to my life. Yesterday, in Jamie's arms, in his miracle world, I had everything. Now Nick is mad. Jordan is getting mad. I'm contemplating breaking Tom's heart and disappointing my grandma *and* I have a bathroom full of baby supplies I have to figure out how to explain.

My fuzzy head hurts. I peek out of one eye and try to center myself. Jordan's stubborn face borders on offended.

I soften my voice. "That's not what I mean, Jordan. You and Nick were there for me, too. Of course, you were, but there was no surprise there. Tom and I hadn't been together all that long. I didn't expect it from him. Remember how he arranged to have the plaque made for the yacht club? And he missed a week of football practice just to be with me. A whole week, Jordan."

"A whole week. What a guy. I'm surprised he didn't secure a magic potion and bring them back to life for you. Besides, that was nearly three years ago. What has he done for you lately?"

My stomach snarls. Bile rises to my throat.

"I saw something in him during that time that maybe he doesn't even know is there. He's a stupid teenage boy. That doesn't mean he always will be. I know he can be sweet and supportive. He was once, right?" I'm grasping, and she knows it.

She directs her gaze right at me. "And how long are you willing to be a stupid teenage girl and wait for him? Jamie's here now. He's not making you wait for anything. In fact, he's the one waiting for you. He's given up way more than a week of football."

My heart drops. No one makes me feel the way Jamie does when I'm with him. Reality skids away and fantasy rides in a white horse every time he wraps his arms around me. It's almost too good to be true.

But I felt that way about Tom once upon a time, too.

"What would people at school say? How would I explain it? Our friends like Tom. They respect him."

"They fear him. It's not the same thing." she says.

"What about Grandma Betty? She likes Tom."

Jordan adjusts herself and goes in full force. "See, now, this is what I don't get. Didn't your grandma meet Jamie over the summer?"

"I mean, sort of. She knew he was one of the friends I hung out with."

"Well, did she like him? Does she know he's here now?"

"I think she liked him. She invited him to dinner once." He hadn't come. He had apologized but never explained.

"Well, see there. Your Grandma would never invite a scoundrel to dinner. She'll learn to like Jamie, too. Before you know it, he'll be the top guy." She says it with a wink and tempting smile.

We hear the front door. Grandma breezes in and sees Jordan and me on the couch. She steps her bright, happy self right to me and touches my cheek.

"You must be feeling better. Oh, I'm so glad you let Jordan do your hair. By the way, I saw Tom at church. He was so worried about you, so I told him to come right over."

She takes a breath and examines my appearance. She pulls something from her purse and holds it out to me. It's a peach-colored lipstick. "Your hair always looks so good when Jordan does it. Here. This will help."

"Thank you, Grandma Betty," Jordan beams and tucks a strand behind my ear. She's straightened it into a sleek long ponytail that she's draped over one should, but there's always those few misbehaving strands. Jordan's eyes settle for a second on mine until a satisfactory grin spreads on her face. It wouldn't have surprised me one bit for her to pop a bow on my head and hand me over.

Then the spell is gone. Brutal reality rolls over me. "Tom is on his way." I mouth the words to Jordan.

"Break up with him. Why the hell not?" Jordan whispers.

Why the hell not? My mind flashes back to an hour ago. I was on my hands and knees, swabbing the bathroom floor with my precious pink towels when my hand had bumped up against a disgusting glop of smushed up paper. I'd sopped up my pros and cons list that Jordan had thrown to the floor and tossed in the trash along with the rest of everything I thought I knew about what senior year was gonna be.

If Jordan had read that list, she would have seen one name already circled at the top and the other one, with its sparse list, crossed out. Just because the decision was made, didn't mean it would be easy. Didn't mean I could actually carry out what I knew was best for everyone.

Just because my parents are dead doesn't mean I can find the courage to disappoint them.

The front door crashes open. It's Tom.

"Daisy. Wow. You look like hell." My stomach lurches. Jamie would never, ever tell me I look like hell even if I did. Something clicks all the pieces of my brain together. I set Grandma's lipstick aside and pull the ribbon from my hair. It cascades against my bare back. I'm wearing the halter dress that Jordan says is casually stunning on me. Apparently, Tom doesn't like it. Or he doesn't notice.

My stomach clenches. Tom's hard body nearly bursts the seams of his Sunday sport coat. I swear he gleams like a hardwood floor that's just been waxed. There's something sturdy and old-fashioned about him, like you know he'll be there forever, never relenting in his duty.

A flash of memory cuts through everything. My mom, crumpled on the living room floor and sobbing overdramatically. In one hand, she gripped an empty mimosa flute while the fingers of the other traced a rude gauge on the freshly scarred wooden floor planks.

"For God's sake, Ginny. We'll buff it out. It will be like it never happened," Dad had yelled at her.

"But *I'll* know it was there. You should have been more careful. You shouldn't have thrown it in the first place. Now, it's broken." She'd pointed accusingly at a shattered picture frame a few feet away.

"It's fitting, don't you think?" He'd scoffed at her. A million times I'd seen him wrap her up and *there-there* her histrionics. I'd also seen him turn his back and close his eyes against it, pretending she would calm herself if he poured his drink slowly enough. But before that day, I'd never seen him throw anything.

"I think it was something she ate," Grandma Betty says and pats Tom on the shoulder like she's gonna offer him a treat if he sits and stays.

"Or drank," Jordan says under her breath.

I elbow her gently. I feel her fingers untangle my hair behind me. It reminds me of how my mother used to run her absent-minded hands through my curls while we waited for Daddy to come home, eating popcorn and watching *Back to the Future* in the study and wondering what it would be like to drive that DeLorean into another dimension.

"That's not very nice, Tom. I don't feel well," I say.

"Well, you don't need to get all pissy about it," he says. His smile takes the sting out. He's joking. His expression reveals he's noticed the dress, after all. But then, "Jordan, scoot over." He motions aggressively for her to move. That does it. That single dismissive flip of his hand secures our fate.

I grab her thigh. "She doesn't need to move, but you and I need to talk."

"Talk? About what?" he asks, and I can see by his empty eyes that he's completely oblivious.

"I'm breaking up with you, Tom."

CHAPTER THIRTEEN

The satisfied sigh that comes out of Jordan fades in comparison to the look of shock on Tom's face and the one of disappointment on Grandma's.

"Oh, oh my. Oh dear." Grandma wrings her hands and shifts her weight back and forth.

For a second, all I can see are those worry lines in her face accentuating every sad thing that's ever happened to her. Grandpa dying of that surprise heart attack on his seventieth birthday. Her having to leave Tybee after to be in Chicago near mom and dad and then losing them. The burden of having to finish raising a teenager.

She looks so lost, swaying back and forth in the middle of the polished hardwood floor with the white sheers gently stirring on the windows, blowing in towards the poufy white couches and the seascape prints framed on the walls. Everything is pale and peaceful, and it occurs to me that this break-up scene that's about to unfold is the most dramatic thing that's happened in Grandma's sedated living room.

No one speaks. My words hang there until I wonder if I actually said them out loud at all.

"Have a seat, Tom. Would you like some tea? I think we need cookies. Chocolate chip or sugar?" Grandma asks and finds her way to the kitchen. Pans bang around. She's comfort baking.

"What the hell, Daisy?" Tom doesn't even try to hold his voice down.

"Oh, that'll win her back," Jordan snarks.

"I swear to God, Jordan, you need to shut your mouth."

"Or what? Are you gonna shut it for me?"

I feel her entire body bristle beside me. I want to cheer her on, hold her over my head like a championship quarterback, but I'm frozen. It's as if those words--I'm breaking up with you--sucked every confident ounce of energy from me.

"I might." He inches closer to her.

I clear my throat and wrangle the softest Ginny Fay tone I can muster. "Jordan. I think Grandma needs help in the kitchen."

It's a bad line from every sappy romance ever made. Couples throw it out there to dinner guests like everyone in the world doesn't know what *help in the kitchen* means. We have microwaves and smart fridges now. No one needs help in the kitchen.

For once, she follows my order and marches out. Maybe she can soothe Grandma by talking about the best hairstyles for my face shape.

Tom takes her place on the couch beside me. My stomach tightens. Sweat runs down my cleavage. I curl my lips inward and clamp down, afraid I will take it all back, afraid he will try to kiss me. Just afraid.

"What's going on, Daisy? Did Jordan put you up to this?" His voice shakes. He's full of vibration, like the old Perfection board game I played as a child, right before it all explodes. It's not the first time I've seen him this way, but maybe with Jordan and Grandma so close, it won't be so bad this time.

"I just need time," I manage.

"Time for what? That's bullshit. I give you all the time you need."

"That's just it, Tom. I don't want you to *give* me time. I want my own time without having to seek your permission for it."

"I don't even know what that means. You don't need my permission." His face grows red.

"But I do. On a lot of levels, I do. You have to know where I am. I have to check in with you."

"No, you don't." He stops. He has nothing else to say. Then he remembers, "Where were you yesterday anyway? I texted after game film."

"This is exactly what I mean. See."

"What? I can't text my girlfriend now?"

"No, you can."

"Then what's the problem?"

My head spins. I grab my coffee from the side table and sip it. I should have stayed drunk. Drunk was easier.

He waits for me to set the mug down. He takes my hands in his.

I'm shaking, too. His eyes are fiery black, but his voice is softer now. "Of course, I want to know where you are. Why wouldn't I? I love you, Daisy."

The words hit me. Why wouldn't he? I don't know. Because right now I can only think about where Jamie is and what he's doing and if he's trying to text me and wondering if he's wondering the same about me.

I lose my words. I can't speak because if I say anything, I might accidentally spout out the real reason I'm breaking up. In the silence, lie a million sentiments, and finally, a revelation for Tom.

"Wait. Is there someone else? Is that where you were yesterday?" Lines of anger and disbelief mar his beautiful face. Red and black, like a volcano ready to erupt.

"Is there someone else?" he asks again.

Yes. Yes. Yes. Just say it. What's he gonna do?

"My phone broke." My heart sinks. He'd kill Jamie, that's what he'd do.

"It has to be someone else. Who is it? I'll fucking kick his ass." He jumps up. The pacing starts. That pulsating place in his temple returns. His fists clench, sending undulating muscle spasms up his arms, noticeable even under his sport coat. I imagine the way even his pecs are tight right now. Every muscle in his body is activated. I've experienced it, too many times, in anger but also in passion.

"It's nobody. My phone broke," I whisper.

"Who is it?" He's in my face now, nearly growling.

"I told you nobody."

"You're telling me you'd rather be alone than be with me? That's a fucking lie." He shoves an accusatory finger in my face.

He's not wrong. I'd rather be with anyone than be alone. The realization rolls in my stomach and reaches my throat. I swear I'm gonna hurl any second.

"It's no one. No one. I promise," I manage and clamp my hand over my mouth. *Don't throw up. Don't throw up.*

"Who would put up with you anyway? Your drama. Your annoying laugh. Your insecurity. Who would deal with that?"

"Somebody might." I swallow and breathe in slowly. *Don't throw up. Don't cry.*

"For a while, maybe, because he doesn't know you yet. Because he hasn't had time to get used to it and get over it. I put up with it every day because I'm used to it. Did you ever think of that?"

"Maybe someone else won't think my laugh is annoying." What does Jamie think about my laugh? He's never mentioned it. Does he hate it, too?

"You're a lot, Daisy. You don't think you are, but you are."

"If I am so much to deal with, then why do you want me around? Why aren't you the one breaking up right now if I'm so awful?"

"See what I mean? Overdramatic," he says.

"How is that overdramatic? You just said--"

"I know what I just said. Did you hear *me*? I said I put up with it. No one else will for long. He might think it's cute now. I did too, at first."

"But not now?" Do I really annoy him that much? My own boyfriend?

"I put up with it because it's who you are. If I want to be with you, I guess I don't have a choice, do I?"

My brain is so lost, I don't know what I want. I should be happy I annoy him. Here's his chance to get away, right? But am I that bad? Will Jamie feel this way about me eventually?

"You have a choice right now," I manage.

"Apparently, I don't. Apparently, Jordan has talked you into breaking up."

Please stay in the kitchen, Jordan.

"This isn't Jordan," I say.

"Come on. Like you would do this on your own. You don't have it in you. You can't decide what bra to wear in the morning without consulting someone first."

Oh my gosh. He's right. I do that. I actually have texted Jordan to tell me which bra makes my boobs look best with which shirt. Maybe this *is* Jordan's idea. Even at the beach on my first day back, the first time I was going to leave Tom, she'd pushed things. It was supposed to have been my call, and she had jumped prematurely in.

Break up with him. Why the hell not? Jordan's words pound in my head.

Tom stops abruptly, towering over me. "You know what? You're right, Daisy. I do have choices. Don't think I can't get a girl right now. Any girl I want." He pulls out his phone as a threat.

Something catches in my chest. What would that be like? Seeing him with those muscle-bound arms around another girl? I close my eyes against the boastful, giddy face of the vixen who'd take my place. Do I want that?

Tears come. Determination wanes.

He sits again and tucks away his cell. His hand comes to my face and wipes my cheek. "It's our senior year. It's everything we've planned. We've been together since we were freshmen. Everybody looks to us, you know. Can you imagine? We'd disappoint everyone. We'd disappoint your grandma for sure."

And there it is. That team feeling I have with no other person on the planet. Not even Jamie. Not even with Tom most of the time, but every now and then when he thinks he might lose me…

"I'm sorry, Daisy," he says.

"What?" I hadn't expected an apology.

"I'm sorry. I haven't been there for you since you got back from your island. I was too wrapped up in football and our senior year. I take the blame for that. But I can fix that. Remember, when your parents died, and I didn't go to practice for a week?"

"I remember."

"I guess I just thought we were good right now, and I could focus on football. I thought you wanted that, too. I didn't even think how hard all this senior year stuff would be for you without your parents. I didn't even think. I'm sorry."

He hangs his head and makes a little clearing noise in his throat. Before the movement can register with me, I slide my hand over his football-season buzz cut and around to his chin. I lift his face and look into his obsidian eyes.

"It's okay. I didn't realize it either." It's true. I hadn't until just this moment.

"We're all gonna have to say goodbye at the end of this year. I just never, never thought I'd have to say goodbye to you, Daisy. I don't want to say goodbye to you. I'll do better. I promise."

His apology comes too soon. It feels wrong now to deliver the knock-out punch, but I must. The words are sitting on my tongue. If I don't speak them, I'll have to swallow them, and I don't think my stomach can take it.

"You choked me, Tom. You put your hand on my throat and

threatened me Friday night. I won't put up with that." I should sit up straighter. I should jut my chin to the ceiling like Jordan when she's out-snarked everyone in the room, when she knows she's right. But I don't. Instead, I sink into myself. It's the first time I've ever made him face his own brutality.

His lip curls. His eyes go darker. "That wasn't my fault. I was defending myself."

"What?" I almost laugh.

"You hit me first, Daisy."

"I slapped you. It's not the same thing."

"If I had slapped you, would it be the same thing?"

My brain goes numb. I can't answer.

"You slapped me. What did you expect me to do? Just take it?" he asks.

"I... uh... but..."

"But what?" He raises his eyebrows and waits.

"You insulted my dad."

He is unmoved. "I was upset. I was still excited about the game, and that asshole just about ran you over. I should have gone after him. That's what I should have done. No one should be able to come that close to hurting you, Daisy."

"Not even you?" I ask with no idea where my strength is coming from at this point.

"Not even me." There's a truth at the edge of his expression. He's realized something. Or he's starting to.

He continues, "Don't I deserve a second chance? Aren't I worth at least that? This is the first time you've ever told me you're unhappy. You haven't even given me a chance to fix anything. Is that fair?"

It's not. None of this is fair to him.

"Give me a chance. I'll make it up to you. Don't break us, Daisy. Remember when we used to make fun of all those stupid couples who fight over nothing and break-up all the time and then get back together. Remember what we used to say?"

"Yeah. We're unbreakable, we said."

He squeezes my hands. He's so strong, so powerful. It's intoxicating.

"Unbreakable. That's us. We're not like everybody else. There's too much between us. Even if we broke up, we would still live in each other's hearts." He rests his strong hand on my heart. Its warmth spreads through me. I hadn't noticed I was shivering until his touch makes me stop.

Again, he's right. Even if I were to ride off in the sunset with someone else, a part of Tom would never leave me.

"Give me a chance. I'll give you everything you need to be happy. I promise."

He's begging. He's actually begging. He knows me. He loves me.

Softly, his hand moves to behind my neck and pulls me in. His lips land in tender desperation on mine. I can't resist. All the confusion and uncertainty and history and passion between us comes out in breathless waves. I reach for him and close off any gap along with any possibility of freedom.

A buzzer goes off in the kitchen and startles us apart. Nervous laughter fills the space. Grandma will be in with the cookies. Her expression will have that inquisitive, hopeful edge. She'll want to know we've worked it out.

Tom touches his forehead to mine. "Your grandma would have been so sad. All the cookies in the world wouldn't have healed her heartbreak."

For the millionth time today, he's right. Grandma would have been heartbroken. She likes Tom. She sees him as my future, as a guarantee that if something happens to her, I won't be alone. I'll have someone.

My face is in his hands again and his lips are on mine when Grandma carries her cookies in on a tray. She's put Jordan to work serving the tea. Grandma begins the small talk.

Jordan doesn't indulge. She perches on the edge of a hard chair, glass in hand like she's holding her evening brandy. She's diffcrent though. She doesn't raise her chin to the ceiling once. Instead, her eyes fire hatred and plotted revenge at Tom. My stomach snarls.

"Delicious, Grandma Betty." Tom waves a half-devoured cookie in the air and shoves it toward my face. "Have one."

My body heaves. "No thank you," I manage.

"Come on. You know you like them." He rubs it across my lips.

"Geez, Tom, why don't you shove it down her throat. Along with your tongue," Jordan whispers the last part.

That does it. In a hurl of regret, it all rushes out--Jordan's eggs and coffee and a bottleful of bubbly. It all would have landed in a gushy, violent heap on Tom's lap if he hadn't caught it in his deft, cupped hands.

"Oh god. Oh god," he moans. Grandma grabs the empty tray and holds it under his hands like an alter server and escorts him to the kitchen.

Jordan dabs my mouth with a napkin. "I bet you feel better, don't you? I know I do." Her laugh is too sneeringly delighted.

I can't look at her nor respond. I know she's pissed. I'm a little pissed at myself. If rock bottom is possible at seventeen, I've hit it. However, it doesn't feel like a rock at all. More like a mud hole that I can't crawl out of.

From the kitchen, Grandma's reassurance waves in, mingled with little retching noises from Tom.

"That was brave... so very kind... not every young man would...and you saved my sofa..."

Tom comes back in, white as heaven. Jordan thrusts her arm under mine and tears me from the couch.

"I'm taking her upstairs."

Tom approaches, "I'll take her. Haven't you done enough?"

"Haven't I done enough? You're the one who made her throw up."

"By offering her a cookie? She's my girlfriend. I'll—" Tom towers over her.

"Which is enough to make anyone sick to her stomach. I'll take her up."

"You don't own her, Jordan." Tom's growling now.

"Right back at ya."

There's a literal tug-o-war, each aggressor yanking on my arm as if it's a weathered rope on a grade school playground. Grandma observes with wringing hands.

I finally throw them both off. "I can walk myself. I feel a lot better. Really. You should both go."

I gather our glasses and take them to the kitchen. That's the sign to leave, isn't it? When the host clears the dishes away. Grandma sees them out. I fling a prayer in their direction that they won't kill each other on their way to their cars or that Tom won't run her over with his Hummer.

I help Grandma clean up. We're standing at the sink, washing crumbs off little plates and drying crystal goblets.

"Are you well, dear? Are you happy?" she asks, staring out the window at two robins flitting in a marble birdbath.

"I think so, Grandma." I try to support my voice in a way that sounds sure.

"Sometimes it's hard for a soul to tell, isn't it?"

"Why is that?" I ask. The next question rushes out before I even realize I am thinking it. "Were Mom and Dad happy?"

She stops. One of the robins flies off. The other hops around, looking for something.

"Mostly, I think so. Yes. Of course."

"Mostly?" I stack the little plates back on the shelf.

"Oh, no one can be happy all the time. That's a bit too much to ask, don't you think? Not even Jesus was happy all the time. But He got along alright."

The comparison doesn't sit right. "He did have the job of saving the world, so that would be stressful. The rest of us don't have that burden, Grandma."

The first bird returns. The two hop happily for a second and then fly off together.

Grandma dries her hand and hangs the tea towel neatly over the edge of the sink. "Oh? Don't we?"

She pats my shoulder and retreats for her afternoon nap without a word about this morning's fiasco. It's all cleaned up. It's over.

A nap is a good idea. I'm so unbelievably exhausted. I start towards the stairs when a discomforting thought interrupts me. Upstairs in my pale, soothing cloud of a room waits a lover's cell phone. It's probably overflowing with undeserving sweetness and promises and hope.

I turn around and head towards the den. There's an uncomfortable, stiff leather chair in there that I sit in sometimes when I want to think. Beside it, tucked in the drawer of the side table is a photo album with pages and pages of another life. One where a daddy smiles at his daughter and a mother smiles at Daddy. There are no captured images of sadness or anger or confusion. Everything is perfect. Everyone is happy. Everything is past.

CHAPTER FOURTEEN

The next morning, I'm shaking all over like Katharine Hepburn in one of her last movies, *On Golden Pond*, when her essential tremors were blatantly obvious. I don't have essential tremors. I'm simply trying to move my hoard of baby products out of my room, down the stairs, and into my car in one trip without Grandma noticing. Plus, I'm still dehydrated from my pity party. Also, I think my entire being is attempting to shake away the reality of what I will face when I get to school.

I like *On Golden Pond*, but it's Jordan's least favorite Hepburn movie. She prefers the earlier woman power films. I rewatched her favorite, *Adam's Rib,* last night, trying to suck in some of its girl grit. Hepburn's character, Amanda Bonner, is a defense attorney who creates her own power and then never backs down from it while her husband squirms uncomfortably in his toppling masculinity. If watching all those old movies with Jordan over the years has any lesson at all, it's this. There comes a time in every woman's life where she realizes her own power.

After the movie, I'd finally checked my Jamie phone, then spent the next hour returning his run of sweet texts calling on the stars and the universe and our souls to mix in some kind of romantic utopia. If Katharine Hepburn had had cell phones back in the black-and-white day, would she have snuggled in her pillowy bed trading gushing texts with her secret love? Or would she have blasted social media with a glorious announcement that if men can have a partner and a concubine, so can women?

There comes a time in every woman's life when she realizes her own power. I wish with all my heart that today were that day for me.

But it's not. I shove the trash bag loaded with baby paraphernalia in the back of my MINI Cooper. Maybe I should skip school, say I'm still sick. Grandma would probably believe me. I mean, it's kind of true. I already have a headache thinking about how Jamie and Tom will both be there. They'll both think I'm madly in love with them. They'll both be right.

I need music. Behind the wheel, I grab for my cell phone, but remember I threw it away. I don't dare bring my Jamie phone to school. What if someone saw it? What if Tom saw it? I switch on the radio and turn the actual knob to find something soothing, something girl-powery. I find a P!NK song. She belts out a musical equivalent of the middle finger all the way to school, but it doesn't work. Whatever illusion my mind bore regarding the strength of my spirit vanishes on every rebellious rhythm.

I'm not P!NK. I'm not Amanda Bonner. My inheritance isn't rebellion. It's comfort and conformity.

My parking spot is beside Tom's. I arrive first, but I don't wait for him. I hurriedly slink into school, preparing for a firing range of rumors to hammer away at my reputation. My heart won't register that nobody actually knows anything that could ruin my reputation, let alone reveal the truth to Tom. Nobody but Jordan and Nick, and no matter how mad Nick might be, he will never tell. His journalistic integrity prohibits divulging secrets.

Jordan will never tell because she's a woman who has always known her power. Once everyone else knows what she knows, her power is gone. But I don't want to think about Nick and Jordan and their disappointed smirks. There's no space for them in my thoughts. That room is reserved for the distracting unreality of blue satin and golden skin and green sea glass.

And the empty, dark eyes of my muscle-bound boyfriend.

This is impossible. What was I thinking? East Eggerton isn't that big. They're bound to run into each other which means Tom's bound to pound Jamie's face in.

But he doesn't know.

He will though.

Crowds of properly uniformed private schoolers congregate in the commons, hovering over flyers secured to bulletin boards with shiny pins. I lower my face and slip in behind a small huddle, half-expecting my sordid love affair to be plastered like a colorful billboard above a grey highway. It's ridiculous. I know it's ridiculous because no one *knows*. Still, I can't help but think on those eye-like windows of the apartment towers, glowering down at me, and it feels as if people don't know, surely, they all at least suspect.

I smooth my hair, then my skirt, as if pressing out imperfections will hide them. Maybe I can blend in with the crowd and avoid Tom and Jamie and, well, everyone. Peeking through straining heads, I see what's so important on the bulletin boards. Adulting Day. I'd forgotten.

Adulting Day is what *we* call it. The staff and faculty refer to it as College and Career Readiness and Charitable Activities Day. Several years ago, our parent/teacher association decided we needed to add charitable giving to our college/career day. Not everyone is going to college, they'd argued. I don't buy it. Who in this school isn't going to college? Nevertheless, they added a list of charities who need volunteers and money. Then they initiated a mandatory volunteerism program for students to help us be well-rounded, empathetic, successful citizens. That's the program I have yet to engage in, so I'll need to make up all the hours this year.

The ache in my head invades my whole being. How is it possible I can be failing at life already? I haven't even graduated high school yet.

I reach for the bead hidden under my required white, button-down. Tybee pulls to me. It was so easy there. Jamie's smile sneaks into my psyche. Maybe it can be easy here, too. If I would just make a choice.

"There's my girl." I hear Tom's voice behind me. His arms snake around my waist and turn me to face him. Worry smolders in his dingy, black eyes. He seems twelve feet tall and a mile wide.

"Here I am." The raspy edges of my voice are unfamiliar.

"Are you feeling better?" He slides a hand across my forehead.

"Better?" I swallow hard to keep from cringing.

"From whatever you were sick with yesterday."

"Oh, yes, I'm better. I guess."

Tom takes my elbow and guides me to a chair. He sits beside me. "Are you sure? You still look kind of pale. Should you even be here?"

"Aren't you being attentive?" It's a huge turn-around from yesterday's "you look like hell" greeting.

"I promised you I'd do better." Obsidian sparkles again in his eyes, and his hand is on my cheek. I lean into it. It's such a natural thing, I don't even realize I'm doing it until he rubs his thumb along my lip, and my stomach lurches.

I keep eye contact even though everything inside me wants to run screaming out the door. Is Jamie somewhere watching? The back of a blonde head turns down the far hallway. Is that him? Did he see Tom looking at me like that and caressing my face? Does Nick see? Does Jordan? Are they as disappointed as I am that I can't look away, can't break away?

"I want to do something for you," Tom says.

"You don't need to. Really."

"But I want to."

"Even after I threw up on you?"

He cringes. "Yes. I want to make up for whatever I did to piss you off."

"Really, it's not necessary."

"I'm gonna pick you up after practice and get you a new phone."

"A phone? I already have one."

"You have one?" Tom asks.

"I mean I already have one picked out." I'm stepping in that mud hole again and suddenly aware that the harder I struggle to escape, the harder it's going to suck me in. I'm not very good at this secret life thing.

"Oh, even better. Are you going to cheer practice?"

"Of course."

"Okay. I'll see you after"

We sit for a few intolerable minutes. Jordan and Nick are nowhere in the sea of bodies swimming around us. I don't see Jamie either, thank God. I look for him anyway. I can't help it.

I see Myrtle, leaning against a wall while Wilson George invades her space with manic movements. She's surprisingly stoic, her gaze piercing through his invisibility. She moves a drowsy hand to her face. He pulls it away, and she awakens with turbulent, troubled eyes and a pointed comeback. Something white hot shoots through me. Did Wilson do that to her face? She shakes her head at him, her siren-red hair billowing back and forth until he's lulled into submission and hangs his head. She retrieves her cell phone from her wristlet and swipes at the screen.

Panicked, awkward freshmen nervously scatter across my view on their way to their chosen career sessions. When they clear, Myrtle and Wilson are gone. Everyone else lingers, wading slowly into yet another day of what-are-you-gonna-do-with-your-life. The question sits with me, too.

Tom glances up from a text I hadn't noticed he was sending. "What session are you going to today?"

"I don't know. You?"

"We're all in a room together. Coach will have us in there all day." He slings the words out there.

"Who in a room?"

"The D-1s." He means the D-1 athlete prospects. He leans back and sort of flexes his shoulders. A vague memory of my dad with a newspaper, settling onto the couch after he'd mansplained something to my mom crawls out of my quicksand psyche and settles on solid ground.

Last year the school had installed a new bell system on account of loitering students who couldn't seem to prioritize punctuality. It's not really a bell at all. It's more like a long, whining foghorn. It goes off. We have one minute to get to class. Tom kisses my hand, then my head, and with the most sincere sweetness tells me he's glad I'm better and leaves.

I realize I've been half holding my breath since he first came upon me. I let it out and head to the bulletin board, but I'm stopped.

"There's my girl," Jamie steps out from behind the board, hands shoved in pockets, hair beautifully cascading across his eyes. I can't read his expression.

I freeze. Tom can't be more than ten feet away. Do I dare check?

"Jamie. Hi. I didn't see you there." The starched white shirt and creased pants sit uncomfortably on him. I wouldn't be surprised if they cracked and crumbled away as he moves through his day. It's weird seeing him in Eggerton clothes.

"Have lunch with me." I can't read him. I can't even wrap my brain around the fact that he's here.

"Today?" My heart pounds.

"Yeah. I have a spot in mind."

"A spot? What do you mean?"

His smile finally comes. He glances around. "I'll text you."

"I didn't bring my phone."

His eyes narrow. "I'll get a message to you."

He kisses my cheek and squeezes my hand. Soft flutters fill me. I reward him with my biggest smile. He looks like he wants to devour it along with the rest of me. I wouldn't mind if he did.

He scoots away. Just when I start to relax in the afterglow of his beautiful aura, I panic. Did anyone see that? I scan the empty commons. No one. Well, no one except Ms. Eckleburg who is coming my way.

I have less than one minute to choose a room to hide in for the next two hours. I check the choices on the board. Culinary careers. Financial careers. Medical Careers. Theatre. Journalism.

I remember that Nick's newspaper responsibilities will keep him occupied with speaker interviews and student feedback. I wonder if he has hooked Jordan to help, but I can't picture her as Nick's assistant. The possibility seems only slightly more plausible than her lounging with the other jocks in the D1 room, even if it is the most appropriate placement for her.

What is she gonna do with her life?

Quicksand tugs harder with the realization that I have no idea. Golf, I assume. It's what her mom would want, considering Gloria Baker had destroyed her own golf career with booze and who knows what else. Her dad would support her choosing golf, too. Mr. and Mrs. Baker had adopted Jordan long after Gloria had panned out and he had retired from screenwriting. There was nothing too good for Mr. Baker's little girl, especially since Mrs. Baker had to be reminded she even had a daughter most of the time.

A vague memory climbs out. It's of our freshman year when Jordan didn't make varsity because of rumors of misconduct during try-outs. Someone had suggested she'd lied on her scorecard. It had taken her two seasons to live it down, but she'd managed to keep the gossip from her parents.

"Which one are you considering?" Mrs. Eckleburg reaches me. Her voice is like a salve to my soul.

"I don't know. Guess I'd better decide."

"How about this one?" Her finger points to the last entry at the bottom of the page. Social Justice, Room 310.

"Social justice? Like Martin Luther King?"

Her smile is so sweet. I realize I've missed her and her office with the pastoral mural on the wall and the bowl full of comfort chocolates on her desk.

Just Daisy

She answers, "Martin Luther King and then some. I think this morning's presentation is more on women's rights, though."

"Don't we have them already?" I ask.

"Give it a try. If you are bored stiff, I'll let you change rooms after lunch. Trust me." She says.

I do. I trust her. Besides, a couple of hours in the presence of mighty feminist warriors might cloak my guilty conscience. I hope it will, anyway. I think I'm losing it. Is paranoia a sign of emotional distress? Because as I float down the hall to room 310, I can't shake the feeling that somebody is following me, watching my every move.

CHAPTER FIFTEEN

It's amazing how four walls and a closed door can help a person breathe easier. Sheltered away in a classroom full of bored teens, I can shut out the reality of my two worlds colliding and the nagging premonition that nothing good can come of it. I sit on my hands, forcing my fingers from my intrusive, green stone. Then I see our speaker.

If ever a person's appearance commanded the attention of a room, our speaker's did.

She's no female version of Martin Luther King. She's her own powerful presence. She's tall and toned, decked in a seriously gorgeous bright red Armani pantsuit and no-nonsense Anne Taylor pumps. Not exactly my picture of social justice battle attire. I guess I'm used to Lilly Ernest, a senior in choir, who's sitting near the front, already nodding her head in agreement with everything our speaker hasn't even spoken yet. Lilly wears propaganda under her Eggerton uniform and combat boots when she can get away with it, and kneels, bowing her half-shaved head, every time we sing the national anthem.

Nevertheless, our speaker is impressive. Her impeccable, precise hair rivals any Fox News female, as does her make-up. Flawless.

"I'm Claudia Hip," she says, her intelligent voice welcoming us with weary insistence. We've come to the right room today, she insists. She has one request. Leave everything we know or think we know outside and listen. Really listen.

How could we not? Honestly, she's one of only a handful of African Americans in the entire building. We have no black teachers and only a few dozen black students. It doesn't matter, though. Her confidence owns the place.

She begins, "Next summer we will celebrate the 100th anniversary of the passing of the 19th Amendment, June 4th, 1919. One hundred years. You would think our work would be done." She pauses to stare, unflinchingly into our eyes. "You would think, but you'd be wrong."

For the next several minutes, she rattles off statistics like an auctioneer. In 2017, women made on average 18.3 percent less than their male counterparts. We still lack enough women in job fields requiring math and science and technology skills. Female athletes work just as hard but earn significantly less and garner fewer commercial sponsors. Women are more often sexually harassed at work or sexually abused in general. Millions of women every year report being abused in their own homes. Many want to leave but feel they can't. Where would they go? After all, there are 3,000 more animal shelters in the United States than women's shelters.

"Are you listening?" She asks, her stern gaze boring into us, one by one.

Lucille raises her hand. I hadn't realized she's in the room.

"You have a question?" Ms. Hip asks.

"Uh, yeah. I just don't know what any of this has to do with us." Lucille looks immensely bored.

"You're a woman, aren't you? You're a human being, aren't you?" Ms. Hip says.

"Well, yeah-uh. But why do I care how much less women make? My mom doesn't have to work."

"But if she did, shouldn't she make as much as your dad for the same work?"

"That makes no sense. If my dad already makes enough, why would it matter if my mom makes less? Wouldn't it all be like extra?"

Everyone laughs. Except Claudia Hip.

"The lower pay is a sign of how society still values men over women rather than valuing them both as equal members of society."

Lucille duck-faces and rolls her eyes in response.

Ms. Hip directs her next comment to the general audience. "Don't think these statistics don't include your socio-economic group. Thirty percent of all male batterers are professionals who are respected in their communities. Business executives, attorneys, doctors."

Lucille's hand goes up again, "Okay, but seriously, if these men are beating these women, the women should just leave."

"Many can't." Ms. Hip's voice is softer now. It's no longer a public announcement she's giving. It's heavier than that.

"If he's a doctor, she can just leave while he's at work, right?" Lucille says.

Sometimes the stupidity of Lucille McKee astounds me. I'm not the only one who feels that way. Lilly Ernest scoffs so hard it sounds like she's choking. If she had a protest sign, I think she'd beat Lucille over the head with it. The room snickers. Ms. Hip quiets them.

"Perhaps, but it goes deeper than that. Often, by the time he's physically abusing her, a lot of emotional damage has already been done. He may blame her for his actions. She made him do it, somehow. She made him mad or frustrated. She acted out of line, so what choice did he have?"

Something pricks my subconscious. My breath goes shallow.

Lucille is in it now. "How could it be her fault that he hit her?"

"It's not. He's simply done a good job of making her believe that all the problems in their relationship are her fault. Even if he apologizes and promises to do better, she's the bad one if she doesn't give him another chance, and another, and another. After all, he's promised to do better. And abusers aren't hideous monsters. They can be quite charming and convincing, romantic even. When he's bad, he's very bad, but when he's good..."

He's very, very good.

My chest tightens. My body goes cold, though I'm sweating.

Lucille is still clueless, but she's lost her bluster. She smirks at the girl beside her and mumbles, "Nobody's good enough for me to put up with that."

Ms. Hip doesn't let it slide. "You must have a very strong support system. Good for you. Not everyone does. Sometimes, there is a lot of shame in breaking off a relationship. Fear that people might not believe you. Fear that you'll disappoint family or friends who have never seen the abusive side. Often, the abuser buys into this and convinces his partner that she'd disappoint the world if they break up. Like somehow their entire family or social circle is balanced on their relationship."

Ms. Hip has circled around the room. She's standing over me now. Finally, Lucille settles back in her chair. "How many women live like that?"

"Statistics show that one in four women between the ages of eighteen and sixty-five have experienced some form of domestic violence."

My hand shoots up, involuntarily.

"Yes?" Ms. Hips indicates me.

"You said eighteen through sixty-five. What about younger?"

"Younger than eighteen is considered child abuse. That's a different category."

"What if it's not done by a parent though?" I wish I could keep my mouth from talking. Myrtle's bruised face floats through my thoughts. I want with everything in me to shout, "It's Myrtle, guys. I'm referring to Myrtle." I feel heat crawl up my chest and pray they don't think I'm talking about me.

Ms. Hip answers and moves onto another question, but I don't hear it. The voices in my head are too loud.

She's starting a video now, about their shelter and how they provide more than just safety and all the jobs we should consider if we want to be social justice warriors for women.

After the film, she implores us. "We need doctors, counselors, lawyers. Mostly, though, we need women who are willing to use their voices to amplify the message of equality. Whatever choices you make after high school, make ones that lift women up. Make ones that command respect. Make ones that create pathways to equality, justice, and victory."

The bell sounds for our first break. Everyone leaves the room, rushing, I expect, to the snack bar or the bathroom or to the exit near the band room where they might be able to sneak out for the day, unnoticed. I don't. My body seems frozen. Unexpectedly, a remembered vision flashes in my head of my mother's old poster flaunting Marilyn Monroe lustily laughing wide-mouthed and red-lipped in a low-cut gown that barely contains her bosom. The graphic artist had scrawled a quote in the bottom left corner: *I don't mind living in a man's world as long as I can be a woman in it.*

I used to sit at the feet of my beautiful mother while she primped in front of her dressing room mirror. I would stare at that iconic image, framed in gold and hanging on her wall. I would stare for what seemed like hours, and sometimes I'd drag Jordan in there to look at it.

"Utterly ridiculous," she'd say and turn away disgusted.

A twisted knot of something pulls at my insides. How is it that I never thought about the existence of battered women shelters before? I mean, I know they exist, but I never thought about them, the necessity for them, the people who end up there, the fact that in order for the victims to have somewhere to go, warriors must be there first.

"We're supposed to shoo you all out of here for ten minutes. Sorry." Ms. Hip says. She's placing information on all the desks.

"No worries," I say, but I don't move.

She hands me a business card and a pamphlet. "Here's more information for you. That's my cell phone. Call me if you have any questions."

I glance it over. Glance only because I don't need the information, but I don't want to be rude. On the inside cover, there's a number to call to schedule bringing donations and a list of things they need. A list of basically the stuff I've got stuffed in the back of my car.

"I have some things to donate," I say.

"Great. Call that number to schedule a delivery."

"Why do I need to schedule? Can't I just drop it off?"

"We give every patron a tour, too. If you're going to support a cause, you should know what it's all about. It takes only about ten minutes, but it's important."

"Will you be the one giving the tour?" I have no idea why those words spill out. Why do I care if she's there? I only want to rid myself of my baby hoard.

"I can be. Mention that when you call to schedule." She lays the most beautifully manicured hand I've even seen on my arm. "Is there anything else?"

"No," I say too fast and too hard. "There's nothing."

The claustrophobia of the four walls hits me and I dash. In the hall, Jordan is waiting. She huffs and pulls me by the hand to a tucked-away table. As we sit, she looks around like we're two spies setting the world on fire.

"Are you still mad?" I ask.

She lifts her chin again and addresses me without looking at me, "Of course, I'm still mad."

"Oh." If the entire East Eggerton structure collapsed down on me, I could not feel more burdened, more incapable of crawling out of the rubble I've somehow created of my life.

"Jamie wants to see you for lunch," she says.

"I know."

"There's a perfect spot behind the back shelf on the second floor of the library," Jordan directs.

"If you're mad, why are even bothering?"

"Someone's got to fix you. You're my best friend. It's my job."

"Do I need fixed?" My soul sinks lower.

"Well, maybe just patched up a little." She pushes a strand behind my ear and offers a soft smile.

"Gee thanks. You make me sound as appealing as a blown-out tire."

She laughs without her usual condescension. "It's not quite that bad. You're lovely. Jamie thinks so, too. In fact, he thinks you're as beautiful as an island paradise." She mimics his voice.

She stares wistfully at my face. I close my eyes against visions of sandcastles, melting in the relentless progress of incoming tides, and of sea glass, half-buried and sparkling against an emerging sun. The waves and wind and the music we'd danced to play a deathless song in my mind. Tybee Island, more so than any other reality, could not be over dreamed.

"What are you gonna do?" Jordan asks.

"Meet him, of course,"

"What are you gonna say to him?"

I can't answer. I don't know. Or maybe I don't want to know. I mean, I have to tell him that I'm still with Tom, but how can I? I can barely accept it myself.

The one-minute warning bell, sounding very much like a reticent foghorn, goes off. Once again, I'm stuck to my seat--this time by a pull to the past.

Jordan pushes out her chair to leave, but I reach for her wrist and sit her back down. "What break-out session are you in?"

She offers a confused, haughty laugh. "How do you not know?"

"How would I know?" I swear the world feels so upside down right now, I wouldn't be surprised if she said belly dancing or Uber driver.

"You know everything there is to know about me, Daisy. You're my best friend."

"I didn't know about you and Nick."

She's silent for a second.

"What about Nick?" she finally says with a flip of her aloof hand.

"Are you two dating?"

"Well, we dated."

"Does that mean you are broken up already?"

"It means we went on a date."

"Are you going to go on another?"

She turns directly to me with a bounce in her chair like she's just been flopped around in a bumpy jalopy. "You know what I like about Nick? He's careful. He takes in life as if he's on a perpetual Sunday afternoon drive. I like Sunday afternoon drives." The rigidness leaves her posture.

It's these fleeting moments of vulnerable truth that connect us. Before I let her go, we hear footsteps stomping behind us. It's Myrtle being pursued by Wilson in mid-tantrum. We're invisible to them. Wilson pulses a fist at his side as he slinks behind her. I dam up a wall of words from calling out to her. I swear, if I had a lifeline, I'd lasso it around her curvy little hips and yank her away from him.

"Investments," Jordan says.

"I'm sorry?"

"I'm in Investments."

If I had seen that choice on the list, and if I had thought about it long enough, I would have figured it out. I exhale and hang on to the one solid thing in my life, my Jordan.

She squeezes my hand and leans in. "See you in the library. I'll be the lookout."

I sigh at the idea that the reason Jordan is in Investments is because Bank Robbery isn't a choice. Little rivers of excitement run through me as I picture her as lookout, dressed in black, speaking in code in some French accent. A too big smile takes over my face. Lunch can't come soon enough.

When it does come, I bound up the library stairs. I imagine Jamie waiting for me, decked in a tuxedo with his hands stuffed casually in his pockets like Leo on the Titanic. When I come around the stacks, there he is. He turns to me, his single flap of hair hanging loosely over one eye. It feels like an eternity since I've seen him even though it's only been a couple hours. I race to him, not caring who might see. Jordan won't let anyone see. Neither will Jamie.

I throw my arms around him and tuck my head securely under his chin. He smooths my hair.

"I'm glad you came," he says.

"How could I not?"

"Do you feel better?" he asks.

"I never felt bad."

"I thought you might regret--"

I lift my face to his shining eyes. "Never."

Then he kisses me, soft and sweet and secret. Finally, in a kiss of a whisper, he says, "Come over after cheer practice. I have a surprise for you."

I breathe in every ocean-air possibility of us. "I love your surprises." It comes out in a hushed giggle.

He kisses me once more, and his face becomes happy. The electricity is back, the voltage amped up. My heart beats so hard, I almost don't hear his response. "And I love you."

CHAPTER SIXTEEN

The next few hours are spent taking online personality and career matching assessments. I don't see Jamie for the rest of the day, but Ms. Eckleburg catches me in the hall.
"How did you enjoy the presentation?" she asks.
"Claudia Hip is, is..." I don't know how to describe her.
"Amazing, isn't she? She's my stepsister."
"Really?"
"Her mom didn't marry my dad until we were already adults, but I feel like I've known her my whole life. I grew up an only child, like you. Then five years ago, I gained seven siblings. I'm very blessed."
"Seven. I can't imagine."
"Sometimes life presents pathways we can't imagine on our own, but when we climb them, the experience is nothing less than extraordinary." She looks to me like she is intoning more than just an expression of gratitude for blended families. That's when I notice it. A glorious, glitzing rock of a diamond sitting awkwardly steady on her hand. She's engaged. The fellow who could buy her a ring like that won't need the extra, inferior income of a high school counselor.

I could imagine her path, and it made me vaguely sad for future Eggerton scholars who will never know her.

"Daisy, we need to do something about your lack of volunteer hours."
"I know. I know. I'm sorry."
"It's okay. You've been dealing with other things."

Truly, I hate the fact that my parents' passing gives me a pass for everything. But not an actual pass, just a postponement until my poor little psyche can equal the exertion of other, normal kids from normal families who only deal with asshole fathers and overwrought mothers, not tragedies like crashing cars.

"I'll find something. I promise," I say.

"How about I hook you up with Claudia? She always needs volunteers."

"I'll think about it," I say, and run off to practice knowing full well the disappointment instilled by my response. Right now, the idea of warrioring for anyone, including women and their rights, feels too heavy. My immediate need is to get to cheer practice and make the next hour fly. Jamie has already spooled the universe around his magic heart and presented the only path I want. No need to imagine anything else.

At cheer practice, the squad is already stretching when Myrtle rushes into the small gym, her cheeks flushed and her aura glowing. I'm surprised. She must have made up with Wilson because she looks exactly like a woman in love.

She makes room for herself on the gym floor between me and Lucille. She has her phone with her and immediately shows Lucille something on it.

"Isn't he adorable?" Myrtle squeals. Lucille joins her.

"What is it?" I ask.

"It's nothing." Myrtle smiles at me in a way that suggests she might know something. I try to look away, but there's something I need to ask her.

"How did you like career day? Which session did you end up in?" I say.

Ms. Hip invades my mind. An urgency surges inside me to tell Myrtle everything from that session, to shove the pamphlet and business card at her and make her confess that it wasn't a door that smashed her face.

Myrtle answers with a giggle. "Um, let me think."

"You don't remember?" Maybe she'd used the exit by the band room, like so many others.

She can't stop smiling. "I think it was Culinary. Yeah, that's it. Culinary."

"I didn't know you cooked," I say.

"I don't. If I'm gonna be a good wife someday though, I guess I'd better learn." It's a preposterous thing to say. Myrtle is a sophomore.

"Ginny Fay was a terrible cook."

"Who?" Myrtle asks.

"Never mind," I say and wonder what Jamie's favorite meal is.

Myrtle considers me for a second and then shakes her head.

"Okay, Okay, I'll show you. Look, I got a new puppy this morning. It's an Airedale."

She pulls the pic up on her cell. It's no Airedale. But it is cute.

"So, you weren't actually in culinary?" I ask.

She squeals again. "Not actually. At least not the whole time."

Stretching is almost over. This conversation isn't going the way I want it to. I'm about to miss my chance, so I breathe in and turn to her. "Myrtle, I have to tell you something."

She cocks her head and looks at me wide-eyed. "What is it?" she finally asks.

I don't want to say. It might not be my place. It's probably not the time, either. But it's gnawing at me. I muster all my Southern upbringing. Grandma Betty would smile, offer sweet tea, and passively mention some something-or-other and the message would be delivered. But that kind of charm works only on other Southerners.

I look Myrtle squarely in the eye and dive in. "I saw you earlier today."

Panic takes over her expression. Panic and something else. Her eyebrows arch outward. Her lips bow downward until she begins to nibble on the lower one.

I continue. "I saw you with Wilson. He seemed upset about something."

At once, she lowers her head but raises her eyes to me under a billow of red locks. It's arresting. I feel checked somehow. My first inclination was right. It's not my place.

A voice inside my head, a little sharp with an edge of humble righteousness, reminds me that I'm the captain. She's on my team. I should protect her. After all, we're all in this together. But a lifetime of Grandma Betty provides a very strong undertow.

"But there's a smile on your face now, so I suppose it was nothing?" I say. *Always offer a graceful exit.*

It's a full ten seconds before she takes it. With a flip of her head, the red waves fall down her back.

"Just a misunderstanding. You know how clueless guys can be. Completely clueless and jealous. Mostly clueless. Guys don't like being made fools of." A flash of a look tells me Myrtle may have a little Southern upbringing herself. Either that or it's my imagination and she's not insinuating anything.

"Did Wilson give you the puppy?"

She exhales an inconceivable laugh and continues stretching. Something about the sound of it pokes at me until I want to poke back. The words spill out, sounding more accusatory than I mean for them to.

"Just exactly how jealous does Wilson get? Jealous enough to impersonate a door?"

Myrtle's jaw drops like I've just spoken the most inane nonsense she's ever heard. "No. Wilson would never impersonate a door. He's not man enough for that."

"Man enough?" My stomach goes foul, and I wish with everything in me that Myrtle had attended Social Justice with me.

She opens her mouth as if attempting an articulated response, but only partial stammers interrupted with incredulous groans come out. Finally, she gives up, jumps to her feet with renewed energy and claps us all to attention. "Let's get this party started, ladies!"

If it weren't for my looming date with Jamie, I might have dwelt on our conversation. I feel nothing less than usurped. But I don't dwell on it. Instead, I run through the drills, escape as quickly as possible and drive in a mad rush through commuters meandering home after their manic Mondays, straight to Jamie's place. There's no orange cone to greet me this time, but I locate the parking space anyway, shut off the engine and bound up the stairs to him.

He answers the door before I can knock.

"There you are." He beams like he's been waiting for me his whole life. I throw my arms around him and attack his face with my lips, not caring that I'm a bit sweaty from practice. Memories of his hot skin against mine tremor through my core, and all I want is for him to lead me back to those blue satin sheets. He doesn't. He breaks away and gives me a glass of water.

"I have a surprise for you."

I swallow hard and attempt to calm myself. "That's what you said."

"Are you ready?"

"I never know with you. How can I ever be ready when you come out of nowhere all the time?"

He smiles at me from under that flop of shimmering, blonde hair. "You're ready. Even if you don't know it." At that moment, a wave of something—uncertainty—billows between us. Briefly.

He grabs my hand and rushes me out the door, down the steps, and to his garage. He punches a remote he'd carried in his pocket. The door opens. I know what's behind it, but I hold my breath anyway. When the door raises and the interior is revealed, I swear to God it shines like Tutankhamen's treasure.

"She's beautiful." I hesitate to step into the garage, so he pulls me in.

"You can touch her, you know." There's satisfaction in his voice.

I finally do, running my fingers gently over the smooth golden-yellow paint, across the hood, dancing them all the way to the door handle. As much as I want to open her up and slide inside, it doesn't seem right somehow. I never actually sat inside these cars with my dad. We just marveled at them, like paintings in a museum. He never owned them, either. He owned practical luxuries like his Lexus and mom's Cadillac Escalade.

There are some dreams, Dad would say, that are better left as dreams. Some dreams we aren't meant to own.

Tearing my mesmerized eyes from Jamie's dream of an automobile, I look at him. He's not looking back. He tours around the Mach 1, his studious gaze seeming to reevaluate every inch of it through a new lens. It's that moment when I realize the weight of my approval on his worldview. Little shivers of shock run through me along with my dad's repeated warning. *Some dreams we aren't meant to own.*

"Do you want to drive her?" Jamie asks without making eye contact.

It feels a bit like a trick question. Am I being tested?

"Can I?"

"Of course, you can. It's your surprise."

We slide in. The steering wheel reminds me of the texture of those sea glass beads from the summer, buffed and smoothed clean by the power of water and wind. Oddly, I don't feel transported back in time as I imagined I would at all those Saturday morning car shows. No, it's more like transported to an unfamiliar world. Memories and dreams and hopes and the tug of what might have been and what never will be flood in. I push on the gas.

"Where are you taking us, Daisy?"

"It's my turn to show you something," I answer.

CHAPTER SEVENTEEN

I haven't driven home in over a year, but it doesn't matter. As we fly down the tree-lined street with the open sky above us and the whisper of wind zipping by, I almost forget Jamie's with me. The pure power of the machine tempts me to see exactly how far I can push the pedal, how fast I can go. A muscle in my thigh spasms while I struggle to maintain control. Time zooms and we're suddenly there. We enter the gates, ramble through the twisting road and arrive in front of my parents' mansion. We slide out of his Mach 1. His trembling hand finds mine and, for a moment, we stare at it like tourists do monuments and ancient lighthouses on lovely vacations.

The skewed reality of returning to a beloved elementary school and realizing it's all so much smaller than your mind had made it to be is even more uncomfortable in reverse. The house—my house—is so much larger than I remembered. Everything about it is grand and glorious and dreamy.

There are twelve windows on the front of the house alone: four tall arched ones flank the double entry door; a line of five denote the second floor, and three charming dormers top it off. Technically, there's more to the front of the house, but the rest is set back on both sides. A smaller door that mom used to joke was the servants' entry is tucked away on the right. On the left, a series of tall, majestic windows let the natural light into my father's study.

It's a mirage. It must be. If we step to it, it will disappear like dust on a wisp of startled air. Just as I decide it's a mistake, we shouldn't have come, Jamie lets go and ascends the front stairs. He turns around and, again, he reminds me of that scene from Titanic where Leo stands at the bottom of the stairs like he owns the ocean liner—hell, like he owns the whole damn ocean liner company—and waits for his goddess.

"What is this place?" he asks.

"It's my parents' house. My house, I guess." A heated blush crawls up my neck.

"And you don't live here?"

"I did once."

I join him on the stairs.

"Do you want to go in?" he asks.

"It's been a long time."

"Whatever you want."

I don't know what I want, but it seems silly to stand there, to bring him here and not go in.

"How stupid does it sound if I say I think I've been waiting for someone to share it with. Someone who—" I have no idea what I'm trying to say.

He squeezes my hand. "It's not stupid at all. We've both been waiting for each other, I think."

When I open the door, it doesn't creak, as I am expecting. I mean, of course it wouldn't. Just because I haven't been here doesn't mean no one has. We pay a staff to maintain it, and Grandma visits every other week. She invites me every time. Every time I decline.

The friendly foyer greets us, and I remember how much my dad hated that wallpaper with its lilies falling over a black and white background.

"Well, I like it, Charles. I can't help it. It makes me smile. Daisy likes it. Don't you Daisy?"

"I like it, Daddy." I was ten at the time. I still called him Daddy.

He rolled his eyes and kissed my mom's nose. "If it makes you smile..."

"You make me smile." She embraced him and attacked his face with kisses.

Jamie slouches nervously as if he's about to meet a suspicious father to ask him what time curfew is.

"My mom loved this wallpaper." I spread my fingers across the rough texture, but no hidden emotion transfers from it. It's empty, like a conch shell but without the promise of a seafaring adventure coiled somewhere in its heart.

There's a sadness that comes when you look with new eyes at something which you've built up in the hollow recesses of your own heart.

Just Daisy

"It's nice wallpaper." Jamie's voice is weak and tense.

"Can I show you around?" I feel oddly formal.

"Is there more wallpaper to see?" His smile returns and puts me at ease.

By the third room, the awkwardness wears off, and I sound very much like a tour guide.

Here's where we hung our stockings. Here's where we played chess. Here's where my mom played sad and lonely songs on the piano. Here's where my dad smoked cigars while he pretended not to listen. Here's where they shared long kisses over coffee and forgot I existed. Here's where I sang funny little tunes for them, and they remembered again.

"What's your favorite room?" He asks as the sun sets in the backyard and jeweled tones of orange and purple peek in at us through a wall of windows.

"Out here." I lead him through to the back yard. Or outdoor living space, as my mom called it.

The gazebo beckons us, so we snuggle under its awning and look out at the pool. It's still filled. They fill it every year, just in case.

"It never gets used," I say unnecessarily.

"That's too bad. We should use it."

I smile up at him, shocked at the idea that I'm here in my old home with this dream of a guy. That bigger, more beautiful fish everyone talks about when relationships run their course and people start looking for new adventures.

I settle in the groove of his arm. I count the stars and listen, hoping one strikes its tuning fork on my heart and sings to me the secrets of my current happiness.

"How did you get here?" I mean it as romantic rhetoric, but he laughs.

"You drove my Mach 1."

My own laughter bounces off the roof of the gazebo. "And how did that get here? Seriously. How is it possible that you have a car like that?"

He steps away, injured.

"Why wouldn't I have a car like that?"

"I didn't mean anything. It's just that most teenage boys don't have old classic cars."

"Haven't you realized I'm not most teenage boys?"

A recognizable shadow crosses his face, a lost memory. Of all people, I should understand. Maybe his dad didn't believe that some dreams aren't meant to own.

"Was it your father's?"

He thinks about the answer before he gives it. "He owned it once. Yes."

I link my arm through his and pull him back to me. "Then I'm even more honored that you let me drive it. Thank you. It was a perfect surprise."

"Perfect?" He seems unsure.

"Yes. Perfect. Would you settle for anything less?"

"Not when I have you."

Suddenly, I want to know everything there is to know about him. A million questions swarm inside me. I secure one and present it to him. "How did he die?"

"Does it matter?" he answers too quickly.

"What do you mean?"

"I mean he's gone. Does it matter how it happened?"

"I don't know. I think maybe it does. I didn't know the last time I saw my parents was the last time I'd see them. I think it makes a difference."

"Maybe." That's all he says, but it's not enough.

"How did your mom handle it?" I try to form pictures in my head of Jamie and a mother and father. It's weird. The only thing that comes to mind is him springing from the ocean, fully formed like some kind of mythical god.

"She was sad, of course." Little muscles in his neck shift, visibly shutting off his voice.

"When can I meet her?"

A white, hot energy smolders in his expression when he finally looks at me.

"She's not here."

"She's not here in Chicago with you? What's going on, Jamie?"

"What do you mean what's going on? I'm here for you. What else matters?"

I recall whispers of rumors about New Guy from my first day back, but just whispers. I hadn't paid that much attention. I realize with the naivety of a heroine in a bad horror flick that no one knows I'm here. No one would expect me to be. I could disappear just like that and never be found. I remember the vocal fluctuations and rhythms that work on Tom and adjust my tone.

"She let you come to Chicago? By yourself?"

He closes his eyes, and I can see his lids twitch. His entire being seems like a robot short-circuiting in front of me. Finally, he exhales and looks up at me from under that mess of perfect hair.

"I'm eighteen. I can go where I want. I can do what I want. What I want is to be here with you. She trusts me, Daisy. Do you?"

I'm not ready to answer. "So, she just let you come? Where is she? What about holidays? What about all those senior year things like Homecoming and Prom and graduation? Doesn't she want to be part of it?"

He'd already lost so much in losing his father. I can't imagine the other parent not wanting to make up for everything.

I must remember to hug Grandma more.

An unbelievably genuine smile spreads across his flawless face. "My mother is never in one place long enough to buy into the importance of things like Homecoming and graduation. The world is a big place. Why limit yourself to traditional expectations when you can make the whole world your own?"

I try to process his world. One parent gone forever and the other just gone.

"Do you know how shallow Homecoming is anyway? It's a popularity contest. Why desire the vote of everyone? What does that matter if you can find all the happiness you need in one person?" He leans in. I scoot back.

"But she'll be back?"

He hesitates.

"Of course. What kind of mom wouldn't come back?"

"You didn't want to travel with her?"

"I wanted you."

He takes my face in his hands and kisses me breathless. All at once, I understand what it is to own a dream, to touch what seemed unreachable before. Like a rush of pre-storm wind, it's full of beauty and freedom and danger.

Maybe it is the laissez-faire parenting that allows a dream like

Jamie to exist. Who am I to challenge that? And he's right. It's brought him to me. I have no idea what I'm going to do with such a gift, so I decide at that second not to think about it. Just enjoy the moment, like we are lying on the beach under the stars on our summer island and the rest of the world has disappeared.

For another hour we lounge by Charles and Ginny's pool, making up stories about the constellations and the pioneers who originally settled this area and what the world looked like then and what the world might look like in a hundred years. Something happens to children of lost parents. Either they become afraid of everything and live in a constant flux of panic and despondency. Or they learn to embrace the possible with the impossible.

It took a while, three years ago, for the unreal reality of my situation to sink in. It didn't seem real that they weren't returning from their romantic road trip. Or if it did, it didn't seem real that they were dead. They were simply still on that lovely adventure, driving down long, picturesque roads, stopping off at quaint bookstores and coffee shops, perpetually drawing out their dream. It was the funeral that had made it real. The funeral, and all those awful people afterward standing around our kitchen with half-empty glasses like macabre mannequins at some apocalyptic cocktail party.

But if I could hold onto the vision of Mom and Dad, forever in love, forever on the road to somewhere celebratory and romantic, I could see the promise of hope in the world. Jamie, if nothing else, helps me see that promise of hope. Just his presence makes it a tangible thing.

Before we leave, I kiss him one more time. "Thank you for coming with me. I'm glad it was you. No one else would have understood."

"It will always be me, Daisy. Don't ever forget that."

The rusted-out hole in my heart that empties emotions and intimacy like a bottomless bucket, closes a little.

We are halfway back to Tuolomee when the violent high beams of an aggressive SUV nearly blind me. I scream. Jamie's hand leaves my knee and grabs the steering wheel, jerking us to the side of the road. The beastly vehicle flies by, but not so fast that I can't recognize it.

"It's Tom," I sob and bury my face in my lover's chest.

CHAPTER EIGHTEEN

I've often seen those real crime shows where the falsely convicted guy fights for justice. Ten years, twenty years, must feel like an eternity when a person is imprisoned for something he didn't do. The suffocation of concrete walls and iron bars must syphon every drop of hope from a soul. How could a person live? How could you even want to?

But as I wake up the next morning, a different scenario plays like a dark comedy action movie trailer in my mind's eye. Drums beat a scandalous rhythm to accompany my morning routine. Though the sound is completely imagined, the energy pumping through me is not. As I finish running the mascara wand over my lashes, I realize I haven't quit smiling all morning.

I think on those real crime shows. I don't care to watch the ones where the guy is actually guilty. Those seem anticlimactic, I suppose. But right now, I wonder what kind of energy runs through a criminal's soul when he's going down for something he *did* do, something he never in a million years thought he would, but he did. What overrides every other feeling as he eats his last meal, finishes his last conversation, mumbles his last prayer?

Is it regret? Satisfaction? Pride? Rebellion? Maybe it's all those, but surely, whatever it is, the memory of those past deeds imbues him with an unutterable energy, like the seismic waves of an earthquake from miles away.

On the way to school, I grip the steering wheel hard, trying to recreate the feeling of that Mach 1 in my hands. All I can feel, though, is Jamie's long, warm fingers clasped around mine and the explosion of my conscience when the headlights of Tom's car poured down on us like a helicopter searching out an escapee. I'd been scared, at first, shaken. Then angry. How dare he interrupt my perfect dream? Then empowered. Full of conviction. I won't lose Jamie.

The thing is, even though Tom nearly ran us over, I'm in the driver's seat now. For the first time ever, I have something tempting me away. I'm not just along for Tom's ride.

The driver's seat is a dangerously powerful place to be.

I'm not sorry. In fact, I don't even hesitate when I pull into my painted parking spot beside his. I don't blink when I knock on his driver's side window and his red face accuses me of what I am guilty of a million times over.

He gets out of the car, closes the door, and leans back on it. Damn, he's fine. Where Jamie is light, a sun-bleached Apollo, Tom is dark and brooding with boulder-like muscles that move slowly and gracefully under his button-down shirt. His dark hair is shorn short for football season. My breath comes in spurts as I picture the luxurious curls that will adorn his Ares-like brow by January. Something inside me buzzes when his coal-black eyes flash and his jaw pulsates.

"Do I want to know where you were when I came by last night?" His voice surges.

I laugh, surprised at the authentic sound of it. "You came by?"

"We were supposed to buy you a phone."

I touch his jaw, and it relaxes under my fingertips. His eyes soften.

"I'm sorry," I lie. "I was a little off my game yesterday."

"Off your game?"

"Out of it, I guess." My voice, soft and alluring, caresses his bruised ego.

I've never really examined his pout before, but something about his stubborn jaw and sulky bottom lip moves me. I shift my palm to his cheek and lean in for a kiss because I can. He hesitates at first, then suddenly, as if motivated by a deep, primal force, he wraps both arms around me, his top hand ensnares my hair and his bottom hand presses my hips into him. I should pull away. It's not right, but it's so familiar. As exciting as new love can be, there is nothing more dangerously stabilizing than familiarity. His lips press into mine in an almost violent reclaiming of what he doesn't realize he's already lost. I kiss him back like it's our last time and wonder if it might be.

When he's done, our foreheads stay touching. He breathes heavily like we've done something hotter than simply kiss by the side of his faux military SUV.

"I hate it when you aren't with me." His voice comes out in a raspy whisper. For the first time since he caught my eye over cafeteria lasagna in September of our freshman year, he seems vulnerable, but it doesn't last.

"Guess you can buy your own damn phone, huh?" He hits the lock button on his car fob, collars his arm around my neck and heads in long, athletic strides to the front doors of the school. I'm powerless to resist, and we enter like a king and his conquest.

Nick finds us immediately. He questions me with his gaze which I try not to meet. He gets the hint.

"You guys know what happens today?" Nick asks. I haven't seen him since our fight. I want to hug him and apologize a million times.

"Daisy goes and buys herself a new phone?" Tom snarks.

"Oh, what kind are you getting?" Nick pulls his out.

"Jesus, Nick. You aren't gonna start talking cell phone garbage, are you?"

"What?" Nick's perpetual surprise sits on his face. I love my cousin so much. What would I do without him?

I settle a hand on his arm. "What's happening today, Nick?"

"We vote for Homecoming candidates. It's early on account of so many away games this year." He questions me again with his expression, and I know what he's getting at. It's pretty much a given that we'll be nominated. That we'll probably win. I mean Tom and me. Panic churns inside me.

Homecoming doesn't actually happen for another two weeks. Those two weeks will be filled with a ton of activities. There's the photo shoot of all the nominated couples. Of course, we'll need to coordinate our outfits, so shopping. There's the parade, the charity ice cream social, the pep rally stuff, and then the preparation for the dance. If we're nominated, and if we're coupled up together—and why wouldn't we be—we'll be stuck together for the next two weeks.

I'm pulled back to memories of Tybee Island and Jamie, sitting on the beach, elbows on his knees, staring at the lighthouse and waiting for me to finish with whatever girls' trip stuff Grandma and I were off doing that day. He always waited for me, patient, constant, and sure. But he never had to watch me parade around with another love while he waited.

I try to step away, to create some distance between Tom and me. His grip tightens around my neck, the muscles stiffening like a bodybuilder striking a pose, and I know it's not just my imagination that he's bigger, stronger than when I left him at the end of last school year. He's angrier, too. It's like a constant undercurrent where before a trigger had been necessary.

He would kill Jamie. Tom would pummel Jamie's beautiful face. I cringe. Tom squeezes his arm, directs my face to his and kisses me hard and fast.

"I gotta get to weights," he says and joins a herd of jocks headed to the gym.

I scan the morning crowd quickly, but I don't see Jamie.

"What are you gonna do, Daisy?" Disappointment is back on Nick's expression. I'm impressed. He's better at deception than I realized.

"I guess I'm gonna buy a phone," I answer, sounding too much like Tom. It isn't necessary. None of this is Nick's fault. He's not in the wrong.

Jordan sneaks up to us. Nick lights up. In fact, they both do.

"Hi," he says.

"Hi," she answers.

Then they just look at each other, and I swear, a happy glow surrounds them. I should be happy, but I find myself gritting my teeth. I fidget so hard with the green glass bead around my neck that the chain breaks. It clinks on the floor and a sob pushes forth from me like I've just lost my best friend. It breaks their spell, but before they can move, a figure kneels, scoops up the broken necklace and hands it to me.

"Don't worry. We'll fix it." It's Jamie.

"Hi," I say.

"Hi," he answers.

"You shouldn't be here," Jordan says, but Jamie never pulls his focus from me.

"Why not?"

"Because Tom will kill you," she says.

"I'm not scared of Tom," Jamie comes back.

"You should be," I say, and I mean it. I drop the necklace into the side pocket of my backpack.

"Tom's just a bully. But the universe will not be bullied." He smiles as if we all share some secret, inside joke. And I guess we do because we all laugh.

"How did you like the drive last night?" he asks.

"Amazing. I was still thinking about it on the way to school. My MINI Cooper is not quite the same."

Nick interrupts, "Wait, you drove his car? *The* car?"

Jordan straightens her spine and tilts her head.

"Want to go again tonight?" Jamie knows he's tempting me. I can see it in his face.

"She can't. She's going to buy a phone tonight," Nick says.

"A phone? Why would you need a phone? You have one." If I didn't know better, I would say I saw doubt crawl across him. He shifts himself back and forth, like he was about to take off on a sprint, but he remains in his spot beside me.

"I thought it broke," Jordan says. Pride builds inside me that she doesn't know.

The warning bell sounds.

Jamie leans in and whispers, "How would you like to lunch in the library today?"

I smile from my toes and nod. As Jamie walks away, Nick warns, "Be careful."

"I thought you were mad at me," I say.

"I was. Doesn't mean I'm eager to see Tom massacre you. Or Jamie." He smiles, but annoyance lies behind his eyes.

"I'm sorry, Nick. Honest, I am. You and Jordan went through all the trouble to plan the beautiful secret rendezvous with Jamie, and I messed it all up."

"Is that what you're sorry about?" He's surprised again.

Jordan side-eyes me. I can't quite make out if she's embarrassed for me or intrigued.

"I'm sorry about the gay comment, too. I don't care if you're gay."

He grabs Jordan's hand. "I'm not."

"I know. That's not what I mean. I just mean it doesn't matter. You're my family. I shouldn't have assumed. It wasn't right. I'm sorry."

Finally, he does that head shake thing I haven't seen him do in a while. The one that means how on earth am I stuck in this school, in this decade, with these people, like an avuncular big brother watching the young'uns play with a new puppy. "It's okay. I guess that's what comes from a life with a big brute like Tom. Anything less seems effeminate."

He's not man enough to impersonate a door. Myrtle's foolish words about Wilson float into my brain. I cringe.

"Are you kidding me right now? Tom is the masculinity standard? Tom?" Jordan jumps in.

Nick flashes a "gotcha" smile at her. In our laughter, the world shifts back on its axis and all energy wraps around us. Everything's not perfect, but it's okay. We're okay.

"You guys, I have no idea what I'm doing. All I know is that other than driving that Mach 1, this double life thing I've got going is the most exhilarating thing I've ever done."

"Well, it's not a Sunday drive, but it's something, anyway." Jordan says and squeezes Nick's hand.

Nick retreats to class, still shaking his head at us.

The confession hovers over me like a protective rain cloud as I head to first hour. I'm still reeling from the power of the drive, from the Sunday morning champagne binge, from throwing up on Tom—all with no repercussions whatsoever. I could get used to this driver's seat position, this acceptance that the road trip of life is a one-way street, and maybe it should be thrilling. Maybe I've finally embraced the unpredictability of life. Maybe I've emerged from the safety of that confining cocoon to throw my hands in the air, my head back, and really live for the first time ever. This feeling, this crazy, edge-of-life, expectations-be-damned exuberance might just be worth the crash.

CHAPTER NINETEEN

In first hour, before Mr. Klipspringer warms up the choir, he reads the announcements, including the one reminding us to nominate eight seniors for Homecoming king and queen. After ten minutes of Owen Lees arguing that Homecoming is just a popularity contest and it's antiquated anyway—why does it need to be a boy and girl, why can't it be two boys—everyone has finally marked their ballots.

For a split second, I want to agree with him. I want to shout it out loud that we should not do this horrid Homecoming thing. It's pointless. It's practically demeaning that we parade these four couples around for two weeks like they are some kind of royalty and then dump three of them at the very dance we are supposedly holding in their honor. It ruins the night for them and probably for the winners, too because if a girl were to act too happy about winning, she'd be considered a heartless bitch. After all, the one who didn't win is probably in the bathroom crying, wiping inky tears with a wad of scratchy toilet paper, listening to all her friends swear they didn't vote for the bitch.

But I don't say anything, and I'm finding that, on some level, I don't really care if she's in the bathroom ruining her makeup. That's her road trip, not mine.

I remember last year's dance and that satiny teal dress Tom had picked out for me. I remember how I laughed that, for someone so graceful on the field, he sure clutzed it up on the dance floor. He didn't care. He gyrated all his parts at me anyway. Then he pointed to the balcony where the candidates stood. We watched the announcement of the winners. He laser focused those obsidian eyes on me and said, "Next year, that's us." Then he spun me around, barreling us through lines of spectators like we were rushing toward the end zone of some glorious championship game.

Three loud clicks bring me back as Mr. Klipspringer taps his conductor wand on the stand in front of him.

"Alright. Here we go," he says, and the accompanist hits a chord.

A million hours later, it's finally time for lunch. I know the Homecoming announcement will come near the end. I know that Tom will expect me to be with him in the cafeteria, like always. I know he'll feel foolish when I'm not there. I know he'll say something to make himself sound stupid. And I know that Jamie is waiting for me in our spot behind the stacks.

I run to Jamie. There he is. I swear his aura literally glows like a benediction from heaven. He hands me an almond granola bar and a bottle of water. I take it and then wrap my arms around his neck. That same earthquake vibration from this morning buzzes through me as our lips meet.

"We must stop meeting like this," he jests.

"Never," I smile deep into his eyes.

"Oh, sorry." Someone coming around the corner of the stacks interrupts us. We've been caught. It's Owen.

The buzzing halts and I feel all the blood drain from me. I'm a stone-cold marble statue. I can't move. Only the warmth of Jamie's embrace gives me an indication that I haven't died on the spot.

"No worries," Jamie's voice is sure.

"Hi, Owen," I whisper. I don't know what else to say.

An expression of confused approval washes over his pale skin, and his dull brown eyes turn warm behind his round spectacles.

"No worries," Owen answers. Then he nods and removes himself to go sit on the bench near the top of the stairs like Cerberus keeping watch over hopeless souls.

When I look back at Jamie, his eyes are wild with adventure. "What will they think?" he jokes again.

"Who? What?" I hate the panicky edges of my voice.

"When we can't stand to keep us a secret anymore." He kisses my forehead. I lean into him.

"I almost can't now," is my answer, but I don't mean it the way it sounds. I don't know what I mean, but I don't have time to explain myself before he kisses me again.

We're reminiscing on Tybee when the intercom pops on to declare the candidates. We're announced in couples, as is the tradition. As if to torture me, they announce us last. Tom Buchanan and Daisy Fay.

Just Daisy

Jamie's aura fades. He steps away from me. I barely hear when he repeats, "What will they think?"

"Jamie, I'm sorry. I didn't know. It's not my fault." I want to make this okay for him.

"Turn it down." He's glaring now. He runs trembling fingers through his hair.

"Turn it down? I don't think I can. I'm not sure that's allowed."

"Sure, it is. No one could force you into it if you don't want it. Turn it down, Daisy. You know you want to."

His soft hands are on my arms now and his face is uncomfortably close, but all I can see is what Tom's face must look like and the angry red that, by now, is crawling up his neck.

The foghorn bell sounds.

"I have to go to class," I say, but he won't let go.

In his eyes, I see the unraveling of a web of dreams. His top lip curls up. His eyes narrow.

Stretching on tiptoe, I reach him. My voice, soft as summer wind and gentle waves, I whisper, "Your love manifested us, remember? The universe won't let it die now. I promise. I'll text you tonight."

It's all he needs. He lets go and I join the scattering students running to class.

I get the feeling that he never came down that day. I have no proof, but if I had to bet, I would lay odds that he stayed up there, waiting with his chin on his knees, gazing at the lighthouse in his dream.

Later, Tom catches me on the way to cheer practice. I mean literally catches me by the arm, too tightly. I can't squirm away.

"Let go," I demand.

He looks at his fingers clamped around my arm like they aren't an extension of his body. He drops my arm and stuffs his hand in his pockets.

"Did you hear?" he asks.

"Yes, I heard."

"Where were you?"

"I was in the library."

His black eyes narrow. Does he see the panic flash across me at my complete inability to control the words that come out of my mouth. Would he look for me there now?

"Doing research for my college application essay."

I marvel at how easily the dishonesty flows from my lips like poisoned promises from an island nymph. They do the trick, though, and I'm rewarded with a smile. Tom may have the body of a Greek god, but his smile is pure Hollywood boy band--Harry Styles or Nick Jonas. Jordan would say Elvis or maybe even a young Dean Martin.

I can't help myself. I like Tom's smile. I especially like it when every ounce of his rugged sophistication pours into that smile and, subsequently, into me. I'd lap it up if I could. I'd scoop it into jars like nectar from the gods.

I smile back, too big. My face, I know, looks best in subtlety. I inherited my mother's wide mouth that bares too many teeth if we don't carefully control our exuberance. But I'm not feeling very in control of anything right now—not my words, not my smile, certainly not my mind. A giggle escapes and I wonder if there might have been voodoo on my summer island. I'm not myself. If I am, I certainly don't recognize this part of me.

Tom's hands are on me again, resting on my hips, nearly forming a complete circle around my waist.

"After practice, I'm going home to shower. Then I'm coming over to pick you up and take you out to dinner. Then we're shopping."

"For a cell phone?" I tease.

"For whatever you want."

"Bring flowers for Grandma. I think she'd like it."

The second I hear my request; I know it's a test. How much does he want to spoil me? How far will he go to keep me?

"Whatever you want," he repeats and kisses me before he hurries off to practice.

I hurry off, too. The squad finishes up stretching when I arrive, but I'm not the reason our practice starts off in a jumble of confusion. We are scheduled to work on tumbling and flying today. Myrtle is in charge of the flyers, but she's absent.

"She was here earlier today. I have her last hour," Lucille says.

"We'll tumble first then." I send them to opposite ends of the gym and finish my own stretches when Myrtle comes in, not even hurrying. Late for practice, and not even hurrying. At least I'd had the prudence to arrive in an apologetic rush.

She strides past me and settles to the floor in a straddle, leaning to one side and then the other. Even with her head bent down, I notice her freshly red-rimmed eyes, oddly beautiful against her porcelain skin. I watch as she extends her arms overhead, mesmerized for an instant at her beauty. Where my mouth takes over too much of my face, hers is diminutive, causing her voluptuous lips to push out perpetually. Her eyes are big, though, with irises the color of rusted pennies, but not dull. They glisten, today with held back tears, but often with something sharper, a pointed focus like a hawk or maybe like a lioness stalking her prey. Even her hair is compelling, cascading in loose ringlets over her shoulders, resting on her full bosom. There's a fierce beauty about her, peeking out from beneath layers of longing and jealousy and decidedness.

But when I go over to her to fulfill my captain duties, she's a complete bitch.

"I know. I'm late. So what?" She flings off her warm-up jacket and as she struts away to gather the other flyers, I notice the red grip marks on her arm.

"Those are going to bruise." The words die as they meet the air, meant for no one's ear but mine. Wilson's mad again. What is it this time?

I glance down at my bicep to the spot where Tom's frustrated fist had grabbed a few minutes prior. He'd left no mark this time.

By the time I cross the gym floor, the bases and spotters are in place and Myrtle flies up into the air with aggressive abandon.

Practice continues, and, even with my captain status, I want more. I'm not a big girl. On the shallow side of average height, I could fly like Myrtle. I could. I never have. I never have even wanted to. Better to keep my feet on the ground. Better to watch from a place of security and assuredness. Myrtle and the other flyers soar untethered, yet no less assuredly. Confidence is most authentic when it comes with risks, when it soars untethered.

At the rallies and the games, it's the flyers the crowds go crazy for. They are fairies, flitting spitefully sure above the rest of us, knowing we'll provide sufficient cushion for a glorious landing. Providing the cushion for the landing is a sensible obligation. Sensible and insincere.

But sensible people don't zoom around in yellow muscle cars. Sensible people don't carry the stones of their past while flying down the path to their future. Sensible people drive luxury cars on weekend road trips, but never arrive.

CHAPTER TWENTY

After practice, I hurry out to my car. As I throw my gym bag in, I'm reminded I still have a trash bag full of baby paraphernalia to deliver. I've been carrying Ms. Hip's card in my purse. I wonder where she lands on the sensible scale. What kind of car does she drive?

We need doctors, counselors, lawyers... We need women who are willing to use their voices to amplify the message of equality.

Seems sensible enough, and at the same time, seems like flying. No, not flying. Soaring. Shot from a solid cannon to soar into the unknown, the undreamed. Until now.

By the time I arrive at Grandma's, I've talked myself out of my funk. Ribbons of giddiness run through me. I shower and throw on my good-butt jeans with a cute little halter that matches my eyes. I'm feeling sassy. I leave my hair untamed and add thick eyeliner and double mascara and bright red lipstick drawn on to bow my lips like a kewpie doll. Jordan would be proud.

"What's the occasion?" Grandma asks when I find her in the kitchen searching for leftovers to heat up. She approves of my look. I know because she does this little shoulder shimmy and whistles.

"I've been nominated for Homecoming queen, Grandma." I give her a big hug and remember that all my accomplishments are for her, too.

"How exciting! I'm so happy for you." She doesn't need to add *I wish your parents were here for this.* We agreed to stop saying it out loud a long time ago.

"Tom's taking me out for dinner tonight to celebrate. Then we're going shopping. We need at least three different outfits for all the stuff they have planned for us."

"How nice. Is he nominated, too?"

"Yes. We've been coupled up together."

"Of course, you have. Who would even try to match you two with other partners? A top girl deserves a top guy."

With those words, it was if mom and dad *are* right there with us, Dad slapping Tom on the back and Mom hugging me like we'd achieved something. Like Homecoming King and Queen secured our spots in everyone's minds as the Power Couple. Like it was some rite of passage, not some shallow popularity contest. Hollow pride fills me, but it's pride, nonetheless. In a little less than two weeks if they crown us—when they crown us—there will be glorious cheering and no untethered flying will be necessary.

Grandma gives up searching the refrigerator and tweaks my chin. We sit at the table. I empty out the contents of a manilla envelope delivered to me from an office aide before the final bell. As we look at the events scheduled, she pulls up possible fashion choices on her phone. My heart is full, and I know hers is, too. I wouldn't trade these girlfriend moments with my grandma for anything in the world. Not for my own happily-ever-after island, not for the rarest sea glass, not for lighthouses erected in my honor.

She scans one final piece of paper and lays it flat in front of me.

"Well now, what are you going to put in these blanks?"

It is the questionnaire for the script they use to introduce us at the pep rally and football game. I read the first one.

"What are my plans for after high school?" I groan, but Ms. Hip's red suit and compassionate statistics stick in my head.

There's a knock at the back door. I find myself channeling my inner Jordan, shoulders back, chin lifted.

"Come in," we announce together and laugh.

"Be careful," she winks at me. "You're becoming more like me every day."

"I wouldn't mind that at all."

Tom bounds in and presents a colorful bouquet to Grandma. "These are for you."

"Tom? Why, thank you." She takes them to the sink and then excuses herself to the living room to get a vase.

"I'd kiss you, but you have that red shit all over your lips," Tom says.

"You can't deflate my ego tonight, Tom. I think I look good."

"Oh, I never said you didn't." He holds out his hand like a

chivalrous dance partner. I accept it and raise myself from the chair. "You look amazing. Good enough to eat." He nibbles my neck and I shoo him away before Grandma comes back in, but I'm too late. She clears her throat as she passes us.

Grandma has this wonderful way of busying herself to draw attention from awkward moments. She does this, carefully trimming the end of each stem and arranging them one-by-one in a crystal vase.

"So, Tom, have you filled out your questionnaire yet?" Grandma asks.

"What questionnaire?" He sounds clueless.

"This one." I scoot it over on the tabletop, in front of an empty chair. We sit down, so he can look at it.

"Oh. No. Can't I just give it to you to fill out for me?" He asks me.

"Sure, I guess. I won't know all the answers, though."

"Like what? What don't you know about me?" He winks. I blush. It feels like old times, like when we used to fantasize about this.

I scan the document looking for something I don't know. It creeps me out a little that, in fact, I do know most of them. Probably some better than he knows them. Definitely better than I know my own. I find an iffy one.

"Like this one here. Who is someone you admire and why?"

He scrunches his face, like thinking too hard gives him a headache.

"I don't know. What are you going to put down for yours?"

"Claudia Hip." The name pops out before I even consider an answer.

"Who?" he asks.

"I've never heard of her," Grandma says.

"Why would you use someone no one knows? Who is she? One of Jordan's dried up old black and white movie stars?"

"She's a local lawyer who runs a women's shelter downtown," I answer.

Grandma places the flowers in the middle of the table, blocking Tom's direct view from me, and pulls up a chair.

"Yeah, what I said. No one knows who that is. You'll just confuse people," he says.

"She's someone who is making a difference in our city. She's a woman who is willing to use her voice to amplify the message of equality. Did you know—" I try to recall the stats.

"No. No one knows. No one cares. How do you even know?" He dodges his head back and forth in an attempt to make eye contact.

"Adulting Day," I answer.

"Adulting Day? Are you saying you want to be a lawyer now?"

In my mind, a picture flashes of a green campus dotted with venerable buildings and the elevated philosophies of storied people who went on to amplify the message of equality. It's the picture from the pamphlet I'd rescued from the garbage the day Tom tossed it there.

Tom's muscular fingers pry apart the tips of the foliage as he tries to clear a pathway between us. I move the vase right just as he leans that way and then left as he does the same.

Finally, he stands to tower over me, Grandma, and the flowers. "Why didn't you go to the Culinary session? It would be more useful."

I want to be offended, but my grandmother's hand rests on my thigh under the table and my mother's soothing voice as she molds my father's thinking to her own sings in my head.

"I don't need to study culinary. I have Grandma Betty for that. Right, Grandma?" I say.

"Of course. Would you like some pineapple upside down cake?" she asks Tom.

He's tempted. He loves Grandma's cooking.

"Save me a piece." Then he winks at her this time. She blushes. I cringe.

He continues. "Why don't you just put your grandma's name? Everyone would know who that is. Everyone would understand that."

I squeeze Grandma's hand, kiss her cheek, and say, "That's the first smart thing you've said today, Tom." I hop up. "Are we ready to go? I'm hungry. Grandma, can we bring you something back?"

"No thank you. I think I'll order a pizza. My show is on tonight," she says with the excitement of a bunch of jocks preparing to watch the Super Bowl, only I know her. It won't be a sporting event. It will be some reality TV show where middle class iGen-ers pretend to be rich and accept roses from eligible bachelors.

A smirk builds up inside me. It's sad, isn't it? The world's obsession with the happy ever after, the perfect romance. Then it hits me. That's exactly what Ms. Eckleburg must have found. What about

Ms. Hip? Just because she goes by Ms. doesn't mean she isn't married. I remember her glorious manicure, but I don't remember a ring. Maybe amplifying her voice at the shelter is too real for that dream.

Still, true love holds universal magic, doesn't it? Why wouldn't the world be obsessed with the dream of perfect love. It's not like it doesn't exist. Some folks have it for a lifetime. My grandparents did. My parents did. Who wouldn't want it?

Mom and Dad wanted it for me, too. They'd picked out Tom, practically. They had approved totally. They had seen him as my ticket to happy-ever-after. Across the table, Tom is busy on his phone. For a brief second, I'm not even in his world.

"I'll be right back," I say even though I know he won't hear me. He doesn't hear me when he's on his phone like that. He's not very good at juggling what's right in front of him and whatever is in that phone.

I take the stairs to my room two at a time. I pull open my desk drawer, grab my Jamie phone and send the message I know he's waiting for. I send a second one with loads of heart and kissing emojis. Then I send one more of my subtle smile and shining eyes and hope that's enough. I know how far he'll go to have me. How long will he wait to keep me?

CHAPTER TWENTY-ONE

Even though I'm starving, Tom and I shop first. He buys me the phone. We choose five coordinating outfits, just so we'll have options. He prefers to have options, he jokes. Makes him feel powerful. I don't tell him that I understand exactly what he means.

We stay in the last outfits we purchase just to try them out and head to Chicago Yacht Club.

"I haven't been in a long time," I confess in a cloud of nostalgia. I stare at the wall plaque honoring Charles Fay.

"I know. I thought maybe it was time you came back." Tom stands with me a moment, just looking at it like it's Raphael's *Portrait of a Young Man* hanging in someone's living room and not a wood and brass plaque. His hand moves to touch the words, tracing his finger over each letter as if he's emblazoning them there anew. Is it pride he feels? Maybe it's grief. Maybe I'm not giving him enough credit.

When the spell breaks, he instructs the host to sit us near the windows on the still-opened patio, near the fireplace. He orders sparkling wine.

"I apologize, sir, but I'm going to be required to confirm your age."

Tom flashes a smile in response. "I'm Tom Buchanan."

"I know your father, sir." The waiter gives an apologetic nod, disappears, and returns promptly with two effervescent flutes.

The celebratory wine glitters like little jumping diamonds, much more sophisticated than a cheap bottle from the grocery store guzzled in a bathtub. I shake away the thought. As far as I'm concerned, it never happened.

"I think the stars fell right out of heaven and landed in a glass just for me," I giggle and the sound of it joins the bubbles tinkling off the crystal, bursting in the air.

Tom hands me one and takes up the other.

"To us," I spout and lift my glass.

"No, that's too cliche."

"Cliche?"

"Yeah. I want to toast to you."

"Toasting your girlfriend? That's not cliche?" I want to ask him if he knows what the word means.

"Daisy, there is nothing cliche about you. You are one of a kind. If the stars fell from heaven, it's because they couldn't stand not being near you." There's not a single insincerity in his expression.

"Tom, have you been reading Shakespeare again?" My laugh does not land softly, but he's undeterred.

"I know I don't say it enough, but I'm so grateful for you every day. You're the only one who gets me, Daisy. The only one who puts up with my bullshit." His eyes are moist with emotion. My throat catches. I haven't seen moistened eyes on Tom since his cousin tragically crashed into that football career-ending ditch.

I set down my glass and place my hand on his. "Tom, where is this coming from?"

"The other day when you said you wanted to break up, it got to me. I can't lose you. You feel so distant. I miss you now more than when you were on that island."

"I'm right here." The reassurance is as ineffective as a Band-Aid on a knife wound.

Tom continues. "My cousin says senior year does weird things to couples. I don't want anything weird to happen to us. I don't like to be without you. It's uncomfortable."

"Growth is uncomfortable, Tom."

"Are we growing?"

"I think that's what senior year is supposed to be about, isn't it? Jordan says, if we're doing it right, we should be sick of Eggerton by the time we graduate."

"I can't imagine ever being sick of Eggerton."

A dangerous silence falls over us until the waiter comes to take our order. I say dangerous because if I'm not fully engaged in conversation with Tom, my mind goes back to Jamie. Little smiles sneak onto my face. My body and brain get all fuzzy. Also, it gives Tom a chance to gather the few thoughts his jock head will hold.

"You know when I said you could fill out my questionnaire?" Tom asks.

"Yeah. Do you want me to?"

Just Daisy

"If you want. That would be great. You'd probably make me sound better. But that's not what I'm getting at. What I mean is that I realized I couldn't do the same for you."

"Does it matter?'

"I don't know. I wouldn't have thought it did before. When you're not there, Daisy, and I don't know where you are, it's like you have this secret life I don't know anything about."

My face feels like it's on fire. *Wouldn't have thought it did before what?* That's what I want to ask. But I don't. I'm not ready for the answer. Not ready to know my own truth. Instead, I lean in and whisper, "I do have a secret. You want to know what it is?"

"I'm not sure. Do I?"

I keep my composure and lift my glass again. "The secret is that I'm not the only one who puts up with your bullshit. Everyone does. How do you think we got this wine? So, here's to you Tom Buchanan. Not all bullshit is bad."

Uncertainty and relief, two expressions I would never have associated with my Tom wash across him. He raises his glass, too, but doesn't clink with mine.

"I'm not toasting bullshit. Like I said. Let's toast you. To my Daisy, may all the stars of the sky always fall into your glass."

Tom's words sound sweet, but the longer they sit in my psyche, the more they sour. My determination to not feel guilty wanes.

The waiter brings bounteous plates of refined chow and places them before us. Something about his submissive demeanor closes in on me. I notice a gold band on his finger. He's married, and this is his job—catering to bullshitting teenagers.

I set my glass aside. I can't agree with Tom's wish for me. Not with this grown man waiter, husband, maybe father, graciously grating cheese on my entree. Is it fair? Is it right to wish for all the stars of the sky to simply fall into my glass? Shouldn't I have to work for something? And I mean real work, not manifestation, not trust funds, not inherited yachts.

Being in the driver's seat might be powerful, but as I gaze at the boats, I feel my count of enchanted objects has diminished.

If only that waiter had telepathic powers, he would accept my unspoken invitation to sit and dine with us. Sip on stars, laugh with legends, breathe in bullshit. He would know he doesn't need to wait on us. We aren't worthy of serving. He leaves and I nibble at my meal, but all I want is a heaping of Grandma's homemade pineapple cake. Everything else tastes like dust.

The sun sets on the far side of the lake. No stars smile down on us. No mystic love manifests itself in our souls. As I relent and drink down Tom's sparkly elixir, an unnamed anger simmers. I have no desire for shadows of ancient gas balls to fall into my hands. I have no desire to suck on that pulp of life. If I want to shine, I will propel myself into the darkness. I will illuminate the world. I will fly, untethered, and with no team of spotters to catch me.

"I have an idea," Tom finally says, pulling me back to earth.

"Okay." I pick at a parmesan-coated eggplant.

"There's another one of those parties on Friday. We should make an appearance."

He means one of Jamie's parties. It strikes me that Jamie hasn't actually invited me himself. We haven't discussed his parties at all, in fact.

"I can't believe you'd want to," I answer, dragging the eggplant through a river of marinara sauce and plunging it in my mouth to dam up any oncoming deluge of unnecessary words.

"I'm curious. That's all. Everyone is talking about this guy's parties. I bet they're dumb, like a carnival freakshow."

"Then why would you want to go?"

"For laughs, I guess." He munches on his dinner roll.

So far, Eggerton Academy had somehow managed to keep Tom and Jamie apart. Somehow, I'd managed to, also. How on earth could I go with Tom to Jamie's party? Is Jamie even having the party? Am I naturally invited and don't need an actual invitation? Or does he not want me there? I mean, I wouldn't blame him. Maybe it's his way of distracting himself from Tom and me together for Homecoming.

I keep shoveling in bites of eggplant because I can't think of anything to say that wouldn't make me sound stupid. What does it matter now if I choke on my words or choke on my Yacht Club repast? I'm choking either way.

Gradually, Tom looks up from his meal and grins at my stuffed, chipmunk cheeks. He reaches with his napkin to wipe the sauce escaping the corners of my mouth. "Guess you were hungry, huh?"

I nod and blink back panic.

"I'll pick you up at 8." He commands then snorts a carefree laugh and downs the rest of his champagne.

CHAPTER TWENTY-TWO

The next day at lunch, I run up the library stairs two at a time. My jittery, resolved heart can't take concealing Tom's plans from Jamie and hiding Jamie's identity from Tom. This driver seat thing is too much. A restless dream had tormented me all the night before. Stars crashing to the sea and endless crescendos of wave after wave. Jamie and I thrown together and ripped apart on its currents with Tom ramming toward us in his unsinkable SUV.

Jamie is in the library, waiting. I throw my arms around him like he's the last buoy on a rogue riptide. It takes him a second before he enfolds me in his magic aura.

"What is it, Daisy?' His robotic voice fails to soothe me.

I step out of his cold embrace and wipe my face. "It's too much, Jamie. It's just too much."

It's then when I realize his demeanor mirrors my jittery nerves.

"Too much? Of course, it isn't." His eyes are a wide, vivid blue.

"He wants to come to your party, Jamie."

A cool smile finally spreads across him. "Is that all?"

"Is that all? Isn't it enough?"

"So, let him come." He flips his hair aside.

"Let him come?"

"Why not?" He seems annoyed.

"Why not?"

I realize I'm repeating everything he says, maybe because I can't believe it. Maybe to make it real because suddenly I think maybe I've dreamed myself into one of Jordan's black and whites. From a window at the end of our secret aisle, streams of sunshine illuminate tiny dust particles that dance in the light. Jamie's gorgeousness is silhouetted. It's a dream. Jamie here in my world, the one I built with Tom, is a dream. It can't be real.

"Everyone is invited," he says, cool again as if it's the normalest thing in the world to invite me and my boyfriend to his, my other boyfriend's, party. But there's something else that bothers me, that quivers in the corners of my brain, hiding from my conscience because revealing it would make me sound like the shallowest bitch. Unfortunately, the dam is busted, and the words gush out.

"That's not how it works. Not everyone is ever invited. There are just some people who don't make the list. How do you not know this?"

He laughs, "But Tom isn't one of those people, so what does it matter?"

It's all a jumble in my mind. Tom most definitely does not need to be at Jamie's party. If he does go to Jamie's party, he most certainly does not need to see *everybody* there. Tom will never be impressed with a come-one-come-all kind of party. There are rules, unwritten rules. How does Jamie not know?

"It matters, Jamie. It absolutely matters." My soul sinks to a murky, uncertain bottom. I want Tom to be impressed. How twisted must I be? I actually want Tom's approval of Jamie. The tears come again, and I can't stop them.

"Shhh. Daisy. It's fine. It's really fine. It's all going to be—fine." Jamie pulls me in, and my breath loosens.

"He wants me to come with him, Jamie. What am I supposed to do about that?"

"Do it." He's enjoying this. His smile reminds me of our careless days.

"Do it? Do it?" My laugh sounds like a crazy woman.

"Or don't."

"Don't?"

"You know you're repeating everything I say, right?"

Suddenly, I'm laughing, too, and somehow still crying.

"You just seem so cavalier about everything."

"Maybe it's because it doesn't matter."

"Oh, it matters. It absolutely matters." I pace to the end of our covert aisle. Owen sits, perched on his bench, munching on a microwave burrito and peering suspiciously into the first-floor study carrels.

"Then end it," Jamie commands.

I scurry back. "End it?" I tried that once. I'm not sure I'm capable.

"You're doing it again." He's smiling like it's all a big joke, like it's a bad version of a predictable film noir flick, complete with the hapless watchman who's gonna get the crap beat out of him before the end of the scene.

Jamie takes my hands. "Daisy, you know it's just a matter of time. So just end it now."

I stare at that triangle of freckles on his nose. It helps me ignore the quiver of his upper lip. Besides, I know he's right. It's going to end sooner or later. But Tom had been right, too. How can both be right? It's all being held together with the silken sinew of a spider's web. Miraculous. Beautiful. Deadly. Deceptively strong and easily destroyed all at once.

"Jamie, I can't. Not in the middle of Homecoming." I feel myself disappearing like the photograph in *Back to the Future*. How much of me is left? Just the shoes? Not the mind, because I'm losing it.

"What does Homecoming matter? Last summer, did you care about Homecoming? Homecoming king and queen isn't real." He's yelling now, that library-voice whisper yell.

I want to scream that *he* is the thing that isn't real, that my life was set and planned before I met him, and that nothing about him seems real at all. But he takes my face in his hands and kisses me with more reality than I remember could exist. He kisses me the way I've seen my dad kiss my mom a million times. The way I've imagined a true love would kiss, and in a way I didn't know was really real until Jamie.

When we come up for air, there's none to take in. I'm breathless but unchanged. He waits for me to say something, so I do.

"Homecoming is real to Grandma. I can't disappoint her." It's only a partial lie. Not the disappointment part. That part's real. Maybe the Homecoming part is, too, but something about using that excuse for that purpose isn't honest.

I remember with cloudy certainty a bit of advice my father had given Nick one sweltering day while roasting on the side of our pool. He'd said, "Dishonesty is a trait you never blame deeply in a woman." Nick had repeated it to us later when Jordan had that golf scandal, and I didn't speak to him for a week.

A wash of understanding blurs Jamie's beauty for a moment. "No, you can't disappoint your grandmother. I wouldn't want you to. So come to the party."

"I have to bring Tom."

"Then bring Tom. Like I said, it's only a matter of time. I've waited a lifetime for you already. I can wait a few more days."

"A few more days." I shake my head at my inability to form original speech. "I think you've taken over my brain or something." I sigh while he smirks like some kind of maniacal puppet master. He peers his hypnotic vision out from under that layer of blonde.

"I'd rather take over your heart," he says, his voice soothing again, and hopeful.

Before I can break the news that he already has, we're interrupted. It's Owen. He steps around the corner of the stacks, wiping cheese off his face with the cuff of his white sleeve.

"It's him. Downstairs. Better wait it out."

Well, what do you know? Maybe Owen is not so hapless after all. But my impressed reaction over Owen doing his duties doesn't last. By now, my stomach has gotten used to not eating lunch, and Tom has gotten used to my MIA lunch hours and the excuse for them. Nevertheless, I think I'm gonna hurl. Desperation and guilt roil around in my gut.

Jamie gives me a little peck on the cheek. "I'll go first. Owen, take care of her." He hands me over.

The railing is just far enough away that I can't see Jamie descend the entire staircase. I can only see the last few triumphant feet of his jaunt as he saunters out of the library, cool and casual and confident.

Weirdly, a vision of that drunken hobo plowing through the bistro window invades my mind. I blink it away and come back to my unnerving present situation. What in the world is Tom doing in a library? Is he looking for me?

Owen pulls a candy bar out of his backpack. "Want some?" he asks.

"No, thanks though. Really, thank you."

He shrugs. "Sure."

Playing lookout has obviously been the most natural thing in the world for him, and I have no idea why.

"Jamie knows your name," I vocalize my surprise to Owen.

"Oh, is he not supposed to?" He looks around for the answer. A book catches his attention. He pulls it off the shelf. "Have you seen this one? It's so... real."

"Is it not supposed to be?" What the actual hell is wrong with me? It's bad enough when I can't stop the flow of drivel coming out of my mouth, but whatever short wiring has caused my brain to only be able to form only words someone else has already spoken is a million times worse. Talk about sounding stupid.

Luckily, Owen is oblivious. He laughs like I've told the cleverest joke. He knocks on the hard cover and fans the pages. "Of course, it is. Of course." Then he sits down right there on the floor and begins reading to himself.

I watch the library door. Just as the foghorn warning bell sounds, I see Tom's hulking frame strut through to the hallway. Even from a backside view, I discern an arrogant agitation, more so than usual.

CHAPTER TWENTY-THREE

It's Friday. Our bye week, so there's no game. The frantic anticipation of tonight's party weighs down on me, but as 8:00 nears, all I can think about is what the hell was Tom doing in a library. Which his dumb because there is so much more to worry about.

It's so weird driving to Tuolomee with Tom. I make him stop twice, once for gum and once for bottled water.

"What the hell, Daisy. If you don't want to go, just say you don't want to go."

"I don't want to go."

"Too bad. We're going." He turns up the volume on some sick rap so loud, my ears burn.

I turn it back down. "Why are you in such a snit to go?"

"What the fuck's a snit?" He laughs.

"It's a Grandma Betty thing. It just means like hurry. Why are you in such a hurry to go?"

"There's something I gotta see." He definitively cranks the music until the car vibrates. Or maybe it's just me whose shaking.

I clamp my hands together and squeeze them between my thighs. I clench my jaw, too, to keep my teeth from shivering out of my head even though it's not cold. In fact, I'm sweating through my dress. It's one Tom picked out for me on our shopping trip, one I know Jamie will like. Which is nuts.

The party is not in Jamie's apartment. It's in the pool area and the clubhouse and the sand volleyball pit. I swear it's like he owns the place, like the whole complex really is a castle and he is the king of it all. We park, and I can't get out of the car fast enough for Tom. When I finally fix my lip gloss, fluff my hair and pretend to rebuckle my shoe, Tom is about to bust.

"Let's go." He grabs my hand and we practically run to the

Just Daisy

clubhouse. Only I'm in heels and he's a D1 recruit, so it doesn't go well. My ankle twists.

"Ow. Slow down."

He stops for half a second. "Look at this place. Lit up like a goddam carnival. Holy shit. Look at that."

Tom points to Jamie's Mach 1 parked near the club house. Why it's not in the garage, I have no idea. Tom looks down at me with an accusatory glare.

"What?" I ask. What I really want to do is fess up like a guilty convict.

It's obvious, though, that he's not looking for a confession. He's here to send a message. He grabs my hand again. We're finally at the door. Tom slams it open. I peek around him.

"I see Jordan," I say and push away from him. I'm not sure he notices because two seconds later he's already grouped up with his jock head buddies, and he's already drinking. He used to drink only in the off-season.

Jordan examines the room, holding a cup, as usual. "Everybody who's anybody is here. And even some who aren't."

I look around. It's quite the concoction of folks. Owen stands awkwardly in the corner, pointing and laughing and sipping on something that makes him wince. A couple of freshman skanks desperately shove their ambitious little chests at a gang of Lacrosse players who egg them on. I don't see Jamie anywhere, but Myrtle lifts her head off Wilson's shoulder from where they are draped on a loveseat when she sees someone near the keg. I follow the unmistakable focus of her gaze straight to Tom's. I know that look. It's the way he's looked at me a hundred times when there's no getting out of it, we'll end up in bed before the night's over. But it's not me he's looking at. He shifts his focus and kind of nods at Wilson, laughs at the two of them, and turns back to his boys. Myrtle tears up and trounces off to the bathroom.

"Did you see that?" I ask Jordan.

"See what? Those double doors?" asks Jordan. "That's where the real party is." She gestures to a pair of ornate French doors that separate the main area from a private dining room.

"You mean the dope smokers are in there?" I'm not a prude, but I've honestly never understood the point of weed. Besides, it smells like musty, rotted kale and Grandma's perfume.

"There's a lot more going on than just smoking. Any little pill your heart desires is just sitting there in piles waiting to be plucked up. For free." Her eyes mock scandal and gossip.

"Piles?"

"Okay, maybe it's more like little baggies, but they are free."

"You went in?"

"Just for a peek. You wanna see?'

"No. How did all that get in there? Does Jamie know what's going on?"

Jordan cocks her head and scrunches her nose at me.

Myrtle comes out of the bathroom, glances over to the same spot as before, narrows her eyes, raises a brow, slips between the French doors, and disappears into a foggy haze.

Jordan's gaze nods over to the gaggle of jock heads by the keg. "Tom's doing a good job of ignoring her, don't you think?"

"I don't know what to think," I mumble.

"Come on, Daisy. This isn't news."

I know the rumors. I've discounted them for years. Even the few times I thought it might be true that there's someone else, I never imagined the other woman to be *Myrtle*. For a second, I think the fumes from the party room have escaped and attacked my brain. I can't think. I can't breathe. This must be what it feels like to drown in a tidal wave.

Images of Myrtle's black eye and finger bruises on her arm rush at me. *Wilson isn't manly enough to impersonate a door.* My hand reaches for the glass bead hanging around my neck on a jerry-rigged chain. Little rivers of betrayal and dreams cascade like white water rapids through the jagged pieces of my soul.

My knees go weak. Jordan catches me. "It's not the end of the world, Daisy."

I study Tom and his arrogant friends. They point and laugh too loud at Owen in his introverted world against the wall. A sophomore member of the dance team floats by. One of them smacks her ass. She giggles, then slides by, but not before Tom's hand juts out, grabbing her crotch as she passes. Two guys jeer and high-five. Tom's chest is puffed more than all the others. I really, really think I might throw up. The girl he's just molested only rolls her eyes at him. That's it. The thought that later, after the party like after every party, Tom would want to put his hands on me disgusts me nearly to the point of anger.

And all she did was roll her eyes. Which, I guess, isn't much different from when I close mine.

"He gets what he wants. Period." The words sit there on a formidable cloud that blows out every dream that's ever floated by.

Jordan shifts her drink to the other hand and holds it like a crystal-glassed cocktail. "He has always gotten what he wants. Doesn't mean he always will. You have a say, too, you know."

My mental fog clears a little. "Where's Jamie?"

Jordan examines the air above us as if the answer is written there. Then she wrinkles her forehead at me and nods to the French doors.

"Jamie's in there?" I ask.

"High on life, I assume."

"That's not funny."

"It's a little funny." Her pout is obvious until she spots Nick come in.

I want to say hi, but I don't think I can formulate words. Jordan and I separate. She to Nick, and me to find my big fish. I don't care if he's in the party room. I need him. I need the security of his arms, his aura, his faith in the universe.

Before I get to the doors, he emerges. He closes them behind him.

"You smell like weed." It's an accusation more than an observation.

"I'm the host," he answers, surprised at my indignation.

"What's going on in there?" I strain my neck around his tall shoulders.

He studies me before he answers, "Where's Tom?"

"He's over there somewhere with his little boy fan club probably telling dirty little boy jokes."

"Have they got out their measuring sticks yet?"

I smirk. "When do they not have them out?"

He rests his hand on the small of my back, and my insides melt. When he leans in and whispers in my ear, I'm totally gone.

"Let's go upstairs."

"Absolutely."

He steps away. I watch him nod and joke with people, meandering his way across the room. My brain searches for an excuse to leave. Then I realize, no one is watching. Not even Tom. He's doing a pretty good job of ignoring me, too.

Everyone is drunk. The couple that just stumbled out of the French doors and into me are worse than drunk. They barely make it to the couch. Another partygoer falls through the doors. It's Lucille. She's surprised to see me. She's happy I'm here, she slurs and sloshes beer on her dress. "Izn't thiz juzz the bezz pardy-uh." Someone comes and helps her to a chair.

Two of the small-breasted, short-skirted freshman girls plant themselves on either side of Wilson. He's still on the loveseat where Myrtle left him. They smile and laugh and then one bursts out crying. Wilson frowns and hands her his drink which she downs and then she falls asleep in his lap.

Across the room, Jamie catches my attention. He's about to leave. I'm about to join him when someone stumbles backwards into the food table. Trays of shrimp and canapes go flying. Owen catches himself against the wall. Poor Owen. How drunk was he over there talking to himself in his introverted corner?

But he's not drunk. One of Tom's linemen looms over Owen. "What the fuck is wrong with you? Look what you did. Aren't you gonna clean it up?"

Owen struggles to climb out of the refuse. The bully shoves him back into it. Tom steps in. "What happened?"

No one says anything. Time stops. Then Tom, in an untrustworthy gesture of gentlemanly kindness, extends his hand. Owen hesitates then reaches out to accept the help up. Only Tom swipes it away at the last second. Then shoves his foot at like he's pushing aside roadkill. Owen curls in and frowns.

"What a faggot," Tom's words spew out like vomit.

The jock heads huddle and three of them take a turn, not beating him, really, just poking and prodding, indicating that they could, if he were worth it. Nevertheless, the sad, brutalized cry that lurches from Owen reaches into me, and silent, paralyzing sobs push out of me. I try to move to help, but I'm too late.

Jamie pulls Tom and his three goons off Owen in one swift move, so hard that two of them crash over a group of bystanders and they all go down like bowling pins. Tom tries to grab Jamie the way he's grabbed me a hundred times, by the neck, but Jamie's too quick. He ducks and weaves and comes back up with his long, swimmer's reach. He blocks Tom's grip with one hand and punches him right in the gut with the other.

Tom doubles over, deflated. My feet move in that direction. Not fast enough. Before I'm halfway across the floor, Tom lunges at Jamie so fast it seems like one of the superhero movies playing out right in front of me. The jock heads are holding people back. I don't see Nick or Jordan. Maybe they bolted when they had a chance. Tom holds Jamie's collar bone with one hand and punches him repeatedly in the stomach with the other, lifting him clean off the floor.

I run to him. I pull out my cell.

"Stop it, Tom. Stop it. I swear I'll call the cops."

He doesn't stop. He can't. I've seen that hollow look in his eyes before. The only way to end it is to escape.

"Jamie!" I shout, shocked by my own desperate tone.

At the sound of my voice, Jamie straightens up. It's all very Iron Man-ish. Jamie's eyes are calm, like an eerie, unnaturally toxic swamp, like nothing can hurt him. His long arm shoots out and around Tom's neck. He headlocks him, but Tom's two goons are on him. They pull him away.

"I'm calling the cops," I yell. People rush toward the door, abandoning us to the scandalous lovers and comatose drunkards and oblivious pill poppers.

"Don't do it!" It's not Tom who shouts the order. It's Jamie. Tom's dark eyes move back and forth between Jamie and me in knowing condescension. Then he smiles and snorts a short laugh. His anger subsides. He's amused.

My fingers freeze on the screen of my phone. I stare at Tom, "I'll do it. I'll call the cops right now. I swear."

Jamie, free from the goons now, puts his hands on my shoulders so gently, I want to cry. "Don't do it. Put the phone away, Daisy."

So, I do. At the same time, I push away the nagging vision of little baggies of pills and platters full of weed or however they serve it. I quickly remember Myrtle slipping through those doors. I scan the main room for her, but she's nowhere. Neither is Wilson. I hope he's saved her. I hope someone can.

When I turn back around, Jamie has gathered Owen from the floor and is escorting him out the door. He looks back at me. He wants me to follow, so I do this thing that I've become pretty darn good at. I pretend. Jamie's drug room isn't a thing. It never happened. It doesn't exist.

I shove through the numb fools still blocking the doorway, past Tom who angrily brushes off consolations from his team. I don't care if he sees me go. I follow Jamie up the stairs to his apartment. He shows Owen the bathroom to clean up and offers him a change of clothes. Then we're alone in his kitchen, where I saw him that first time since we said goodbye on Tybee.

He's battered and bruised, and it's my fault. It's all completely my fault. I have to fix this. He's uprooted his entire life for me, and all I've given him is a few secret moments in the back corner of a library. And why? Because I feel some sort of obligation to Tom? When has Jamie ever made me feel obligated? All Jamie has ever made me feel is loved.

My arms wrap around him. I sob and sob and sob in relentless waves of primal understanding of manifesting universes and aligning stars and miraculous possibilities. "It's you Jamie. It's always been you. In this stupid, hopeless wreck of a world, you are the realest, surest thing I've ever known." I don't even know what I'm saying, but it doesn't matter. My big, beautiful, manifested fish knows exactly what I mean.

"I've known that since the moment I saw you," he says.

"Since before," I remind him.

A million memories pass between us. Finally, he says, "It's time, Daisy."

And I know exactly what he means, too. I just pray I have the strength to do it because I know something about destiny that Jamie doesn't. You see, destiny doesn't answer to the wishes of just one person, it answers to everyone who wants it enough to grab it. And Tom gets what he wants. Period. When he doesn't, he punishes everyone around him until we all give in. He won't stop next time.

Then, like a siren calling to a sailor, Jordan's voice plays in my head. *You have a say, too, you know.*

The sobs subside, but not the tears. I've always had a voice. I've known that for forever. What I never really understood is that I have a say.

There's a feeble knock at the door. Nick and Jordan come in with Myrtle draped between them.

"She's not okay," Nick says. He takes her to the bedroom. Jordan goes to the kitchen to make coffee.

"What did she take?" I ask Jamie whose wide eyes shift between all the people in his apartment as if he never imagined they could all be there at once.

He rushes to help Jordan with the espresso machine. "Get her some water," he says, and Jordan obeys. She grabs the kitchen trash can just as he points to it. They're like a practiced tag team. They disappear into the bedroom. They've done this before. Maybe not for Myrtle, maybe not with each other, but they've done this.

Nick comes out to the living room. We wince at the retching sound coming from the bedroom.

"I'm sorry. I'm so sorry," Owen has found his way to us. He's putting on one of Jamie's pink shirts.

"For what?" Nick asks.

"God, I'm so sorry."

"There's nothing to be sorry for, Owen," I reassure him.

He strides into the living room and stands in front of a grand, marble topped fireplace, reestablishing his breath and his self-respect. "Look at the place. He's thorough, you know. He's thought of everything. It makes you wonder if one brick falls out of place--"

"Owen," Nick taps his shoulder and offers an espresso from the kitchen.

"I'm really sorry, guys."

Jamie and Jordan finally join us. We all stand in a circle like campers telling ghost stories around a fire, only no one is talking.

"She can stay here," Jamie finally says.

"I don't know that she'd want to. It would be embarrassing. People might talk," Jordan offers, and I wonder who she's really protecting.

Jamie turns to me like we're alone. "I'll take you back home while she sleeps it off, if you want."

"Daisy did come with Tom," Jordan cautions.

"I don't care," I say.

"She doesn't care," Jamie echoes.

"Tom might care." Jordan's trite tone hurts my psyche.

"Who cares if Tom cares," Owen and Nick answer in surprising unison.

Pride breaks into Jordan's demeanor. "Well, I certainly don't."

Jamie turns sincerely toward me. "What about Homecoming? What about your grandma?"

His words find all the cracks in my facade. I wish he hadn't said it.

Nick's kind eyes search mine. "Homecoming will make for quite a story."

Finally, Jordan decides on a plan. "You know he'll come looking for you, so I'll just tell him you're riding with me. That he was acting like a pig, and you didn't want to sully your sundress."

"Yes!" I hug her and she folds in on herself like she's afraid I'll wrinkle her. I keep hugging anyway.

Urgent, violent pounding on the door makes us all jump. "Daisy. I know you're in there."

I freeze. My blood runs cold. My guilty brain sees visions of Tom's bulging muscles pummeling Jamie to death. He could do it, too. He'd been surprised by Jamie's quick reflexes earlier, that's all. Tom's vicious testosterone, when ignited, can explode in terrible ways.

"It's Tom." Owen says what we all already know.

While I'm thinking of what window to escape out of, Jamie valiantly and calmly opens the door.

Tom's stormy eyes rush over us. He reminds me of the sky before the funnel cloud touches down, dark and brooding and ready to rain terror.

"That was a cheap shot, asshole. A coward's punch," Tom seethes.

"Not from where I was sitting," Jordan's smirk is back. I want to hug her again.

Tom ignores her. "What the fuck do you care about Owen, anyway? You two lovers or something?" Tom juts his chin in Owen's direction who immediately turns tomato red.

"I'm the host. Everyone is welcome. Unless they cause a problem. You and your friends caused a problem." Jamie is all control.

Tom screws up his face and mocks, "Everyone is welcome. That's your first problem." Then he grabs my wrist. "Come on, Daisy."

Jamie steps to him. "I wouldn't, bro."

"Bro?" Tom's disgust is palpable.

I break loose. "Go home, Tom. I've got a ride." I should end it right there. I should dump him and push him out the door and never speak to him again. If it weren't for the vision of him punching Jamie, I would.

Just Daisy

Cued by my words, Jamie drapes an arm around my shoulders. A vein pulsates in Tom's temple. His eyes burn, and I swear to God his face goes purple.

"I don't fuckin' think so, dude." He reaches for me again, but Jamie pulls me back.

A groggy whine comes from behind us. "Tom? Tom baby?"

Now, Tom's the one who freezes, except his eyes that dart doubtfully between me and Myrtle, Jamie, and Jordan.

"You've got an interesting group in here, don't ya, asshole?" Tom stares at Jamie.

Myrtle stumbles toward us. She reaches for him, hair as wild as her eyes, skin pale as ash. We all step together, closing off her path.

"What have you done to her?" Tom's protective voice accuses Jamie. I can't tell if he's gonna punch someone or cry. He tries to push us apart.

"Don't be dumb, Tom. She's riding with me. So is Daisy," Jordan intervenes.

My gaze dashes to Jamie. His eyes pull me into our deep, blue ocean. I can't look away.

Tom's voice is gravelly. He hisses the words. "Is that right, Daisy? Are you riding with Jordan?"

Jamie's expression asks the same thing. My voice curls in the corners of my throat. *I have a say. I have a say.*

"No. Not this time. I have a different ride."

Jordan's jaw drops. Her face exudes pride, but if I didn't know better, I'd say it was pride tinged with jealousy. I look back to Jamie. He's beaming. The world is ours and, finally, no one else matters.

"Tom. Tom." Myrtle breaks through and lunges for him. He steps away and she falls to the floor where she wraps her arms around his ankles.

"For God's sake, Myrtle." He shakes a leg free. He reaches for me again.

"Why is it always Daisy?" Myrtle cries. "Daisy, Daisy, Daisy."

She literally crawls her way up his leg like a dancer might do to a pole. We all stare. Someone should help her. Someone should pull her back from him. He pushes her away, but she boomerangs back to him, only this time she's sick. All that she's swallowed in the last hour shoots from her mouth and onto his chest.

"What the fuck. Not again." he yells. He peels her off him along with his ruined shirt and flings them both to the ground.

Jordan laughs first. I try not to because I share Myrtle's mortification. I can't help it, though.

"You'll regret this," Tom says. His eyes, black holes in our universe, take us in. All of us, but land on me. With a slam of the door, he's gone.

"It's not fair," Myrtle moans. Someone's gotten her a towel, and she wipes her mouth with it. The color returns to her cheeks.

I go to her, helping her to a chair, but she won't take it.

"Leave me alone, Daisy. Just leave me alone."

"She's only trying to help." Jordan comes to my defense.

"Am I supposed to be grateful or something?" She takes the water Jamie offers her. After her purge, she's coming back to life.

"What a bitch," Jordan whispers. Nick shushes her. She looks at him like she wants to tee him up and hit him with her clubs.

"Yes," I finally manage. "You should be grateful. Or something."

A tear traces down her cheek, but she's hardly a magnet for sympathy. She raises a pointed finger at my face. "I don't owe you anything. Not my gratitude and not my friendship. Certainly not my loyalty."

I'm shocked. How could *she* possibly be mad at *me*? "I never asked for your loyalty."

"Oh, but you do. Every day. You're the cheer captain. We're your minions."

"Minions? Would a minion--"

"You can stop with the pity looks, too," she cuts me off but addresses the room.

We're all in a semi-circle, half surrounding her in the middle of Jamie's living room. Except Jamie--he's off to the side, waiting for the storm to pass, I suppose.

"I don't pity you, Myrtle," I say.

"Oh yeah, then what?"

The bruise on her face has dimmed to a greenish yellow. My eyes can't stop staring at it. She rubs her fingers on it. Another tear falls.

"Maybe I understand you," I say. Jordan scoffs beside me.

"Do you have any idea how stupid that sounds? *You* understand *me*? *You*? The golden girl? The one everyone's in love with," Myrtle says.

Just Daisy

It's not the response I was expecting. I feel Jordan stiffen. In my peripheral vision, I see her chin raise. Nick crosses his arms. Owen rubs a hand over his chest where, if he had on his own shirt, a pad and pen would be.

She forges on, whipping her hand through the air. "They all love Daisy Fay, even if you don't love them back. Even when you love someone else. They are all still in love with Daisy Fay. So, you collect them like trophies, like trinkets in a locked box that you keep out of reach of everyone else until they rot into nothing, but you don't care. You hoard their hearts anyway." She talks faster and higher.

"I... I don't do that."

"You do. And they're all still in love with you. No matter what." She's spent now, sagging like an empty puppet.

Our semi-circle loosens.

"They all?" I ask.

She counts them off on her fingers. "All. Tom. Nick. Jamie. They're all in love with you. And you don't deserve it." She points an angry hand in Jamie's direction.

"Nick's my cousin, Myrtle."

"Oh." From her expression, it's clear she didn't know. Jamie's out of his corner now and coming toward me. He doesn't care who knows of his love for me. The universe approves it. Myrtle's pout quivers like a spoiled toddler with an empty birthday pinata. She steadies herself and looks past me for a second. Then her eyes lock back on mine.

"Jordan." She spits the word out like venom.

"Jordan's my best friend. Of course, she loves me." Jamie's behind me now. Serenity courses through me at the simple touch of his hand on my back.

Her face shifts, brightens. She glances behind me again and laughs. "Not loves you. *In* love with you. It's not a secret. Everyone knows."

An involuntary sound like the last secret being torn from a betrayed spy, heart wrenching and telling, rips out of my best friend.

One of her old movies could not have overdramatized it any more clearly. The world stops. I turn to face her. Her dark eyes flashes open with fright then clamp down again.

Nick is stone. Owen's face rotates, wide-eyed like an owl back and forth between the object of his desire and his desire's heartbreak.

My breath stops.

"Jordan?" I ask.

She raises her chin and escorts herself to the door. "Find your own ride, Myrtle. You pathetic lush."

After an elongated silence, Nick follows her. I try to follow, too, but Jamie stops me. "Give them some time," he says.

"I have to go to her." I rip free from him, but he grabs me again by both shoulders. His face is in mine.

"Give her time with Nick. It's between them. It has nothing to do with you."

"But--"

"Stay here with me where you belong. Jordan's a big girl."

I step away from him and the door. I'm lost. Jordan needs me. Doesn't she? Or do I just need for her to be okay, so I'm okay? It would be so easy to stay, to let Nick handle it.

By now Myrtle has lost it. Her maniacal laugh fills the void left by Nick and Jordan. I want to slap her, but that greenish shadow on her face stops me.

Instead, I say, "Jordan's right about you."

"And I'm right about Jordan. And I think it's hilarious that you didn't know. I wonder how much they'll love you now. Look around, Daisy. They're all gone."

When I was a young girl, I sat with my crying mother as we watched a news story about a toddler who'd fallen into an abandoned well. This is how the child must've felt. Claustrophobic, alone, scared. Stuck. Jamie moves his arms around me like a lifeline, and I grab on.

I don't remember much of what happened after that, but I do know that it was Owen who, after pacing the floor in an obvious attempt to discover what on earth to do with himself, slipped Myrtle away with a fistful of grateful cash from Jamie, a tip for the driver.

"Do you think it's true?" Jamie asks me when they're all gone, and he'd made a few calls to someone to clean up the party refuse, and we are lost in our blue satin and foggy dreams.

"I don't know," I answer.

"Do you think it matters?"

"That she likes girls? No. Not to me, it doesn't. That she might feel some way about me that I don't about her? That, if it's true, the whole world knows, and Myrtle of all people was the one who broke the news, yeah. That matters a lot."

CHAPTER TWENTY-FOUR

I stay with Jamie for the weekend. Everybody ignores everybody. I don't dare even peek at social media. I don't want to know. I look into Jamie's ocean eyes and have everything I need for happiness.

On Monday, I'm late for school, but it turns out not to matter. Ms. Eckleburg had set me up with Ms. Hip after all.

"She'd love to have you this morning if it's okay with you. I've already checked with your teachers."

It's more than okay. Unlike last Monday when the gossip wheel was all in my imagination, scandal would be spinning today. As Jordan had observed, everyone who is anyone was there Friday night.

Jordan. How was her part in the scandal going to go down? Something twists in my gut that I should know. That I should dive into the murky gossip swamp and drain all the gunk away from my best friend. She would for me, but I don't know how.

Ms. Eckleburg loads me up with permission slips and time cards and sends me away.

I set my GPS for a part of Chicago I never go. The shelter lies, nondescript, between a dry-cleaner and a vintage wares store. I've been instructed to come through the front door since I have donations. Even so, the only spot I can find to park is a block away. I nab it fast and lug my bag down the street.

Ms. Hip greets me. "Hello, Daisy. I was thrilled when Tessa... I mean Ms. Eckleburg called me about you." She's wearing a pantsuit this time, grey with tiny white stripes through it, not as fancy but still sharp. She deposits my bag on a table where a freckled-face young woman with vibrant brown eyes and a soft smile inventories it.

"It's baby stuff. That's all," I say.

The young holds up a package of pink, paper baby booty streamers. "How thoughtful of you. Sometimes people forget we celebrate here, too. Birthdays, graduations, baby showers."

"I just picked it up at the store." I feel some need to justify their existence.

"Let me show you around and then we'll get the paperwork out of the way. We're so glad you're here," Ms. Hip says.

"So glad," the young woman echoes.

Ms. Hip whisks me away through a tour. It's much bigger than it looks from the outside. There are a few rooms for women and families. Well, single moms and their kids. There are men's shelters and family shelters in the city, she explains, but no men are allowed here.

"We offer sanctuary for women with nowhere else to go. Then we help them find a more permanent place. We have programs for women who need job training or education. We provide financial literacy classes. You'd be surprised how many women know absolutely nothing about their own finances. They haven't been allowed to."

"Allowed to?" I ask. My parents left me a fortune. I don't know how much, but I know it's enough. Guilt pours over me that a man in a suit and Italian loafers manages all of that for me from the top floor of a skyscraper.

"We'll start you up front with Consuela. You'll still need to sign a confidentiality agreement."

"Of course. I'm sure no one wants people knowing they had to come here."

Ms. Hip stops me. "Is not about hiding in shame. It's about protection. These women have nothing to be ashamed of." Her eyes are nearly black, too, but not like Tom's. Soft greys spill around the edges like a whisper of another life she might have lived once upon a time, but it's over now. In that moment, the intense sincerity of her words blind me to anything else.

"It's not their fault," I say in an attempt to convince myself.

The sincerity of Ms. Hip's smile matches her words. I don't know if she's ever been a wife or a mother, but she should be. I'd curl up in her lap in a heartbeat.

We go back up front where Consuela has some volunteer papers for me to read and sign. "Don't sign anything you don't fully read and understand. Ever," she says as if she's been there, done that. I'm on my second page when the door hesitantly opens.

The woman who glides in looks half done. Her blonde hair,

porcelain makeup, fake eyelashes and matte, peach lipstick could rival an Instagram model. But her grey slacks don't match the green blouse which sits on her, haphazardly buttoned. The shoes, too, don't go with anything, although they're lovely little ankle boots, probably purchased at a price even I might have balked at. I saw some like them in a window once. She carries in a basket of things. On top is a flashlight, Nike running shoes, and an old cookbook.

Ms. Hip greets her. "Let me help you with that. Consuela here will be glad to fill out a tax receipt for you."

But the woman won't let go. That's when I recognize her. Ardita Fitz-Peters lives two blocks down from my parents' house.

"It's not a donation. Please, I need help," she whispers.

"Of course. You're in the right place." Ms. Hip gestures to Consuela who immediately walks Ardita in a half-embrace down the hall to a private room.

Ms. Hip turns to me. "I apologize. We try to advertise that the front door is for donations only. It's safer that way. Sometimes they come through anyway."

I'm there for another hour, learning their inventory system for donations. They'll have to teach me all over again in my next session because I can't concentrate. A fiery ember burns in my brain. Ardita Fitz-Peters. Ardita Fitz-Peters. Mama used to call her Ardita Fitz-*Perfect*. Even Ginny Fay with her doting husband and dreamworld mansion envied another woman's perfection.

The Fitz-Peters house looms as big as ours. The lot is bigger, though, with a hill that the home sits atop. On repeat in my mind is an imaginary vision of Ardita straightening her long, blonde hair until she hears handsome Dr. Fitz-Peters' Cadillac turn down the road. Then she grabs what she can—a laundry basket, a flashlight, her family's cookbook—and beats it out the door. Or maybe he was there when it happened. Maybe he'll come after her. Maybe he'll cut her off, and the contents of that basket will be all she has to start a new life.

I think of the Italian-loafered man sitting in his tower, counting my money. I'm so angry. When the volunteer coordinator finally stops talking, I secure a pen from her desk to sign my timecard. My fingers hurt. I've chewed the nails to nubs, and I don't even bite my nails. I guess I just needed something to destroy in protest.

Before I can leave, I hear a rustling down the hallway.

"I insist. I really insist," Ardita's tired voice floats to me. Then she's back up front, softer now and coming toward me.

"Daisy, I thought that was you. I just wanted to say I'm sorry."

I don't know what she means. Sorry for what? For marring my image of her perfect life? A dry, cynical laugh sticks in my chest. "There's no need to apologize."

"I was at the funeral, but I never had a chance to tell you myself how sorry I am for your parents' passing."

"It was a long time ago." I want to make her feel better.

"Still, your mother was... well, I'm sorry you don't have her anymore."

I don't return to Eggerton Academy. I'll serve the detention. I don't care. Let Lucille or Myrtle run cheer practice. I don't care. At first, I head toward Tuolomee, but it doesn't seem right. Jamie will be at school. Although, I can't imagine him actually sitting in class. He seems more like a permanent fixture of the library's upper floor.

Even if I went back to school, it's not Jamie I want to see. I need my Jordan. I need to info-dump on her about the inequity and the inquiry of life. I need to flail my arms and curse. I need her stoicism to calm me when my rant is over. But it's not possible. I consider going to Grandma's to sink into my soft bed, but after spending my day in the shadow of Claudia Hip and Consuela, softness seems an inappropriate response.

I turn the car around and head to the Fay house.

CHAPTER TWENTY-FIVE

At the end of *Back to the Future,* when Marty McFly finally makes it back home, but everything is different... I'm channeling that moment.

I punch the code and as I walk through the front door into the lily-covered entry, the familiar ghosts that greet me every time dissolve into old memories like faded photos pasted carefully but now crumbling on a yellowed page. Promise hangs in drafty corners and I follow it to my mother's dressing room.

On a tall shelf hidden under some sweaters she thought she might wear again someday, I find it. I pull down the box, open it and wrap my steady hands around the floral cover of her journal. Dropping the box to the floor, I turn to the entry I've tried to unremember in the last three years and read it again with fresh eyes.

I've given up everything and it's never enough. I've given up even myself. What do I have left when that's gone?

I want to cry. I want to sob ferociously, but my enlightened heart won't release the tears. Instead, I turn to the utterly ridiculous golden-caged Marilyn Monroe and remove her from the wall. Should I smash it? Should I throw it in a fireplace and incinerate it, letting its ashes take the shape of wives and mothers and sisters and daughters moving with transcendent effort through cigar smoke air. Intense obligation presses in on me. I raise the framed print above my head and bring it crashing down through that air, but the memories fade and I stop myself before it hits the ground.

Whirlwinds of convenient suppressions tumble through me. Mama's unhappiness. Mrs. Fitz-Peters' book clubs. My own lies. And Jordan's.

Suddenly, I'm really mad at all of them. Especially Jordan. I truly, truly, truly do not care what her sexual orientation is, but to find out from Myrtle something I should have already known! Maybe I did know, but it didn't matter so deeply that I never even thought about it. But from Myrtle. Myrtle, in a rush to hurt me, to bring me down a notch, to punish me for my privilege. A privilege that doesn't look so pretty from the inside. A privilege we're all faking our way through. It's not golden. It's not safe. I'm not even sure it's real.

I look at Marilyn again and recite out loud the words I've read a thousand times.

I don't mind living in a man's world if I can be a woman in it.

Marilyn Monroe was from another time, from a world I could never know. She was from poverty and a mentally ill mother, from an orphanage and a poor education. She came from drugs and depression. She came from war and desperation.

She used the tools she had to make it in a man's world. And she did make it, for a while. She doesn't deserve to be trashed. She doesn't deserve to be locked in a forgotten closet.

Without thinking, I carry her downstairs. The portrait of my mother and father had been removed from its throne atop our fireplace mantle a long time ago, taken to the funeral home and lost. I prop her in their place.

Next to the fireplace, stacked beside a crystal vase lies a bundle of my mother's dainty scrapbooks. I thumb through the pages until I find the picture I'm looking for. It's the last book club with the neighbor ladies. My mother flashes a foggy grin and beside her is Ardita Fitz-Peters, displaying a tray of giant cookies. Half a dozen ladies crowd behind Ardita's kitchen island. That old cookbook lies on the corner with someone's half-empty cocktail glass sitting on it. There are no other books in the photo. Lots of cocktail glasses, but no other books.

I peel off the photo and rest it against Marilyn's gilded frame. Then I curl up in my father's overstuffed chair and swallow down uncried tears until all the woman-power black and white movies, and all panicked breaths calmed by Ms. Eckleburg, and all the notes my mother sings to me in my head align with my soul like planets prepared for an epic reordering of the universe. Inside my bag still crisscrossed on my torso, is my laptop. I pull it out and type in the university I've memorized from Mrs. Eckleburg's brochure. A screen opens asking me for my name, address, school, and intended major.

... make ones that lift women up. Make ones that create pathways to equality and justice...

Just Daisy

    Without hesitation, my fingers type in the word: Pre-law. I complete as much of the application as I can. As I close my computer, I know there's one more piece of unfinished business. I need my best friend to know that it's not always about me.

CHAPTER TWENTY-SIX

"I didn't know if you'd come," I yell across the yard to Jordan when I get back to Grandma's.

She's leaning on the passenger side of her car, arms across her chest, nose pointed to the sky, elusive and aloof.

"Have I ever not come?" Her voice is low and unexpressive.

We meet in the middle of the yard. It's 4:00 on a sober Monday afternoon, and the grey air foretells a damp evening.

"No. You've always been there for me. Always. I can't think of a single time you haven't been since grade school when you saved me from all those stupid boys on the playground."

"Well, they were stupid. And someone was gonna get hurt the way they were throwing that football through the swing set." She plants a hand on her impatient hip and sticks it out, very much the way she did that day when we were nine and didn't know yet that we were best friends for life. Except for the color of the plaid uniform and her angular haircut, she's her nine-year-old self.

I laugh at the playground memory, still the superciliousness of her present demeanor eats at my subconsciousness. I, the perpetual mess, always needed the best friend to fix me, to save me from myself, even in grade school. She'd said it herself often enough. But all along she was trying and failing to hide the most important things. She'd trusted no one. Not herself. Not me. Certainly not the crusty, white-bread, wholesomeness of Eggerton.

In my mind, when I texted her from my parents' house, this conversation had gone smoothly, but now I don't care about smooth. Life roads are bumpy, even with the donut stores and running water.

The words burst out. "Why didn't you tell me yourself, Jordan? Do you think it would have mattered?" The words sound harsher than I intend, but they're out there now. There's no sucking them back in.

"Is this why you wanted me here?" She turns away.

"No. Yes. I mean, sort of. I want everything settled. I don't want weirdness between us. I want to be there for you."

She looks at me in silence for an awkward minute, then does that single shoulder shrug she makes when she doesn't care what people think. "Maybe I knew it wouldn't have mattered and that's why I never said."

"It's not fair to me. If I had known you were in love with me--"

Her vicious laugh cuts through my words. "In love with you? Is that what you think?" She sneers. I hate being on the receiving end of her disapproval, but I'm in it now.

"Myrtle said--"

"Myrtle's a bitch. She's a careless little ho who smashes through people and then retreats back into her miserable little pill-popping head, leaving the refuse of shattered reputations behind her. She doesn't deserve our consideration." She states it so matter of fact, my head begins nodding in rhythm.

"Wow! You've really thought this through," I say.

"Nick helped with the wording."

"Nick helped? Are you guys—"

"Nick and I are what we always were. We're friends. Friends work things out." Her chin lifts.

"That's what I'm trying to do. I want things right between us. I want to be there for you like you always are for me."

"Really? Is that why you followed me Friday night? Because you wanted to be there for me?"

"I wanted to. I did. Jamie said maybe you needed to talk it out with Nick. That it wasn't my place."

She narrows her eyes, her perfect brows somehow retaining their perfection. Glamorous. Even in the breezy afternoon, edging on cool except for the warm breeze confusing the clouds as they pass by the sun, she's all glamour. Jordan, the glamour girl and Nick, the gumshoe reporter. They couldn't be more perfect.

"Maybe Jamie was right about that part. It might have been weird with you there," she admits.

"But I did want to follow you. I wanted to be there for you. I still do."

She studies me. I let her. She won't find anything insincere.

She inhales, holds it a second, then releases. "Okay. You can start with not believing everything Myrtle says." She says it like she's announcing a declaration to the universe. I saw her face that night, though. I know it's not a total lie. But our friendship needs the whole truth now, not only the bits she's willing to share.

"But part of it's true. That you like girls. Just not me." I contort my voice, softening the edges, offering a safe heart opening.

Her defiant eyes flash everywhere and finally land on me. For a moment, I think she might stick out her tongue like she did to those stupid boys that day on the playground. A hot wind, blown in from another time, wraps around us. Jordan's hair flips here and there and settles around her like slow motion in a spy thriller movie. She hooks her pinky around the few strands stuck between her lips and frees them.

"Of course, I like you. I'm just not in love with you. Sorry to disappoint. As for girls in general, what's not to love?" A beautiful smirk forms on her hard face. Jordan really does need one of those long Hollywood starlet cigarettes. She was born in the wrong generation.

"So, the thing with Nick?"

Her mouth softens to a pout. "Nick is the most decent human I've ever known. Other than my dad, anyway."

"Oh, I'm sure he'd love being compared to your dad."

"That's just it. I should be head over heels for Nick. What girl wouldn't?"

"Your eyes do light up when you talk about him."

She sighs and leans back on her heels. "Do they?"

I nod.

"But there's also this junior girl on my golf team." She frowns. She actually frowns.

"So, basically, you're stuck. Hmmm... Sometimes, it's hard to choose, isn't it?" The wind continues to whip, only my hair doesn't dance and stick to my movie star lips. It wraps around my neck and flicks into my eyes. At one point, I'm sure I inhaled a few strands. I wrangle it into my fist.

"Oh no, you don't. Don't compare my situation to yours. I made my choice. I chose Nick. What I didn't choose is for Myrtle to--" Her eyes go glassy. Suddenly, I want to punch my fist into Myrtle's other eye. I wince against the thought and blink it away. Instead, I think of less violent remedies. If the situation were reversed, if I were in turmoil as I usually am, and Jordan was looking to mend things, I know what she'd do. What she's done a million times.

"Jordan, I think we need a movie night." I link my free arm through hers and start toward the house.

"Marlene Dietrich?" she asks.

I cringe. "Okay. Marlene Dietrich."

"In German."

"Can we at least have the captions in English?"

"Deal."

And just like that, the world is right. Different. But right. In fifteen minutes, we've popped the corn, poured the tea, and are curling up on the couch. I twirl a strand of ratty hair and ponder on the weird sensation balanced between us.

Balanced. That's the weird sensation. Like when the teeter totters to that level place and no one dares move or your hang time might crash.

"You know, Jordan. I think liking boys and girls would make for a very complicated love life." I point the remote at the screen and push play.

"Or an adventurous one." The words curl in the back of her throat, deep and genuine.

Adventurous. Tybee had been adventurous, something from a teen movie. "Adventurous romance is complicated."

"How is your dream boy, Jamie?"

A hollowness fills my brain. I can see his face, but he feels a million miles away, like Friday never happened. Like I didn't spend the weekend in his bed, lying to my grandmother and avoiding my life.

"I don't know. I actually haven't thought of him all day."

In a rush, guilt and obligation crash over me. I can't breathe. I close my eyes against the opening credits of *The Blue Angel,* a story of misdirected obsession, and focus on Jamie's ocean eyes. Slowly, they come back to me. He's no longer half a world away. He's a text away. A car ride away. A thought away. The world is ours. Now that he's made it that way, how can it ever be anything else?

I think of my Jamie phone, tucked safely away in a bedside drawer. I gave Jamie my weekend, but my Jordan needs me now. Satisfaction smiles across her face as the credits give way to the first scene. She might need Marlene Dietrich more, but she needs me, too.

Deborah Linn

    I hold up my glass of tea. She clinks it with hers. Unlike my mother who'd given every bit of herself away, there was still enough of me to go around. The text could wait. This moment right here, right now would never come again. I couldn't wish it away. Not even for blue silk and ocean eyes.

CHAPTER TWENTY-SEVEN

"All I'm saying-uh is that you could've told someone you weren't coming-uh." Lucille's eyes roll so hard, I think her head might topple right off her body. She acts all holier-than-thou because she actually came to school the Monday after the party fiasco, so she ran cheer practice. And I didn't.

"I was working on volunteer hours. Ms. Eckleburg already okayed it with my teachers."

"But here's the thing. You didn't okay it with us." Her hand is on her hip. There are twelve "minions" lockstep behind her. Myrtle stands in the back in smug satisfaction.

One day. One day is all it took for her to turn them all against me.

"Thank you for stepping up, Lu. I knew I could count on your leadership."

I could have knocked her over with a fairy's wing. She was expecting pure bitch, I'm sure. Salivating for some little morsel to validate whatever pathetic story Myrtle has told them.

The thing is, they can't really touch me. They were all at that party, too. And they were all drunk. I wasn't. Whatever lies Myrtle has told to turn them, my truth is more powerful.

Lucille opens her mouth to spout another stupid comment. I want so much to interrupt with "Did you enjoy the party Friday? You seemed like you did. Was that a lacrosse player I saw you disappear with?"

Instead, I link an arm through hers and force her over to our stretching spot. Twice I ask her advice on a new cheer move. It helps, but still, no one is disappointed when I call practice short. I have somewhere to be, which is good for them, so their gossiping can continue. It's fine, though, because Jamie is waiting. He has another surprise.

When I arrive at the Fay house, he's already there, sitting in my dad's overstuffed chair that held me just yesterday. The breeziness of him in light wash ripped jeans and rosy V-neck tee settles into the stiff worn leather like a casual houseguest. The heart of the room beats differently with him here. Less haunted, I guess.

"How did you get in?" My laughter floats to the high ceilings and lingers there like a voyeur.

"I remembered the code," he pulls himself up and embraces me with a happy kiss.

"How sneaky of you," I tease.

"I prefer clever."

"Yes, very clever."

"Are you hungry?" he asks and leads me to the kitchen to sushi and some yummy frozen drinks like the ones we had when Cody and Ella celebrated with us.

I take a sip. "Nice. I see you've made yourself at home."

"Of course. Why shouldn't I?"

"You absolutely should." For some reason, a memory pops up from that time my dad's friend bought a draft horse on a bet that he could turn it into a racing champion. The poor thing was snubbed so hard by the elite equine, Dad's friend handed him back to the farmer without even requesting a refund.

Jamie loads our snacks and drinks on a tray and carries them out back. "Let's come out here. You said it's your favorite place."

"It is. You remembered."

Only the gazebo is not how *I* remember, nor how I have ever experienced. Jamie has miraculously entwined it with Back-eyed Susans and Seaside Goldenrod. He's hung a fishing-net hammock and surrounded it with clear jars filled with sea glass beads and candles. He jumps under the awning and sets the tray on a side table. He moves a hand in front of him as if he's presenting masterpiece.

"For you," he says with a bursting smile.

"It's Tybee." I squeal.

"Yes." He gathers me into him and kisses my happy face.

"What's this all for? And when did you have time? I was just here yesterday."

His smile fades. "By yourself? Did you come alone?"

"Yes. I needed to think."

A hesitation. A thin crack in his perfection. But he recovers.

Just Daisy

"Well, think about this." He takes me by the hand to the back of the gazebo and pulls back a beaded curtain. On the ground is a beach of sorts, a spread of sand where shells and green glass spell out one word. H O M E C O M I N G?

Behind us, he's pushed a button. It's not music that starts, but waves and seagulls and the sounds of our island.

"Jamie. This is amazing. You've brought our world to us." I can't stop smiling.

"I want everything to be perfect for you. And now that we're together, we can go to your important Homecoming dance together. No past holding you back. No waiting. No king and queen. Just you and me." His triumphant voice cascades over the words like Poseidon declaring victory. Only something's not right. The spoils of war are missing.

"Wait, what do you mean no king and queen?"

"Well, now that you've given it up. There's nothing stopping us."

"But, I haven't given that up."

Everything about him goes limp.

"You're... you're... not with Tom. You don't need that now. *We* don't need that."

"No, I'm not with Tom, but being Homecoming queen isn't dependent on that."

He's pacing now, like that day in the library. "Are you sure? Because that's what it seems like."

"I'm my own person. I shouldn't have to give that up for us to be together." I reach out, try to touch him. He pulls back.

"You mean you *want* their approval? Why would you want their approval? It shouldn't matter." He's grasping now, panicked for me to throw him a life raft, but I don't see the need. This shouldn't pull him under.

Uncertainty swirls in a vicious whirlpool in my brain. I'm not sure I do want their approval. I'm not sure I don't want it, either. The only thing I'm sure of are my mother's words. *I've given up even myself. What do I have left when that's gone?*

He stops pacing. "Daisy, Daisy, look. Sit here." He guides me to the hammock. The porcelain doll routine constricts me. I feel more than placed on a shelf. I feel boxed in, waiting for a salesclerk to shoot a price on me with his tag gun.

"I want to show you something. I was going to wait, but—'" He slides his shirt off and drops it to the ground. A square of white gauze is taped to his wide, bronzed swimmer's chest. He looks like a cowboy who's been treated for a gunshot wound to the heart. Slowly, he peels back the tape and the bandage to reveal a rather large tattoo. A vibrant daisy with my name scrolled across it mars his perfect physique.

"That's my handwriting." Before I realize I'm even moving, I'm to him, tracing the art with a skeptical finger.

"Clever, right?'

Sneaky, I think.

"Isn't it perfect?" he asks, rotating a smile between it and me.

"Jamie, I—"

"And look." He pulls his cell from his back pocket and shuffles through some images. "Here's what yours will be."

He shows me a lighthouse—our lighthouse—with his name in sea glass green twined around it. He touches my chest like the image is already emblazoned there.

"Jamie, stop this. It's too much." I take his cell and toss it aside.

"What do you mean, too much? I don't understand. What's too much? Nothing's too much for you. For us." The frantic pace of his words cut into the syncopation of the faux waves and wind.

I rein in my voice to soothe him because I know I can. I'm practiced at it. I'm weary of it.

"Okay, maybe not too much. Maybe too soon. I mean just yesterday I finally decided on a college to apply to and now you want me to permanently ink your name on my chest?"

Sad wrinkles gather on his brow. He turns from me and leans on the railing to stare at my pool, the surface of it now shimmering in the setting sun. "You decided on college. What college? Where?"

"Cornell."

"Cornell? That's in..that's... where's Cornell?"

"It's in New York."

"You want to go to New York?" He pulls at his flop of hair, repeatedly soothing it down and picking it up again, twisting it through his fingers.

"It's one application. I guess it doesn't have to be Cornell. There are other places." I don't know where the words come from. What other places? Those garbage-covered, discarded pamphlets pop into my brain. I fight the ridiculously unproductive urge to run back to school and dig them out. They wouldn't be there. They're last month's trash.

My gaze moves back to his chest. The tattoo is fresh, smothered with Vaseline, inflamed angry red edges around the daisy petals. I want to touch it because it seems made of plastic, like one of those car window clings that remove easily with a flick of your fingernail.

I retrieve his shirt and slide it back over his head. I don't want to look at that tattoo because I know it can't be peeled away. The only other choice is to cover it up. Do that thing I'm so good at—pretend it isn't there. The muscles in his back ripple like the gentle tides of our island as I smooth his shirt in place.

"It's okay," the words hover under his breath like the promise of rain. "It's okay. I can do New York. We can do New York. It will be okay."

He turns to face my parents' pool, but his eyes focus on something on the other side of the water, maybe on the other side of everything. For a moment, I'm within and without. I'm looking down on us like an angel, sending approval or understanding. But I'm here, too, wondering if he's really okay with it. He's a million miles away and the waves spray sea salt in his face and the air smells like seaweed and a lighthouse calls. I don't know why he's so sad when I'm right here. I'm not with Tom. What is he searching for when I'm right here?

A nervous giggle bubbles up inside me. Jordan's snarky *utterly ridiculous* rattles in my brain, and suddenly, it all feels a little silly. The tattoo. Homecoming. It's not life and death. It's just high school.

I return the smile to my voice. "Jamie, this is all lovely. The beach, the hammock, the flowers. But can we just get through our senior year first? You're miraculously somehow here. We're together just like you said we would be. Let's do Homecoming and then we can maybe worry about everything else. Homecoming first. It's fun. I promise."

"I'll wait," I hear him say.

"What?"

His face is to me again, bright and soft. "I can't be in there when they call your names on that stage, but I'll wait. I'll be in the parking lot, and after you're done doing what you need to do, you come find me. I'll wait for you."

I'm up for air. I exhale and find refuge in the crook of his arm. The night wind breezes around us.

"It's a good compromise," I say, my eyes shining at him again. "Thank you for all this. It means more than you know."

I leave him long enough to gather a couple sushi bites. Playfully, I place one on his tongue, then pop one in my mouth. It's clean and fresh.

"Mmm." He smiles around a mouthful.

"This is so good." And I don't mean just the sushi. Rhythms of moon-pulling tides rush over us. If I close my eyes, I'm there again with the island sky, the vast stars, and my beautiful fish.

But even with closed eyes, the image of my name in my handwriting permanently tattooed on his chest threatens to strangle the night like the fibers of a fisherman's net.

There are times when hope is a palpable thing. It sifts between us like a medley of sand and salt that dries on your body after an ocean swim, a buffer of friction from a frolicking wave. The difficulty comes in discerning whether hope offers a true manifestation of your heart's desire or a false promise of something that never really should have been in the first place.

CHAPTER TWENTY-EIGHT

For the first time, I bring my Jamie phone to school on Friday. I really don't know why. A compulsion, I guess. A lucky compulsion because Jamie's not in our spot for lunch. We texted yesterday, but I haven't seen him since Tuesday. I think he's staying away on purpose, giving me room, protecting his haunted heart.

I admit, it's been much easier to couple up with Tom for Homecoming stuff without wondering if Jamie's looking on. Tom's not talking to me, but he does a good job of playing the crowd. It's not lost on me that I benefit from his show. Only Grandma's happy picture-snapping eases the guilt. That and the fact that the second our Homecoming week activity is over, he glares at me with disgust and walks off laughing with his flavor of the day who selfies her good fortune all over social media.

The little nook in the back of the library's second story aches with missing Jamie. Even the sunlight that used to filter through the skylight, illuminating particles that float through our secret air, hides behind a cloud.

I ache a little, too. But Jordan and Nick are with me.

"So, how big is it exactly?" Nicks squints his eyes as if trying to picture in his mind's eye the exact dimensions of the tattoo.

I splay my fingers and stick them in the air. "Bigger than my hand. It takes up half his chest."

"And it's *your* handwriting? You're sure?" Jordan's tone is half-impressed, half-creeped out.

"Yeah. He took it off a government assignment I left in my textbook. Romantic, right? My name, my handwriting, his heart." Doubt tinges the edges of my voice, no matter how hard I try to hide it.

"Sure. absolutely," Nick says, but his head swivels back and forth in an aggressive no.

"And the design for yours?" Jordan asks.

"His handwriting. Very clever. Don't you think? Romantic and clever."

"Those aren't the first words that come to mind, Daisy." Jordan's eyes enlarge. She shares a look with Nick.

"What was that look?" I ask.

"What look?" They respond together.

"Fine. If you aren't gonna tell me what you really think, I'll ask someone else."

I notice Owen sitting on his bench and motion for him to bring his lunch over. There's no need for a lookout now.

"Where's Jamie?" Owen asks.

"I don't know. We aren't joined at the hip. We're our own people." I say.

"Yeah, it's not like they have matching tattoos or anything." Jordan offers, her laughter mingling with Nick's. Owen joins in, though I can tell he's clueless.

"Maybe he's at the dermatologist having something removed," Nick says.

"You guys aren't funny. You know this, right?"

Owen clears his throat, "Why don't you text him?"

That's when I remember the compulsion and grab my Jamie phone from my purse. I text him while Owen stares at me. He's grown so used to his watch-out post, he's not quite sure what to watch out for now.

I miss you.

Sorry

Everything ok?

Sure. Had an appt.

Are you sick?

It's all good beautiful.

He follows that with a run of hearts and flowers and kissing emojis.

"Apparently, he has an appointment," I say.

"Dermatology?" Jordan asks.

I scrunch my nose at her.

Just Daisy

"Did his mom call him out? If his mom didn't call him out, he'll have detention." Owen finishes up his habitual burrito.

"I doubt she did," I say, a little sad that there's no one to call him out. How does that even work? Can he call himself out?

Owen leans casually against a shelf. His goofish face bears a small cut surrounded by a blue bruise from last Friday night's altercation. It draws attention from his big, owl-eye glasses that usually takeover his whole countenance. Oddly enough, the bruise isn't marring, just interesting. Like battle scars scratched into saintly monuments whose unfortunate location make them victims of angry mobs.

"Seriously though, Daisy. I have to ask," Jordan says.

Here it comes. "What's that?"

"Did the universe manifest it like Rev. Dimmesdale's A in *The Scarlet Letter,* or did he go to an actual tattoo artist?"

"You aren't funny."

Nick chimes in. "The universe didn't manifest Dimmesdale's A. It's a sign of his inner guilt. It came from his own soul."

"Actually, it was a form of self-mutilation. I wrote my essay on it last year. Got an A." Owen confesses, and we all laugh.

"Still not funny," I say, feeling lighter.

"But I did get an A," Owen assures us.

"I'm sure you did, Owen. Nick says you're a brilliant writer." I say.

Owen beams. His smile brightens my whole being. I reach up and wipe a stray cheese drop from his chin.

"By the way, Tom's in the study carrel again," Owen says.

"What's he doing down there?"

We scrunch down and peer over the railing like a group of slapstick detectives.

"Maybeeeee, studying?" Owen says.

I laugh. "Now that's funny."

We watch Tom poke the keyboard and narrow his eyes at it like an old woman threading a needle. Periodically, he reclines, tipping the chair back on its hind legs. He smirks then scowls then shakes his disbelieving head.

"He has a laptop. Why is he on the library computer?" I say.

"So, not studying?" asks Owen.

"Uh, probably not. Although now that I won't be writing his papers for him..."

"And not porn unless he wants to get kicked out of Eggerton," Nick says.

"Nick!" I jab him.

He jabs me back. "What? People do."

"Really? In the library?"

"They snagged Walter Chase leering at anime porn just last year," Jordan agrees.

"Is that a thing? Anime porn?"

There's a shared moment of grimace, and we scan our attention back to Tom.

"I gotta know. I'm going down," I say.

"Okay, but wait a minute." Owen rests a hand on my shoulder.

"What is it?"

"You sure he's not into anime? I wouldn't want you to walk into something…"

Jordan and Nick snicker. So does Owen. He's finally in on the joke.

"I'm sure." I pat his shoulder.

I straighten up as if I've been looking for a book all along. I grab one off a shelf to appear studious and glide down and around behind then cover Tom's eyes with my hands. I know it's a risk.

"Guess who?" I say.

He jumps. "Geez, Daisy. What are you doing?"

"Being scholarly. What are you doing?" I hold up the book for proof. It's on Ruth Bader Ginsburg. Silently, I congratulate myself on the random choice. Or was it the universe? I shove it under my arm to check out later.

"Why do you care?" he turns to the screen and scrolls through.

All week, it's been weird being near him but not *with* him. It's also weird not immediately being thrown at his harsh words. A new normal, I suppose. There's a chair close by. I pull it over and sit beside him and lay my purse on the desktop. "Hey, Tom. How about a truce?"

His face is stone and his eyes go dark. I lower my register, knowing what it does to him.

I continue. "Seriously. Let's not stay mad. I'm sorry for how everything went down," I say, and I mean it. As brutish as he can be sometimes, he didn't deserve that kind of break up.

Hope glimmers around him. I've gone too far. I need to clarify the intent of my apology.

"We have the parade Saturday morning. It's our last ever Fall Homecoming parade. Let's try to enjoy it. Let's try to find a way not to be gossip fodder."

There is no confusion like the confusion of a simple mind. He has no idea what *fodder* means.

"Let's just find a way to not be the thing everyone's talking about. Or if they are talking about us, let's at least control what they say. Let's show them that even if we aren't together, we're still unbreakable," I say.

He softens, but a surly smile lurks at the corner of his hard lips.

After an awkward silence and glance up at Owen hopefully poking his nose over the ledge, I hone in on my real reason for being here. I look at his screen. "So, what are you working on here? An essay?"

He sighs. "Eckleburg is on my ass about this common app. Don't know why. Pretty sure the football coaches don't use common app."

Years of rusty memories flash across my mind. Yes, it had been Tom's plan to ride off into the NCAA sunset with me cheering him on to a Heisman trophy, maybe even the NFL draft. But somehow it had become mine, too, even if it was one I didn't create. At some point, I had bought in. Last Friday night, when I'd clung to Jamie in the face of Tom's violent machismo, I hadn't realized what all I was leaving behind. A hollowness nibbles at the edges of my liberation. Life is a process of giving up parts of ourselves until our reflections flit like strangers through a packed terminal.

"Common app," Tom grumbles and fills in a few more blanks.

I'm shaken back to my mission. "But you have a computer. Why are you using this one?"

"Mine broke," he answers.

Did you throw it again? I want to ask, but I don't. It's not my business, and even if he did throw it, it wasn't at me this time.

"Also, I needed to find a book. I have to be on here to get to the library catalog. A lot of good it does me. I still don't know where this fucking book is."

"Wow. You really are being scholarly." Tom, doing his own homework. Who would have imagined?

He looks thoughtful and holds out a slip of paper with a call number on it. "Hey, can do me a favor. Can you get this book for me?

I need it for English," he says. I realize it's the first time he's looked me in the eyes in a week.

"I'll be right back." I was a library aide my junior year. Retrieving the book is not a problem. I find it, a reference book on Greek theatre. I get back to him right as our foghorn warning bell sounds.

"Thanks. Mrs. Beluga wants proof that I have an actual book for research. I don't know how a book is gonna help me, though. There's no search engine in a book." He rolls his eyes as if Mrs. Beluga's request is the dumbest thing he's ever heard.

I want to tell him it's called an index, a table of contents at the very least, but he really seems to be trying. Senior year is for growing, right? Maybe he had listened to me, after all.

"Sure, Tom. It's all good."

He exes out and gives me a sad, lingering look. "I may not look it, but I'm really pissed at you right now, Daisy. Like really pissed. But I'll get over it and you'll get over him." He squeezes my knee and kisses my forehead and leaves.

My brain is numb. No snarky bit about the party? No arm grabbing or cursing Jordan? Only a reverberation in my brain of his promise to do better if I'd just give him a chance. After all, he loves me—

A tapping vibration brings me back. It's my Jamie phone from inside my purse where I had set it beside the computer.

I open my texts. They're all gone but the one that just came through.

Are you sure?

Am I sure? About what? I swipe out of our texts and back in. They're still gone. I must have accidentally deleted them.

A strange sensation like what a Catholic must feel in a confessional overcomes me. I glance around. Is he here? Did he see Tom kiss me? Does he mean am I sure about us?
The bell rings. I'm late.

Of course, I'm sure.

I send a quick, big smile selfie with the message. He sends one back. I see that he's in his Mach 1. My fingers itch to grasp the wheel and drive fast, ripping through every foul memory and anxious doubt and just drive and drive and drive.

Out of library aide instinct or Tom caretaking habit—I'm not sure which—I pull up the internet browser. Tom had only minimized the screen but hadn't logged out. His information would be vulnerable to the whims of the next student. I go to log him out when I see the tabs. Common App, Library Catalog, and something else. I click on it to reveal an old mugshot of the scraggly bearded face of a man who'd run his car through the front window of a bistro.

CHAPTER TWENTY-NINE

If there is one thing East Eggerton parents know how to do, it's throw a party. What is a HoCo parade but one long party moving down Covington Road past bakeries, coffee shops, bookstores, and wine bars? Cecil Cohen's family rented and outfitted a party bus to file in behind the football team. I'm not sure why the family would want to advertise their contribution to the delinquency of minors in a parade for all to see. I guess the policemen blocking traffic from interrupting our stream will know who to pull over later. Or not pull over, the way palms are greased around here.

Nevertheless, it's a beautiful morning for a party in motion. I'm walking to the place for candidates to gather when I see Tom leaning against a crisp, white Porsche convertible. Jamie's Mach 1 would have been cooler, but a 911 Carrera soft top isn't bad, either.

I'm not sure what I expect from Tom, but his greeting derails my confidence.

"You are a ray of sunshine." He takes both my hands and kisses my cheek.

I take a twirl in my yellow boatneck dress with a flowy skirt just as a rogue wind blows through, threatening to expose everything underneath. Tom quickly catches me and scoops me up into his arms. My hands involuntarily swoop around his neck.

"That was close." He cocks his head and the familiar naughtiness in his expression triggers something inside me.

He sets me down in the backseat, then jumps over the edge to join me. "The driver is on his way. We'll start in five minutes."

That's all he says, but he can't tear his eyes from me. I swear, he has a thousand words locked behind those dark eyes. I want to open the spillway, relieve his torture, give him a soft place for those words to land, but also, I shouldn't. It would be familiar, but it might not be right.

"Here's some candy for yas." A broad, dark man in a crumpled, navy suit hands us a paper bag and steps in behind the wheel.

"Thank you," I say and almost ask if I could drive. I'd rather sit behind the steering wheel than on the back.

"You look like a princess today. Ready, princess?" Tom's hungry eyes stay on me.

"Ready," I say, a little tingly for all the attention that's awaiting us. A little sad for the attention that won't be there, that hasn't been there since his Tybee-themed HoCo proposal. The flowery texts haven't stopped, but I haven't seen him either. Jamie assures me it's nothing. Jordan and Nick do, too. I can't help but to worry, though. The last time I'd seen him, I'd sort of rejected him. Postponed him, if nothing else. How long will he wait? How long should he?

Tom senses something. "Remember what you told me? It's our last ever homecoming parade. Let's enjoy it. Let's do this for each other."

And just like that, my foggy aura lifts. This is Tom, after all. We may be broken up, but we can't erase our history. We are a part of who we each have become. And what we have become is seniors, celebrating all the traditions of our school and family and community. That's reason enough for a celebration, isn't it?

Our driver pulls in behind a limo carting kings and queens from the last decade, taking this opportunity to relive their past. Periodically, Tom snakes his arm around my shoulders and points to people we know. We throw them candy and smiles and wave like celebrities.

"Remember when we were on that side of things?" he whispers in my ear.

"Yeah, I do. It's a fun tradition."

"This side is more fun, don't you think?" He tosses morsels to a couple of nerds in Minecraft t-shirts who scramble to gather the goodies. One boy carries them back to two small children who look at him with sad, excited faces. He gives up his haul and makes his friends do the same.

"That part might be more fun." I point to our driver.

Tom side eyes me, impressed and surprised. "Agreed." He pulls out his phone.

I lean over and tap the driver. "Hey, do you think we could trade places?"

"What are you talking about?" His voice is gruff and paranoid.

"Seriously, could we?" I offer the sweetest smile I have.

"My boss would have my ass," he grunts.

"I'm Tom Buchanan," Tom says. Tom's dad owns the finance company that owns the dealership. That owns half the businesses in our suburb and a bunch more in the city. Tom shows the driver a text. "That's from my dad."

The driver stops and quickly gets out. So do we. Before Tom has a chance to weasel himself in front of the wheel, I slide in. The driver sits back on our previous perch.

"This is ridiculous," he says when Tom hands him the candy bag.

"I know, right? I should be driving." Tom jumps in beside me and we quickly catch up to the parade.

As we slink along, confused frowns stare at us from the crowds. We wave like nothing is out of place. By the end of the block, our driver is laughing, too. He's taken the magnetic sign from the car door—the one with our names on it. He holds it overhead with one hand and points to us with the other.

We drive past Grandma Betty who holds her hand to her surprised face and Ms. Eckleburg who clings to her fiancé's arm and drops her jaw when she sees us. We see swarms of old men in old letter jackets from back when that was a thing and fledgling families and flirtatious freshmen and business owners thankful for the crowds this Saturday morning. I spot Nick and Owen at different spots, snapping pictures for the yearbook. Nick shakes his head at us, but a smile tugs at the edges of his disappointment.

"Hey, isn't that the place you used to go to dance lessons?" Tom asks, pointing over my shoulder to a bright-windowed building.

"Yes. Zelda's Dance Academy. It's a yoga studio now. I heard Zelda went nuts and died in a fire."

"Holy crap."

"I know. So sad. Hey, remember that place?" I nod to a lot that at one point was nothing until a man named Michaelis shined it up with a food truck coffee bar a few years ago. It's still really popular.

"We were his first customers at the Grand Opening."

"Only because you sneaked me out of the house at four in the morning, and we slept in your Hummer until he opened."

"There's the smoothie place. Remember when that employee spilled a carton of orange peels?"

"Oh my gosh. Yes. They scattered all over the floor like trampled refuse from an overturned garbage truck. Everyone bolted. Poor guy."

We're both quiet while the parade bore us back into our naive history.

"We had some good times, Daisy." His soft voice caresses my soul.

"We did, Tom. We sure did."

"Look out!" Our driver shouts.

I press the brake in time to barely miss a tall, dangling clown on stilts poking the ground with a dancing shoe and teetering on the brink of complete catastrophe. He rights himself and bows at us with a righteous smirk as if the whole thing had been part of the act and he hadn't almost tumbled into our car.

Our driver groans like his world has just come to an end, but Tom and I can't help laughing. Close calls do that, don't they? End in laughter.

When the parade ends, Tom and I thank Mr. Driver. Tom shakes his hand and I hug him like a prodigal daughter. Then we hightail it, still laughing, before some school official can come reprimand us. He walks me to the edge of the parking lot where I'd left my car.

Suddenly, he turns to me with the force of all those unsaid words. The air abruptly changes. All laughter leaves him. His eyes are on fire, his voice on edge. I've witnessed this before. I'm not sure if he's gonna kiss me or hit me. I fight the urge to run.

"He can't have you, Daisy. I won't allow it." The pacing starts. And here we go.

"It's not for you to allow, Tom." What was I thinking? I should have known we wouldn't make it through the morning.

"Goddamit, Daisy. You know what I mean."

"Yeah, I do. You think you own me. That I'm yours to boss around." I fling my hands as if that will make my words make more sense.

"I know I don't own you. I don't want to boss you. If I did, I would have been the one driving the Porsche." He manages a half-smile. I do, too, but only for a moment.

Adjusting the notes of my voice, I say, "You can't just force us to be together, Tom. You can't just order the universe to do your bidding." At the sound of the words coming out of my mouth, an inner gasp occurs—a realization of a similarity I hadn't noticed before. All air evaporates, and for a second, I can't breathe.

"We belong together, and you know it." He's sure now. Not angry. Not even simmering. Just sure. Solid and hard as a judge's declaration. It's a hardness I never knew how to resist before. I never wanted to. There's security in that kind of definitiveness.

I catch my breath. "We belonged together at one time. I don't know that we still do." I find a firm undertone. I can be definitive, too.

"So, you're saying you're over us? Already?"

I chew on my bottom lip in an attempt to build a dam for a million unsaid words. I want to will him away, but he won't budge, and I can't answer him without making myself sound stupid.

Spinning in my head like sugary threads of cotton candy are wisps of memories. My father's plaque. The night I first gave myself to Tom after a giggly walk in the rain. The way the evening air mixes with grass stains and football sweat when he sweeps me into a hug after a victory. An ancient lighthouse on a pristine shore. My name forever inked over the heart of my big, beautiful fish.

I stare into the obsidian depths. I've never seen him this still. Have I broken him? Finally, he starts to turn away, but I call after him. There's something I need to know.

"Tom, would you ever consider getting a tattoo?"

He scoffs. He's back to me in two steps. "What?"

"If we were still together. Would you have ever considered getting a tattoo? Like maybe my name on your chest?" I drag my newly manicured finger along his left pec, knowing without a doubt how hypocritically flirtatious I seem.

His jaw could not have dropped further if it had been unhinged. "Are you serious right now?"

"Would you?"

He peels my hand from his chest and cups it between his. "What would be the point?" His face wrinkles like it's the most ridiculous idea ever to bounce around his brain.

"I don't know. A sign of your undying affection or something." I seriously can't believe how stupid I sound.

His eyes go fuzzy and everything about him softens into a billowy cloud. "It's not what's written over my heart but in it that counts."

He slides his hands over my shoulders as if trying to discern the realness of me. Then he grabs my waist and jerks me to him with a rush of tempting masculinity.

My face is so close to his, I feel the heat of his cheeks on mine. I could embrace him if I wanted. Breeze all his hurt away in a soft kiss.

"We're not over, Daisy. This isn't over. It never will be." His lips press into mine, claiming what's his.

When he's done, he says, "If it was over, you would have pushed away. You didn't."

He turns and walks in the other direction, back toward another life.

My brain is still a cesspool of self-recrimination when I get to my car. If I was expecting to drive straight home and hide in my forgiving, comfy bed, I was a fool. I'm not alone. Jordan stands not three feet away, chatting with Nick who somehow trailed the side streets to beat me here. I would have preferred a reprimanding school official.

CHAPTER THIRTY

"So that was interesting." Perpetual surprise, as always, sits in Nick's eyes.

"Interesting doesn't even begin to describe it," Jordan says to no one in particular. She examines an invisible bird in the air. Even with the snarkiness, she's so cute right now, I have to wonder if she isn't still trying to impress Nick. She's got on these geometric leggings with a cherry-colored crop sweatshirt.

In syncopation, Jordan and Nick turn their parental gaze at me. Judgment presses down. It's obvious they saw the kiss. No getting out of this one.

"It wasn't my fault, guys. I didn't know he was gonna kiss me. I didn't want him to."

"Then why did he?" Jordan asks.

Jordan shifts her weight. Nick tries to ignore the hints of midriff peeking out from her shirt.

God, life is complicated.

"To prove a point or something" I say.

"What point?" Nick leans in, as if asking the pivotal question in a celebrity interview.

"That we aren't over. That I'd have pushed him away if we were." I mumble.

"So not everything he says makes him sound like the moron he is, I guess." Jordan flings the barb out there.

Suddenly, I understand Tom's calm library confession of how pissed he is. Sometimes there's too much emotion to feel. You know it's there, but all you can do is name it and move on. I secure my keys from my bag. "Are you guys here to interrogate me or punish me?"

"Neither. We were gonna invite you to the dance. You and Jamie, that is. Now that you're not going with Tom. You're not going with Tom, are you?" Nick asks.

"Of course not. But I'm not going with Jamie either."

Jordan's eyes grow big. I know what she thinks.

I clarify, "Jamie doesn't want to go to the dance. He doesn't want to see me partnered up with Tom on stage. I can't blame him. I don't want to see me partnered up with Tom on stage or anywhere else," I say even as his kiss still burns on my lips.

"So, Jamie's not coming to the dance?" Nick asks, as if it's newsworthy.

"He's gonna wait outside until after the crowning. I'm supposed to join him as soon as I can after the announcement is made."

"You're gonna be crowned and then leave?" Jordan asks.

I throw up my hands and then flop against the side of the car beside her. "I don't know that I'll be crowned. I think people kind of hate me right now."

"No one hates you for leaving Tom if that's what you think. Maybe for hogging the new guy already, but not for leaving Tom." Jordan says.

"Besides, final voting happened before the party fiasco. Good thing, because otherwise..."

"Very funny, Nick," I say.

Nick makes a move to scoot in beside Jordan, but stops, still not sure of his place. We stew in our predicaments for a bit.

"Hey, you got our votes anyway. And Jamie's. So, there's three," Jordan says.

"Oh, then I'm forever in your debt." I joke.

"Good because we need a ride. Owen brought us, but he's already gone," Nick says.

I roll my eyes at them and push the unlock button on my key fob. "Is that what this was really all about? Y'all just needed a ride?"

"If that's okay. I mean even though neither one of us are in love with you. We don't have your name tattooed on our chests, but we did vote for you." Jordan laughs. Nick joins her, and it sounds so very, very good, better than saltwater taffy and fresh-squeezed boardwalk lemonade on a summer day.

"Seriously, guys, if I had something heavy, I'd throw it at both of you. I'm glad y'all are enjoying the unraveling of my life."

Jordan pokes a polished finger in the air. "Entertaining. That's the word I was looking for. Not interesting. Entertaining."

"Morbidly so," Nick says.

"You guys still aren't funny," I yell as we all tumble into the Coop.

A memory travels from a lost city somewhere in the geography of my former youth. It's of Jordan and Nick and me, high on milkshakes and French fries, blaring girl power songs on the way to Grandma's then forcing Nick to watch Katharine Hepburn marathons until he pretended to fall asleep. We switched to Marvel movies and suddenly he found his second wind.

We pull into George's garage for gas. Jordan and Nick hop out to go in and grab a drink. From my peripheral vision, I see a flash of yellow.

I turn to it. The glorious Mach 1 pulls in on the other side of the gas station, behind the building. From this angle, I can see only the tail end.

Jamie. My happy heart dances. I've missed him. I haven't been away from him this long since Tybee. I truly didn't think I'd see him before tonight. He must have come to the parade to find me. Another surprise. I finish pumping and return the nozzle. Then I walk a wide berth to the other side of the lot, so I can sneak across the front of the store to the corner to intercept him. Surprise him for once.

I peek around the corner. I see him, but he's not alone. In the passenger seat sits a young guy. A freshman, maybe. I can't make out his face. I'm still too far away. He's wearing a ball cap and aviators.

In an extended hand, he offers an envelope to Jamie. Jamie takes it and passes back something small enough to be concealed in his grip. The exchange is made. The boy looks down just as Jamie's hand goes up, knocking the cap. It topples. The boy moves to adjust it, but it falls and a bountiful mane of red locks cascades out from under it.

Even with her emerald eyes hidden behind dark glasses, her identity is unmistakable. Myrtle has purchased a high, and Jamie has just made a deal with the devil. Bile rises to my throat with the realization that I've sold something here, too. Willingly, easily, crumbling all my realities into ash.

"Daisy." The voice comes from behind me. I turn around. It's Nick.

"Nick. Did you see?"

Jordan comes out and sees my face which must be pale as a corpse because I know every ounce of blood has drained from it.

Just Daisy

"Are you okay?" she asks.

I shake my head and hurry back to my car. My friends follow me. They scramble in and shut the doors.

"Daisy. What's wrong? How is this any different from what Jamie has at his parties?" Nick had seen and hadn't cared.

"What happened?" Jordan asks, for the first time in her life not pretending to know everything before everyone else.

I answer Nick. "It's not any different. But somehow, it is. A party is one thing but making one-on-one deals in the back of a dirty gas station alley?"

"Ohhhh. Was there a deal going down?" Jordan says.

"Yeah, Between Jamie and Myrtle."

"She really is a bitch, isn't she?" Jordan seethes.

"Guys, I can't pretend I didn't see this. At the party, it's just a party, you know? No one really knows or cares what's going on."

"It's easier to pretend not to know at big parties. It's the small gatherings where there's no privacy," Jordan muses.

"There's none behind gas stations either, apparently." Nick and Jordan banter like a stand-up comic act, but I'm not in the mood for their jocularity.

"This is different. He's not just hosting a party and letting people make their choices. This time he's going out his way just to sell drugs to a sophomore. A sophomore. I thought he was here looking for me."

Jamie's car turns out of the parking lot and goes the other way. He never sees us. We never see Myrtle emerge. She must be parked behind the station, too. A seriousness falls over us. I'm wondering all over again—just like at the party—if it's my obligation to go find her.

"Maybe it's just weed," Nick says, but we all know it's not.

"Just weed wasn't what Myrtle puked up that night at Jamie's. After how bad she was, how could he be selling her more? Is this where he gets all his money?"

Jordan's dark eyes flash regret and judgment. "So, no rich mom travelling the world?"

A vivid remembrance finds its way into my brain. *My mother's dead.* I swear it was one of his earliest confessions on our first night on the beach.

"Wait. Surely, it's not all true. All those rumors..." I say.

The bottom of that old, familiar, aching bucket that stores the lessons of my life rusts through again, draining out pebbles and sand and stars and miracles.

"Don't sell him short, Daisy. He might still be better than the rest of us put together. Find out for yourself what's going on." Nick's voice takes on the assuredness of his "amazing" explanation he'd given on our bristling drive home that day.

Jordan reaches out. "People pretend to be things they aren't for a lot of reasons. It doesn't make them bad."

I turn on the ignition and try hard to pretend it was something other than what I'd seen. I pull into traffic and switch the talk to party dresses and corsages. But something has shifted inside of me. I'm too old to lie to myself and call it anything but what it is—deception. I don't want it anymore. Not from my friends, not from myself, not from Jamie. If he really is lying about everything, I'll have to—.

But I know myself. I'll tolerate almost anything to not be alone.

CHAPTER THIRTY-ONE

By the time Grandma Betty discovers me sitting cross-legged in the middle of my mother's living room and anxiously thumbing the edges of her journal, I'm already done crying.

I had delivered Jordan home where her mom had greeted her, lopsided and stumbling, exuberantly announcing that this was her baby's last ever football Homecoming. I'd offered to stay. Jordan had simply tightened her jaw, pressed back her shoulders, and declined. I squeezed her hand before she marched past her mother and shut the front door behind her. Nick and I had driven in silence to his house. His mom had waved cheerfully at us through the front window. His dad was cutting his own grass with the latest Cadillac of lawn mowers from one of his hardware stores.

"Classic Carraway," Nick had said when we'd pulled up. And then, "Nice socks and sandals, Dad," as he'd jogged inside.

And now, here I am, weighing the hand-drawn words that once made up the interior thoughts of my mother's psyche.

Grandma Betty sits down beside me on the floor. She is still pretty spry. It must be the Zumba or the Pilates. She secures her capable arm around me and leans her lovely head on my shoulder.

"Oh my, Daisy."

"I'm okay, Grandma. Just remembering."

"Next week it will be three years," she says.

"Sometimes it seems like yesterday. Sometimes it seems like another lifetime ago. Sometimes it seems like they're going to rush through the door laughing out loud with too many shopping bags."

A sigh seventy-five years deep comes from her. "I could help you feel better and tell you at least they were together when they went, that they loved you and loved each other to the end. There are a dozen sentiments that we have both heard before. But I'll say them over and over if any of them will ease your pain."

We hold each other in silence until my stomach growls.

She says, "We need to feed you. Isn't your dance tonight?" She knows perfectly well my dance is tonight,

"I'm pretty sure there's sushi in the fridge," I say.

"I have some goodies from the farmer's market in my car," she offers.

We hop up and head to the kitchen. She points to the fireplace mantel with Marylin and Ardita Fitz-Peters as we pass. "I noticed someone had done some redecorating. Are you stocking the kitchen, too?"

Fifteen minutes later, we've made a bountiful feast in the breakfast nook. Three kinds of cheeses, sausage, zucchini bread and apple butter, and some apple cider rounds out our meal. Grandma cuts little sticks out of carrots and yellow squash and mixes some family's homemade granola into chunks of ripe melon. We forget all about the sushi.

Our dinner conversation evades memories or plans for the future, even plans for tonight. It's just two girls chatting. It's wonderful and weightless. But the clock on the stove on the other side of the kitchen displays the time like a neon advertisement, reminding me that I'm running out of it. Nick and Jordan will be picking me up from Grandma's soon.

Grandma follows my gaze. "It's getting late. We need to take you home and get you all gussied up for your big night." She's giddy.

She'll be expecting Tom. She doesn't know yet.

"Grandma. I have a confession to make."

She stops gathering crumb-covered plates and instead smooths the crease I feel deepening between my eyes.

"A confession? Sounds serious," she tries to make light.

"I broke up with Tom." I push the words out before my heart convinces me they aren't true.

"Oh my." The crease is on her forehead now. She looks, blankly, in front of her as if searching for advice on the flowered wallpaper of the breakfast nook.

Suddenly, she perks up, scoots plates and forks and cups together and carries them to the sink.

"Surely, it's not as bad as all that," she says while she rinses and stacks.

"What do you mean?"

"Surely whatever happened can be reversed. When he sees you tonight in the gown he picked out for you with your hair just the way he likes it, he'll take you back. Of course, he will."

Her voice, reminiscent and vague, makes me wonder for a moment who she's talking to.

I carry leftover cheese to the counter. "*I* broke up with *him*, Grandma. I'm not asking him to take me back."

She gestures to the cabinet with the baggies, a directive for me to save the cheese. I obey. It's the least I can do.

After interminable silence, the duration of which the oven clock noted as two minutes, she finally turns to me. Drying her hands on a dish towel, she faces me with a sternness I literally have never seen in her.

"Daisy, don't be silly. Of course, you want him back."

"What? Why?"

"You know how much your parents approved of him. You know..."

"But, Grandma—"

"Your father, especially. He and Tom were like..." Her voice trails off.

"They weren't like anything. Tom and I hadn't been together that long. I mean, I know Daddy liked him and all, but he'd only been around him like a dozen times."

The words gush out of some cracked piece of my heart, and it's as if my mind registers them for the first time. Dad never knew Tom. Not really. He knew of him. How did I not understand this before?

Grandma's still remembering, "... and your mother liked him so well. A little Charles, she'd called him. A stouter little Charles. I like him, too. He's so much like your father. People respect him. When he walked into church last week, you'd have thought they were there for him, not Jesus. They're all so proud of him and how he leads his team. And he shook all their hands and... "

My stomach lurches. Even at church. A quick and fractured image of Dr. and Mrs. Fitz-Peters taking their turn as door greeters, welcoming the busy and the tired to their holy weekend respite, flashes in my mind. The way his hand never left her back, the way she never raised her demure eyes, his loud "Let's get together," his roving eye.

A thought rumbles through my tortured psyche to my lips, "Maybe Mom and Dad only liked him because I liked him, but that was before I knew. Before I got it."

She crosses her arms and bends her neck so—I swear—it seems as if she's standing on the edge of the sinkhole watching me get sucked under, wondering if I'm worth the toss of a life preserver.

"Before you got what, sweetheart?" But her tone says she's exasperated, tired of trying. I knew she would be eventually. I do that to people. I wear them down and wear them out. Maybe that's what's so good about Jamie. I just haven't worn him out yet. But it will happen, won't it?

She's waiting for an answer, so I say, "I have to show you something."

I go get Mom's journal from where I had left it on the couch. I'm back in the kitchen, and before I can even open it, she's tsk-tsking me with a disapproving shake of the head. I thumb through the pages, anyway, looking for the entry. I've memorized it. I don't need the page, but somehow, I want to reassure myself that I haven't made it up. That those actually are her words.

"Here, here. Look." I hold open the book for her. I recite my mother's words. "I've given up everything and it's never enough. I've given up even myself. What do I have left when that's gone?"

She rolls her eyes with a different kind of sigh. "Let me show *you* something." She takes my hand and leads me like a child to the living room where she pulls out one of Mom's photo albums. She places it on the table, slowly turning page after page.

She stops on an image of Daddy toasting something with an entire bottle of Tito's. She rubs her fingers over it as if willing it to come to life. "My son. My handsome son." She turns the page to one of the three of us, golden and wind swept, coming in from the beach. "And his doting wife and beautiful daughter."

Grandma's eyes illuminate with laser certainty that she alone owns our history. She always has. "Just what does it seem that your mother's given up? Can you find a single picture that shows anything she was lacking?"

Grandma goes back to softly turning pages.

"She obviously felt she had," I risked.

Now Grandma's cold hand is on my face. Her sure, sweet smile envelops me. "Your mother was always a bit over dramatic." My heart sinks. She turns again to her book of family history. "Tom will take you back. Just like Charles took Ginny back. Every time."

"Every time?" The whisper comes out so breathless, I don't know if she hears me until she slams the book a little too solidly.

She replaces it carefully on the low shelf and pauses to take in the book club photo and the Marilyn print. I hug Mother's journal to my chest, terrified to let go of it, afraid it may fade away like the ragged edges of memories of birthdays and Sundays and the sound of her voice.

"Never mind. It's getting late."

"What do you mean by every time? Was Mom not happy? Did she try to leave? What do you mean?"

Grandma ignores me as I frantically follow her back to the kitchen.

"Grandma!" I stamp my foot, feeling too much like a three-year-old, but it works.

She turns to me. When she answers, her voice is slow and controlled. "You know what your father always said, don't you? It's a blessing that a woman can choose whom to love. So, choose the top guy. Tom is the top guy."

She tweaks my nose and loads leftovers back into the canvas bag.

"Actually, mom said that," I say.

She stops. Maybe she's concerned. Maybe the memories are fading for her, too. "Are you sure?" Her back is still to me.

"Mom would say it's a blessing. Dad would say top guy."

If it's possible, I swear her whole being softens and straightens all at once, as if a calm and confident authority overcomes her. "You see, they were in agreement. And so am I. Tom will take you back. How could you possibly want anything else?"

And then she walks away. When she gets to the front door, she calls back to me. "See you at home. I've set out your dress for you."

There's nothing left to do but follow her home. Before I lock up, though, I slip Mom's journal into my bag. I can't bear to leave it alone in that big, empty house. I set the alarm and pull the front door closed. Putting one foot in front of the other, I make it to my car, buckle in, and steer back down the familiar road. I was wrong. There still is one more thing to be done. It will be awkward, unpleasant and in another time, perhaps it would have been better left alone. But I wanted to put things in order. I would not trust the obliging, indifferent sea of time and innuendo and social cues to sweep my refuse away.

I had been unfair to Tom. How would I have liked it if he had broken things off with me in that way? If I had walked in on him with Myrtle's desperate arms cloying around his muscle-bound neck, and our friend group looking on as if I somehow should have known. It wouldn't have been fair to me. It wasn't fair to him.

If the universe listens at all to the secrets we hold in our hearts, the ones we don't even realize exist, then I need to do this. I need to make things right.

CHAPTER THIRTY-TWO

There's a particular feeling that comes from walking on the shore before a storm. It's different from a Chicago rainstorm when the air smells of Midwestern dirt and cut grass. When a thick, grey-green, ominous wall falls in upon the city, making you want to run for cover. On the beach, the feeling is more exhilarating, a promise blown in on a strong wind that there are exciting things hovering in the next hour.

We're in Nick's car—Jordan, my cousin, and me. That wet dirt smell is in the air, the clouds are, indeed, bruising up to a greyish tint. It will rain at some point tonight. But the mood is defiantly beach storm. I feel like a brave mermaid, dashing and diving in the raucous waves, too close to a pirate ship, daring one of them to scoop me up in his net.

There must be a reasonable explanation for what I saw in the alley. Jamie's texts in the last hour were normal, exciting, romantic. Don't I owe him a chance? Don't I?

But as I ask myself the question, all I can hear is Tom's voice asking me the same thing.

Nick pulls into the parking lot of the hotel hosting our dance in their finest banquet hall. Tiny droplets fall from the dusky sky, reflecting off the windows like enchanted glitter. We're late. The party has already started. Grandma had still been snapping pictures as we backed out of the drive, certain she'd gotten through to me.

"Wait until you see the decorations. It turned out pretty good," Nick says.

"I can't wait," I say, looking around for the Mach 1.

"Look, there's Jamie's car." Jordan spots it first.

My heart flutters. He's waiting, just as promised.

We park and go in. I don't even have a second to acknowledge Jordan and Nick's decorations before I feel an urgent tug on my wrist.

"You're here." It's Tom. He lifts my hand and pulls it through a dainty wrist corsage of baby rosebuds and ribbon.

"It's... lovely."

He stares down at me as if questioning his very existence. Then he intertwines his fingers in mine. I try to pull away, but he squeezes tight.

"I have something for you," he enunciates loudly in my ear. Only the words don't come out as clearly as I'm sure he had hoped, partly because of the deafening music, partly because of his booze-soaked breath.

He pulls me through the crowd. I grab Jordan. She grabs Nick. They have no choice but to come along. The ocean of bodies parts for us as if we have a trumpeter and bodyguards, a full entourage, but it's just us. Tom doesn't stop in the middle of the dance floor, like I thought he might. He crashes on through, clear to the other side of the room. When we get there, I know why.

Jamie stands poised with urgency against the wall, his hands in his pockets. He's out of place, certainly out of his element, but beautiful, not unlike a sand-buffed shard of glass that when hung on a golden chain becomes a jewel. He doesn't see us at first. He's concentrating on something Wilson just said. Between them, sagging on a white chair is Myrtle. Her robust curves covered in gold beaded red lace sink into each other like an inflatable lawn ornament some has pulled the plug on.

My breath stops. Tom steps protectively to her, then catches himself. I'm not sure he'd expected her presence. Wilson's face goes red. His fists clench. He points his finger at Tom, like an inch from his face. Jamie's hand settles on Wilson's shoulder. Myrtle bounces up and softens her catlike eyes toward Tom then pouts her lips and inhales with a seductive sigh so that all the space between us seems filled with her aura.

Tom is stone. We all are for a second. He squeezes my hand. The familiarity of it confuses me.

"I thought you weren't coming." My words reach Jamie before I even realize I've said them.

"I thought you weren't," Jamie answers, but he's not talking to me. He's looking at Tom.

"Now why would I not come? That's seems a little stupid. Daisy and I have been planning this night for years." There's no questioning the level of Tom's drunkenness now. There's no slurring speech with

Just Daisy

Tom. If anything, he becomes more punctuated, more easily agitated. It's always hard to tell when he's crossed that line, but I recognize it now—that simmering, arrogant anger.

Jamie looks at me, confused. "You said he wasn't coming."

"When did I say that?"

"The other day when I missed lunch. You texted."

"I didn't though."

"You did. I even asked if you were sure. You said of course."

I drop Tom's hand and shift my body away from his. I look to Jordan and Nick, but they can't help. It's Tom, or rather Tom's knowing, inebriated laugh that clues me in.

Jamie pulls his phone from his pocket to scan the texts. He needn't bother. I know what the texts will say. And I know it wasn't me who sent them. It was Tom. In the library. With my cell phone while I was fetching him a book.

I smack Tom's arm. "You texted him to come, didn't you? You took my phone when I was trying to help you."

"It doesn't matter, Daisy. I'm here. He can go." Jamie's voice is soft, like wind blowing stars around on a quiet night. I want to melt into them, but I know better. It's not that simple.

"Oh, I'm not going anywhere. Not yet, *bro*." Tom's bleary eyes narrow on Jamie.

"Well, Tom. I had no idea you were clever." Jordan snarks. Tom's whole being sways in her direction like a tidal wave.

Before he can descend on her, Wilson steps in, his voice low and fierce, "Of course Tom's here. This is his show. Isn't it Tom? This is where you get everything you want. Except one thing. You don't get her." Wilson hooks Myrtle's waste and jerks her to his side. She squirms.

"Tom, are you just gonna stand there?" Myrtle sobs.

"I'm not doing this here, Myrtle." Tom waves a hand in her direction like he's dismissing a house servant. She scatters. Wilson follows her.

"Doing what?" I ask "What exactly are you not doing? What the hell is going on?"

"Just clearing a few things up, that's all. Like your situation, James Gatsby the Third. Why don't you clear that up for us, *Jamie*?" Tom practically spits the words out.

Jamie falls back against the wall. Only he looks more trapped than cool. "I don't know what you mean. I'm here for Daisy."

"Oh, I know you're here for Daisy, you freaky stalker. You'll do anything for Daisy. You'll even pretend to be a teenager for Daisy." Tom's laugh borders on insanity.

"You don't know what you're talking about. I moved here with my mom. She's on assignment overseas. That's all."

"On assignment?" I ask. He'd never said that before.

"He's lying, Daisy. Just like he's lying about everything else. He's not even a teenager. Yeah, that's right. He's not a high school student. He's twenty-one. A full-grown-ass man."

I want to shake Tom like an insolent toddler. "You are so dumb right now, Tom. He goes to our school if you hadn't noticed."

I expect Jamie to brighten at my sticking up for him. He doesn't.

"No, he doesn't. I'm mean, he's been there, but he doesn't go there. Not like the rest of us. Any of you have him in class?" Tom looks around at the gathering crowd.

I want to shout that I've seen him practically every day. Then it hits me. He already knows. With Owen as watchman or not, Tom knows.

I scan the crowd for someone, anyone, to claim him. Surely, someone has him in class.

Tom inches closer to Jamie. "What's your first hour?"

I feel my face grow hot and my eyes widen. *Please have an answer. Please have an answer.*

Jamie droops a little, hiding behind that sheet of perfect blonde. His cool vanishes, replaced by an excitedly tapping foot. "I don't have to answer to you, Tom."

"But you might want to answer to her." Tom flings me forward so hard, I fall into Jamie. He catches me. All that energy he'd been holding in place zips through him and pulsates in his desperate face.

Tom continues, "I don't need your answers. I know all about you. You're an imposter. A phony. A fraud. A high school drop out with a GED and an arrest record."

"Don't listen to him, Daisy. He's trying to confuse you," Jamie's eyes plead with mine.

I can't respond. I can't even breathe. Tom is unstoppable. His words spew so quickly, I can't process them. I hear pieces...

"Stalker... pretends to be... stolen... warrant... creeper... I've contacted his dad about his parties and his drugs and his impersonation of a teenager. Who does this shit? Seriously, who does this?" His voice, strangely, grows quieter, calmer with each accusation.

Jamie grips my shoulders. His face is inches from mine. "It doesn't matter. None of it matters. The universe pulled us together. You love me. You love me. Tell him you love me."

I do. I love him. Clarity overcomes me. All at once I truly understand that depth of Tom's control freakishness. If nothing else, I believe Jamie just so Tom won't be right. I turn to face him.

"Jamie's right. I love him. I do."

"Love him? Right." He laughs.

"I do. You know why? He's never, ever, not once raised a hand to me in anger. He moved halfway across the country for me. For me. I don't believe you, Tom."

"You have got to be kidding me." Tom's laughter fills the claustrophobic air.

"It's no joke. She loves me. And I love her. And you're nothing. You two never existed. In a year, in a week, she won't even remember you. Tell him, Daisy." Jamie says.

My throat catches. Jamie's gone too far. I can't say Tom never existed. I can't agree to that. For a moment, everything was clear, but even with Jamie so close behind me, it's all washing away like love letters drawn in the sand.

"Everything about him is a lie. Just wait until his dad gets here. You'll see." Tom slides a flask from his suit jacket and finishes it off.

Instinctively, I thrust my hands at Tom's chest. "His dad is dead, Tom. God, that's low. Even for you."

He won't stop laughing. "Is that what he told you? His dad is most certainly not dead. He's a drunk. Practically homeless. Just recently released on parole for manslaughter. Seems he drove his drunk ass through a plate glass window. Killed a girl. And that car, that ridiculous joke of a car he struts around in, it's not even his. It's stolen."

"What?" I shove my face inches from Jamie's.

"He's lying, Daisy," Jamie answers.

"Tell me the truth, Jamie. Is it your car? I thought your dad left it to you when he died."

"Oh, it's his dad's, all right. But since his dad's not dead..." Tom laughs.

We're encircled now. Even Jordan and Nick have morphed into the collective audience, salivating at our freak show.

I grab Jamie by the front of his pink shirt. "Jamie, what's going on? Is your dad alive? Is your mom?"

"What does it matter? I don't need them. *We* don't need them. We have each other. They might as well be dead. They're dead to me."

"What does that mean? Are they alive?" Flashes of two black caskets and flowers, flowers, flowers, and cards that must be answered by the despondent hand of a fifteen-year-old orphan and her disconsolate grandmother, and all the hollow-hearted parent events that mine never attended shoot through me like a swift, sharp arrow.

Jamie doesn't say anything, and he doesn't need to. All pretense washes away. The internet mugshot flashes in my mind like strobe lights at an illicit rave along with remembrances of his reaction to my parents' house and his "appointments" and his random disappearances and patchy family history. The next few seconds crash together. Nick and Jordan tag team Tom to shut his mouth, but his face is too close to mine. So is Jamie's. Both of them rush at me with pleas and proof, then rush at each other with threats.

Finally, Jamie wins out. "Daisy, you love me."

Waves of Tybee memories wash over me. "That was never in doubt."

"And you never loved him."

I don't know if the music literally stops, or my entire body shuts down, but everything goes silent. It's as if the world, the universe and all its manifesting powers await my answer.

I have a voice. I have a say.

"It's not true. I can't say I never loved him." To deny it would be to do what I've done all along—pretend. I'm done pretending.

I look into Tom's obsidian eyes and see something so solid; I can't pull away.

Jamie presses me again, his voice as shaky as my resolve.

"Remember the first day you came to my place, to see where I live, to see who I am. Remember. We made love, Daisy." He lowers his voice to a whisper, but it doesn't matter. The secret's out.

Tom breaks our gaze. "You fucked her? You fucked my girlfriend?" His temples bulge.

Jordan interrupts, "Mind your toxic masculinity, Tom. It's getting a little rank, like your breath."

Just Daisy

"I didn't *fuck* her," Jamie defends with such indignation, I want to throw my arms around him and kiss all the doubts away.

"Well, I have. More times than I can count," Tom answers.

Tom might as well have shot Jamie with a gun. The luminous beauty of him snuffs out like a thousand dousing rainstorms gushing down all at once. He can't recover. He won't even look at me.

"Say it isn't true, Daisy. You've never been with him." Jamie's golden hair hides his face. His voice comes out so choked, the sound is foreign to me.

Someone breaks through. It's Ms. Eckleburg.

"There you are. There you are. Thank goodness. They need you on stage to announce the winner." She corrals us to the stage.

"Don't go up there, Daisy." Jamie is bright again, bright and determined. "Let's just go. You don't need this. You don't need him."

"Let's go, Daisy." Tom slips his hand under mind, gentler than I've felt him for a long time. "It's our time. It's what we've dreamed about since freshman year. Remember when I bought you that toy tiara and we pretended it was you and me up there? My princess, I called you. Now, it's time for you to be my queen. Let's do this." He bends down and kisses that spot on my neck that makes me melt every time, the spot Jamie never did discover.

I look at Jamie. "What do you have first hour, Jamie?"

Without blinking, he answers, "French. Parlez vous France."

"No, you don't. I have French first hour," Nick says.

"We don't have the same teacher."

"There's only one French teacher," Nick announces very newspaperly.

Somehow, those words from my dear, truth-seeking Nick, illuminate the surface, and my soul paddles up to it. I physically exhale this loud cleansing breath, and all toxic untruths and half realities of my world expel with it. My chest shakes with an absurd little sobbing laugh. All color vanishes from Jamie. His skin, his eyes, even his lips go ghostly pale. Has he been a specter all along? I look to Jordan for support. She's posed with one elbow perched on the other arm that's resting under her bust. Her dainty, powerful fist touches her chin. Her eyes shine with amusement and concern, but even she doesn't seem real.

I can't stay here, sucked into the middle of all of them. This time I'm the one who leads. I march Tom to the stage and up the stairs.

"That's my girl," he says.

I turn on him. He's two steps behind me, so I tower over him. "Just because I'm taking the stage does not mean I chose you over him."

"Oh really? He's a grown ass man pretending to be a teenager, Daisy."

"Well, at least he's a grown ass man."

Ms. Eckleburg shuffles us in line with the other candidates. I barely remember what she says as she introduces all of us one more time. I'm too busy planning what I'm going to say when she calls my name. And I know she will. After all, I've been planning this for years, right? I mean, I've manifested this version of my own truth without even trying. I've pulled this universe to me. But I have a voice. I can change it with one word. I can destroy if I want.

"Your Homecoming King and Queen are." She opens the envelope. "Tom Buchanan and Daisy Fay." Mrs. Eckleburg does a good job of acting surprised.

The crowd applauds and their fierce solidarity in the support of hierarchies and cliques floods the room. But I have a voice that they haven't drowned out yet. They haven't even heard it yet.

All sound morphs into a vacuous space. Tom steps forward. Mrs. Eckleburg hands him the boy's crown, satin and gold like something from a Mother Goose cartoon, and he places it on his head. She presents the sparkling tiara to him on a satin pillow. She nods to me and smiles as she descends the stairs. She's swallowed by the crowd. Tom kisses my cheek and raises the tiara above my head.

I jerk it from his hands and step to the mic.

"What the hell, Daisy?" Tom erupts.

I ignore him. I hold it up like an angry fist, and, finally, have my say.

"I can't accept this. No wait. What I mean is, I don't want to accept this. I haven't done anything to earn it."

Nervous chuckles spatter the air.

"Seriously, why did you vote for me? Because I'm your favorite? Did you vote for me because my parents died, so you feel sorry for me? Or was it because I'm Tom Buchanan's girlfriend?"

A little cheer goes up from the football team.

"Well, all of those are dumb reasons. If you want to vote for Tom, vote for Tom. Although, I'm not sure he earned it either. But honestly, I don't want your vote. I'm withdrawing my name."

Jamie has found his way to near the front. I can see his face brighten with dim hope. But this moment isn't about him. Not really. He's nothing more than a side effect. I pull my focus back to the crowd.

"Ladies, why do we do this? Why do we hitch our wagon to some man and expect him to make our dreams come true? Why am I more valuable to you because I dated him?" I make a face and hook my thumb over my shoulder.

Faces peer up at me like I've suddenly started speaking in tongues.

"Even without him, what value do I have? What difference have I ever made in your lives? Most of you, I don't even know."

I see Lucille, sneering at me while she adjusts the micro-skirt on her strapless scrap of a dress.

I wave my hand to her. "Lucille, did you vote for me?"

Her face freezes. Her eyes shift. "Well, yeah."

"Why? You don't even like me."

"Well, I don't like you now-uh. That's for sure."

I look down to those flirty freshmen whose virginity will probably be gone by the end of the night. I point to one. "I don't know you." And another. "I don't know you." I see a familiar, pimpled waif and move my finger in her direction. "I think I have you in choir, but I've never spoken to you. I wouldn't. You're kind of geeky. I mean I would speak to you now. I am speaking to you now, right? But in class, yeah, I would never do that. Sorry."

Her eyes go big, her face flames red and she disappears inside the crowd with a distinguishable look of pity on her face. I've gone to far. My undammed words are damning when they are supposed to be setting me free, setting all of us free.

"I'm not trying to be mean. Most of you, I don't speak to you because I don't need to. I am the golden girl. We were the golden couple for no other reason than we somehow made East Eggerton look good. The cliche quarterback and his cheerleader girlfriend."

A few in the crowd start to turn away. They aren't getting it. "Ladies!" I command. "Don't be cliche. Don't be just some quarterback's girlfriend."

"He's single now. If you want him," someone shouts from the crowd.

"Not for long," a feminine voice chimes in, accompanied with whistles and catcalls.

Frustration gnaws at my psyche like a hungry tigress on an antelope carcass. "I'm begging you, right now, to stop pretending. Stop buying into this tradition of elitism and patriarchy and hierarchy."

"I think she's high," someone shouts.

Why aren't they getting it? How had Ms. Hip worded everything? Marylin's quote of not minding being a woman in a man's world beats at my brain. I ignore it. I don't buy it.

My throat tightens. My voice goes higher and faster. "Listen. I'm serious. We need to stop giving away our power to someone else's traditions. We need to break this ridiculous cycle of putting people on pedestals, of basking in our privilege, or sucking up to the patriarchy. We need to break it. Now."

They've turned off the mic. I toss it to the floor. I notice Ms. Eckleburg strain through the crowd to get back to the stage.

Desperate, I position the jeweled band above my head and snap it in two. The tether to the old-world snaps, too. Liberation washes over me like a baptismal river.

I wait. I wait for a hundred silenced voices to ban with mine and say enough is enough. I wait for the chant of Daisy Fay or Break It Now or something. Anything. There's nothing but dreadful, humiliating silence.

Humiliation is not what I'm going for. Jordan stands front and center. Her enormous eyes are glassy. She grimaces.

Finally, someone speaks, but it's not who I expect. Tom raises his voice, "Well, I for one appreciate your vote and your belief in the traditions that make East Eggerton Academy the prestigious place of achievement that our fathers made it and our fathers' fathers before them. They've handed us their legacy. Who are we to break it?"

He's mocking me, now, and the crowd loves it. A few claps go up. Someone yells, "Preach it."

I can't stand it. I want to tarnish his luster the way he did Jamie's. The way he has done mine a thousand times.

I turn to him. "Nice speech, jackass, but there's just one problem. East Eggerton wasn't founded until 1983, so I don't think your father's father handed you anything from this school. And your dad graduated from Westside Academy. You're making yourself look stupid."

Just Daisy

I feel rather than see the masses move in. No way are they gonna miss this. Obviously, Tom knows it, too. He's playing the crowd again like he has all week.

"Not as stupid as screwing a grown ass, drug dealing, convict stalker who's pretending to be a teenager just so he can get in your pants. Talk about stupid." The alcohol on his breath is worse, if possible.

"I didn't know. Okay? Besides, you weren't exactly a saint yourself. Don't forget, I know all about your affair with—" Suddenly, I don't want to say it. I don't want to bring her name into it. She's a victim, too, in a way. I glance down and find her at the edge of the stage. Her big eyes resemble luminous orbs floating on a turbulent sea. Her face is pale and her mouth gapes like a frightened fish, gasping for life.

"Who? That whore? She's not an affair. Hell, she's a rite of passage." He snorts and sways.

I look back to Myrtle. The muscles of her flawless face contort into shock and shame as most of the football team hoots laughter at her.

"You're disgusting, Tom." They aren't the right words. I don't mean he's disgusting for being with her. But they're out there, and I can't take them back.

"At least she's not a convict."

From the corner of my eye, I see a flash of gold and red as Myrtle dashes for the door and the weight of what I've just done paralyzes me. Myrtle is a victim of Tom's just like me. Maybe worse than me. I had finally found my voice, and I had used it not to lift women up, but to tear one down simply so I would feel better about my own mistakes.

As she approaches the exit, I notice a figure who has weaved his way through the crowd, leave with her. It's not Wilson. It's someone else who doesn't belong in our world. The expression in Tom's aggressive eyes tells me he's seen it, too. Red splotches creep up his neck. His eyes go cold.

Hanging my head, I examine the two sparkling halves of broken dreams in my hands. There should be more pieces. It should be shattered to bits, but it's not. The sharp edge of the snapped-off metal band mesmerizes me, and I can't stop thinking about how with the tiniest drop of super glue, it would look whole again, like nothing ever broke it to begin with.

By now, Ms. Eckleburg is back on stage. Slowly, so slowly that I hope no one will notice that I'm moving, I tiptoe to her and return the broken parts

My plan is to slink down the stairs and be swallowed up by anonymity and humiliation.

But Tom's not done. He hasn't seen the counselor retake the stage.

"And as far as my father's legacy goes, my dad's at home with my mom, keeping her safe, where he should be. So, be careful before you ride off into the sunset with your creeper and his stolen clown car. You might just get your dad's legacy after all."

In one giant lunge, I'm to him. My hand shoots out and smacks his face. Then his hand shoots out and punches mine.

I don't wait for anyone to come to my rescue. I jump off the stage and shove through the crowd, and I mean shove because they apparently don't part for queens who decline the throne. I escape out the door into a messy downpour of torrential rain where my ruined mascara runs rivulets down my cheeks, mixing with blood from my broken nose.

CHAPTER THIRTY-THREE

The sky pours down, the clouds taking on fantastic shapes as if a universal cataclysm was on the brink of formation.

I sneak a peek behind me, expecting some pursuit. There's none. Music blares. Laughter echoes against the empty spaces of their already tired souls.

But at least I'm not alone. Ten feet in front of me, standing at the edge of the sidewalk that leads from the banquet hall, Myrtle stares out into the rain, a slingback heel hanging from each hand. Water is already pooling in the scooped neck of her glorious dress. Flood lights meant to illuminate the grounds bounce off beads threaded through her paper-thin, lacy gown in sad, dazzling bursts. She shivers against the wind.

"Myrtle." I'm sure I sound more desperate than I mean to.

She spins around. Between her head full of drenched red ringlets and rain-soaked make-up, she resembles one of those clown dogs from a cheap circus. Without a word, she tosses aside her shoes and runs, sobbing, into the night. I don't blame her. I'd run away from me, too. But the rain hammers harder. She isn't dressed for it. Her gown might as well be made of tissue paper, she's barefoot, and we're five miles from town. I start after her, but a bright yellow flash of a car slides to a halt in front of me.

Jamie jumps out. "Daisy, please. I can explain."

"Can you, Jamie? Can you really? I don't even know you."

"You do. We've known each other since before we even met. I waited for you at our lighthouse, remember?"

The words sound so dumb, I can't believe I ever thought they were anything else.

"What I remember is a stupid little girl who believed ever single stupid line you threw my way. Every single stupid lie, I mean."

"I didn't mean to lie."

"You didn't mean to? How hard is it *not* to say your parents are dead when they're, in fact, not?"

"That's what I want to explain. My mom left years ago. I wouldn't recognize her if she was standing right in front of me."

I feel like a dirty, wet mop that needs wrung out. And it's not just because of the rain that's got my hair sticking to my face and has soaked my satin mermaid gown clear to my bones. My psyche, my heart, even my memories are muddied with the grime of half-truths and fantasy.

He's still talking while my eye chases Myrtle across the parking lot and out into the street.

"My dad. He's, well, he's everything Tom said." The strain in his voice pulls me back to him. I see in his face what the admission sucked out of him.

"Why didn't you tell me from the beginning, Jamie?"

"It's not who I want to be for you. From the second I heard your voice, I knew there was a life waiting for me if I could just get to it. If I could just get to *you*."

I couldn't have felt more socked in the gut if he had punched me. I feel my face. I can't tell what's blood and what's rain, and every bit of me hurts. I'm nothing but a bauble for him. A prize to be won. A trophy to be bragged on.

Jamie glides over and tries to put his arms around me. I stop him. He relents.

"Okay. Okay. Just get in the car. Let me take you home. We can work it out. We can—"

"Can what? Go back in time? Undo all your lies? Even if we could, it wouldn't be enough. You stalked me. That's how you got here. You stalked. You're a stalker. I never told you what school I go to. And then you pretended to be a student when you were nothing more than a criminal, dealing drugs to my friends."

"Daisy, you're confused. You don't understand."

I look past him for Myrtle. All I see is streaks of rain and darkness.

"Daisy, please, get in." The hopeful tone of his voice pulls at me. Rain against his still tanned skin reminds me of watching him emerge from the salty ocean. Wind whips around us, and I'm taken back to my simple dream of a summer when I didn't care what was real. I only cared about what my soul craved to make it whole again.

"I'll get in if you let me drive," I say.

Hope lights up his expression. He hands over the keys. I'm halfway behind the wheel when I hear Tom.

"What the hell, Daisy?" He has followed me out. In two steps, he's to the car, pounding it with his fist.

"Let's go," Jamie yells.

You might get your father's legacy after all.

I gun it across the parking lot. The car swerves on the overwet asphalt.

"Be careful. It's dangerous," Jamie warns.

"I don't care," I answer.

Behind us, I see Tom run toward his Hummer.

You might get your father's legacy after all.

Nick and Jordan have finally meandered out of the dance to find us. Nick's usual surprise turns to outright shock to see me behind the wheel of the Mach 1. Jordan doesn't hide her astonishment.

I shout to them, "We're going to find Myrtle. Tom ran to get his car. I think he's gonna chase us. He's drunk."

Jamie grabs the wheel. "Wait, we're going after Myrtle? I thought we were going to my place."

"Myrtle is out there in the dark, humiliated to death and it's my fault. We're going after her."

"What can we do?" asks Nick.

"Stop Tom. He doesn't need to be behind the wheel."

I step on the gas and fly out of the parking lot, hoping they get to Tom in time. They don't. High beams of his pseudo-military wagon clamp down on us. He's going too fast. I shift gears and speed up. He does, too. My eyes move like lasers, scanning the road, then back to the rearview, then back to the road. Where is Myrtle? She can't have gone far.

Hummer beams hit harder. He's closer. The ground shifts beneath us as the car starts to hydroplane. I'm losing control.

"Daisy, watch out!" Jamie yells.

A red and gold streak breaks from the tree line. I try to jerk the wheel away from her, but the car won't respond. Horror shrieks from my chest. Jamie screams my name. At the last second, the car behaves, we swerve toward the opposite curve. I don't remember braking, but we stop.

Then I hear it—a terrified voice calling out and the sickening thud and crunch of steel and bones and asphalt.

Tom stops. He backs up, steers around her crumpled body, and drives away.

Another car comes screaming toward us. They pull over beside us. Nick, Owen, and Jordan scramble out.

"Oh my God. Oh my God." Jordan runs to me with her arm outstretched and clenches me in a fierce hug.

"Tom drove off. He left," I say.

"We called 9-1-1." Jordan reassures me, stroking my hair and examining my bruised face.

"Call back and tell them we need an ambulance," I yell. We all run over to the body except Owen who stares owl-eyed and shocked from the edge of the road.

I don't blame him. I'll never forget this scene. Her lips are blue. Her skin nearly glows in its paleness while her red tresses spill over her face like blood. Her vacant eyes stare up at us, sparkless and empty.

Nick leans over her. "I think it's too late for an ambulance."

"No. No. I won't allow it. Myrtle, Myrtle!" I shake her. She's cold, damp, and limp.

"Don't move her." Jamie kneels beside her and rests two fingers on her neck. He shakes his head then pinches her wrist between his thumb and two fingers.

"Myrtle. Myrtle." I can't stop repeating her name, as if I can somehow will the universe to bring her back.

"There's no pulse, Daisy." Jamie tries to put an arm around me, but I smack it away.

"Then give her one. You know how to save her. So, save her. Unless that was a lie, too."

He's angry now. He straightens and backs away. "That wasn't a lie. I did save someone's life, my father's. So drunk that he was choking on his own vomit. And another time when he was so wasted, he stopped breathing. He literally drank himself into a freaking coma. And, yes, I talked him off a few ledges, too. But I didn't save him, you know. I got him breathing again, but I didn't save him. He might as well be dead. He's basically just a walking corpse, a waste of human skin."

"But Myrtle isn't," I insist.

"There's no pulse," he yells.

I jump up and pummel his chest with my fist. "Do it anyway. For God's sake, do it anyway. If you can manifest me then manifest this for me. Don't let her die."

Something hopeful inside him urgently jerks him back to me. Immediately, he's beside her, pumping her chest and breathing my million apologies into her soul. Jordan's on the phone again, demanding an ambulance, and Nick is directing traffic as the news of the horrific sideshow has obviously reached the hungry sharks at their prestigious party. At some point, Owen activates his robotic body and joins Nick in the middle of the road, a watchman once more.

I'm all cried out by the time the cops arrive and the paramedics slide her into the back of the ambulance. Wilson, who had arrived with the masses, stands damp and discouraged, staring after the sirens and lights that are hurrying the object of his affection to the hospital.

"B U C H A N A N." I spell the assailant's name for the younger cop. He taps the tip of his pencil on his notebook and steps aside to call it in.

The rain has stopped and a sick, silvery sheen glows eerily from the road. We're standing near our cars. Most of the gawkers have been sent away. The rest of us have all been breathalyzed. Ms. Eckleburg remains, and our principal. Some parental guardians have been called. With the receding strobes of the ambulance and its tired, wailing siren, the last of onlookers pile in their daddies' Escalades. I hear one of them laugh, "I guess the party's over."

A few feet away, Jamie leans on the hood of his contraband muscle car. I hear the older officer with the weird mustache and the dad bod say to him again, "You saved her, son. You saved her."

Jamie doesn't respond. He simply stares at me, waiting for me to meet his eyes.

The cop continues. "Did you hear me? You saved her. But I think we have a few things we need to clear up. This car is listed as stolen property. It belongs to..."

"I know who it belongs to," Jamie answers.

Jordan joins me. "They said they're done with us. We can go."

"Did anyone say when we can go see Myrtle?" I ask.

"No. But I bet it's gonna be a while. She's not out of the woods, yet." Jordan's throat catches. Her face is soft in the post-rain starlight.

"I want to see her just as soon as we can."

"We will. I promise," Jordan says, and she means it. She's never really liked Myrtle, but I know she means it. We're connected now. In some tawdry, cataclysmic moment of unreality, we're all connected. It's almost like a plot out of one of Jordan's predictable old movies, all the moving parts share a secret that none of them ever wanted to know in the first place. Only ours isn't secret. It's tomorrow's front page news. It's today's social media virus.

"Let's get out of here," Jordan prods me back toward where my cousin waits by his car for us.

"Wait, I need to hear this, first." I point to the cop who is still trying to pry information from Jamie.

The officer squints and scratches his wet head. "So, you admit it isn't yours?"

"It's my father's. I borrowed it."

"Borrowed? Then why is it reported stolen?"

"Because I didn't tell him I borrowed it. I guess I figured it would be safer with me than with him. He'd just down a pint of vodka and drive this one through someone's business, too."

Jamie's still staring at me, only now I'm looking right back.

The officer swipes residual water from the car top. "This is quite the automobile not to inform its owner that you've borrowed it."

The younger cop comes up and whispers something in the officer's ear. "Hold on a second, son," the officer steps away to confer with his partner. He comes back holding handcuffs.

"I hate to do this, son, but I'm gonna need you to turn around. Seems there's a warrant out for your arrest. We might have overlooked not telling your dad about the car, but we don't look the other way on when drugs are involved."

Jamie isn't shocked; he's simply... sad. He doesn't resist. He hardly responds at all except to wince with the click of the handcuffs.

Then the officer reads him his rights and escorts him to the police cruiser. As Jamie inserts a leg into the back seat of the cop car, he flops back his damp, dirty blond mess of hair and finds me across the road. He mouths, "Daisy?" right as the policeman's authoritative hand pushes his head out of view.

"Wait!" I run to him, and his face lights up like Apollo himself. I divert my gaze and unfasten the clasp that holds his precious polished glass. Reaching each end of the necklace around his neck, I secure it in place.

"Why?" he asks.

"I hope you manifest a new life for yourself. I really do. But it needs to be an authentic one, not built on lies but built on hope. I think maybe you got those two confused. I think maybe I did, too."

"Daisy, wait. You know this is all a misunderstanding. It's a rough patch. I'll be back. We'll be fine."

"Goodbye, Jamie."

I shut the door, and they drive him away. Nick finds Jordan and me and puts an arm around each of us. He silently guides us to our car We climb inside, and the world outside disappears.

CHAPTER THIRTY-FOUR

My mother gave me some advice before she died. She wrote it by hand inside a card she'd made at a crafting class the last time she visited her family island. However, I didn't find it until a couple weeks ago when Jordan had come over to help me clean out Ginny's closet. It had been on the Saturday of Mother's Day weekend, eight months since that awful Homecoming.

The card read: *Trust your beautiful self, my darling. Love, Mom.*

I try to imagine how my father would have followed up. Would he have tweaked her nose and said, "And trust your beautiful mother, too"? Maybe. On a good day. But it doesn't matter. My mother's advice doesn't need my father's approval to be valuable.

I'm sitting on a sturdy, comfortable lawn chair, drinking in the afternoon sun and a cold glass of Grandma's sweet tea, watching light reflect in happy beams off my pool. In a few minutes, my friends will all be here to celebrate our graduation.

"It's going to be good to use it this year," Grandma says, straightening the towels on the table beside me.

"Absolutely. Might as well get a good summer in before we put it on the market. You really are okay with it, aren't you? Selling the house."

She sits in the chair beside me. "I'm more than okay with it. I'm proud of you. In so many, many ways. Your parents would be, too, you know."

"I hope so." My throat catches, but the cool tea soothes it.

"You've become such a strong young lady."

"I had good role models," I say.

She shakes her head. "I don't know about that. But neither your mother nor I had the same options as you do."

I reach over for her hand and squeeze it. We've had this

Just Daisy

conversation many times in the last few months, but it's okay. I reassure her anyway. "Grandma, it's women like you and mom, doing what you could with what you had that make my choices possible."

She tears up a little. "Beautiful and wise."

"Like my grandma."

She straightens herself and stands back up. "Are your friends bringing their bathing suits?"

Bathing suits. How cute. "Yes, Grandma. They are. Stay here and wait with me."

"Oh, just let me bring out the cookies, and I will. Ardita doesn't quite know her way around our kitchen." She scurries off to the house to help her new business partner. Grandma Betty's Bakery serves all the book club ladies in Barrington Hills. Between Ardita Fitz-Peters' business sense, her family cookbook, and Grandma's baking expertise, I wouldn't be surprised to see them take over Chicago.

The back gate opens. It seems everyone has arrived at once. Nick's parents—my cousins, even though they seem like aunt and uncle—carry graduation gifts inside. We don't get together as an extended family very often. There are so few of us. Something else I intend to change.

"Can we jump in?" Nick says and then doesn't wait for an answer. He splashes us unapologetically.

"Thanks for having us." Mr. Baker rushes in and shakes my hand. His face twists uncomfortably as he searches for some way to make conversation with teenagers. Jordan smiles dotingly on him.

"Absolutely. I'm glad you came." I point him toward the adults, and he graciously exits.

"Where's your mom?" I ask.

"She couldn't make it. She's gonna be away for a while. Ninety days at least." A tear sparkles in my best friend's eye. A serene aura surrounds her.

The rest of our friends tumble in. Owen, Wilson, Lucille. Even Myrtle and her sister, Catherine, show up. One particular junior from the girls golf team arrives in a floral sundress, a large hat, and pimple-free face. Seems she only needed a little Jordan Baker expertise on skincare and make-up.

Nick climbs out of the pool and joins Jordan and me in the gazebo. "How do you think Myrtle will do as cheer captain next year? It's usually a senior. She'll only be a junior," Nick asks, rubbing his arms with a beach towel.

I find her across the pool and catch her eye. She scrunches her new, powerfully stacked bob and raises a questioning eyebrow.

I give her thumbs up. Her smile goes wide. She turns back to her group, laughing.

I answer Nick. "I think she'll be great. Just because the captain always has been a senior doesn't mean it always must be a senior."

"How very progressive of you," Jordan says.

"Is it weird to have a graduation party without Tom here?" Nick asks, scanning the guests as if Tom might emerge from the pool like Poseidon commanding the seas.

Jordan throws back her head as if she's about to let loose in laughter. "It's not weird. I think the whole thing is a smashing success."

"You mean the party? Thanks." I say.

"Yes, the party. Also, the fact that Tom's got his license suspended, his scholarships rescinded, and all those hours of community service. He's lucky. It could have been worse."

"I saw him the other day coming out of a jewelry store. I have no idea who he was buying for."

"Not me. Thank goodness," I say.

Nick continues, "He tried to shake my hand even though he still blames everyone but himself for what happened that night."

"Did you shake it?" Jordan asks.

"I did, but I told him he was wrong and that I hoped he'd understand that someday. I think it shocked him a little."

"I don't want to talk about Tom," I say. "I like my life without him in it. Thank you very much."

"What about Jamie?" Nick asks.

Jordan perks up. "Yes. What about that beautiful beach god of yours? Heading to the island again this summer?"

I laugh. "Okay, first of all, he's not mine. People don't own people. And beautiful beach god? Geez Jordan, if I didn't know any better, I'd think you were in love with him."

Nick chimes in. "We know that's not true."

She does that one-shoulder shrug. "I don't know. He was hot. What's not to love about a hot man?" A sly grin spreads across her face.

Just Daisy

"Oh, Jordan. The University of Texas is not going to know what to do with you, are they?" Nick laughs.

"Does anyone ever?" She winks at him.

"No, I'm not going to the island. And even if I were, everything with Jamie is in the past. I haven't heard from him since they took him back to Georgia. Cornell is my future." The shadows of starry nights standing in this gazebo, tucked under Jamie's arm are almost gone. Only romantic nostalgia remains, but it's nothing I can't handle.

"You finally made that decision? It's Cornell, huh?" Nick says.

"Yes. Did you know that's where Ruth Bader Ginsburg went to college before law school?"

"If it's good enough for the Notorious RBG, it should be good enough for our Daisy. What about you, Nicky?" Jordan slips her arm through his and leads him back to the pool. I link mine through his other side and join them.

"You know you're the only one who gets to call me that, right?" Jordan smiles and kisses his cheek.

"I'm not going to college," he says.

"What? When did you decide this? Are your parents okay with it?" I'm utterly shocked. His family comes from a long line of Yale graduates. Nick's education fate was sealed at birth.

"You said it yourself. Just because it's always been done... Besides, my dad owns hardware stores. Let's face it. He didn't really need that Yale education."

"He's done pretty well for himself," I say.

"Mostly from what he learned from his dad," Nick rebuts.

"So, what's your plan then?" I ask.

"I'm going to write the great American novel."

We stop. Jordan and I stare at him like he's speaking a language we've never heard. I don't know what to say except, "Bravo!" Like it has already been written.

"We're in it, of course," Jordan states.

Who knows? Maybe it already has been.

The carefree laughter of new freedoms and adult adventures burst from my busy pool, drowning out the ghosts of all those stagnant years. It's an innocent sound. Alcohol free. Drug free. Clique free, I hope.

But the innocence won't last forever. I'll enjoy it for now, but I'm eighteen. A high school graduate. We'll all have new lessons to learn in the next four years and the next. That's life, isn't it? The constant tug back to the lessons we thought we learned only to learn them again.

In a swift movement as if she is swinging a champion driver, Jordan whips off her bikini cover.

"Let's jump in, shall we?"

We clasp hands—my best friend, my cousin, and I—and splash into the fray.

THE END

ABOUT THE AUTHOR

Deborah Linn grew up as a frustrated reader, wanting to rewrite the stories to fit her imagination. She now teaches literature and writing to teenagers, encouraging them to create stories to share with the world. She lives in Kansas and often dreams of taking off to an island paradise. Read her blog at KeepingClassics.com.

Check out all of Deborah's books and news at www.DeborahLinnBooks.com